THE TORRENTS OF SPRING AND OTHER STORIES

THE TORRENTS OF SPRING AND OTHER STORIES

BY

IVAN TURGENEV

Translated from the Russian
by CONSTANCE GARNETT

This edition first published in 2008
by Faber and Faber Ltd
3 Queen Square, London WC1N 3AU

Printed by Books on Demand GmbH, Norderstedt

All rights reserved
Translation © Constance Garnett, 1897

The right of Constance Garnett to be identified as translator of this work
has been asserted in accordance with Section 77 of the
Copyright, Designs and Patents Act 1988

This book is sold subject to the condition that it shall not, by way of
trade or otherwise, be lent, resold, hired out or otherwise circulated
without the publisher's prior consent in any form of binding or cover other than
that in which it is published and without a similar condition including this
condition being imposed on the subsequent purchaser

A CIP record for this book is available from the British Library

ISBN 978–0–571–24557–4

CONTENTS

	PAGE
THE TORRENTS OF SPRING, . . .	1
FIRST LOVE, ...	241
MUMU, ...	355

THE TORRENTS OF SPRING

'Years of gladness,
  Days of joy,
Like the torrents of spring
  They hurried away.'
—*From an Old Ballad.*

. . . At two o'clock in the night he had gone back to his study. He had dismissed the servant after the candles were lighted, and throwing himself into a low chair by the hearth, he hid his face in both hands.

Never had he felt such weariness of body and of spirit. He had passed the whole evening in the company of charming ladies and cultivated men; some of the ladies were beautiful, almost all the men were distinguished by intellect or talent; he himself had talked with great success, even with brilliance . . . and, for all that, never yet had the *taedium vitae* of which the Romans talked of old, the 'disgust for life,' taken hold of him with such irresistible, such suffocating force. Had he been a little younger, he would have cried with misery, weariness, and exasperation: a biting, burning bitterness, like the bitter of wormwood, filled his whole soul. A sort of clinging repugnance, a weight of loathing closed in upon him on all sides like a dark night of autumn; and he did not know how to get free from this darkness, this bitterness. Sleep it was useless to reckon upon; he knew he should not sleep.

He fell to thinking . . . slowly, listlessly, wrathfully. He thought of the vanity, the uselessness, the vulgar falsity of all things human. All the stages of man's life passed in order before his mental gaze (he had himself lately reached his fifty-second year), and not one found grace in his eyes. Everywhere the same everlasting pouring of water into a sieve, the everlasting beating of the air, everywhere the same self-deception—half in good faith, half conscious —any toy to amuse the child, so long as it keeps him from crying. And then, all of a sudden, old age drops down like snow on the head, and with it the ever-growing, ever-gnawing, and devouring dread of death . . . and the plunge into the abyss! Lucky indeed if life works out so to the end! May be, before the end, like rust on iron, sufferings, infirmities come. . . . He did not picture life's sea, as the poets depict it, covered with tempestuous waves; no, he thought of that sea as a smooth, untroubled surface, stagnant and transparent to its darkest depths. He himself sits in a little tottering boat, and down below in those dark oozy depths, like prodigious fishes, he can just make out the shapes of hideous monsters: all the ills of life, diseases, sorrows, madness, poverty, blindness. . . . He gazes, and behold, one of these monsters separates itself off from the darkness, rises higher and higher, stands out more and more distinct, more and more loathsomely distinct. . . . An instant yet, and the boat that bears him will be overturned! But behold, it grows dim again, it withdraws, sinks down to the bottom, and there it lies, faintly stirring in the slime. . . . But the fated day will come, and it will overturn the boat.

He shook his head, jumped up from his low chair, took two turns up and down the room, sat down to the writing-table, and opening one drawer after another, began to rummage among his papers, among old letters, mostly from women. He could not have said why he was doing it; he was not looking for anything—he simply wanted by some kind of external occupation to get away from the thoughts oppressing him. Opening several letters at random (in one of them there was a withered flower tied with a bit of faded ribbon), he merely shrugged his shoulders, and glancing at the hearth, he tossed them on one side, probably with the idea of burning all this useless rubbish. Hurriedly, thrusting his hands first into one, and then into another drawer, he suddenly opened his eyes wide, and slowly bringing out a little octagonal box of old-fashioned make, he slowly raised its lid. In the box, under two layers of cotton wool, yellow with age, was a little garnet cross.

For a few instants he looked in perplexity at this cross—suddenly he gave a faint cry. . . . Something between regret and delight was expressed in his features. Such an expression a man's face wears when he suddenly meets some one whom he has long lost sight of, whom he has at one time tenderly loved, and who suddenly springs up before his eyes, still the same, and utterly transformed by the years.

He got up, and going back to the hearth, he sat down again in the arm-chair, and again hid his face in his hands. . . . 'Why to-day? just to-day?' was his thought, and he remembered many things, long since past.

This is what he remembered. . . .

But first I must mention his name, his father's name and his surname. He was called Dimitri Pavlovitch Sanin.

Here follows what he remembered.

I

It was the summer of 1840. Sanin was in his twenty-second year, and he was in Frankfort on his way home from Italy to Russia. He was a man of small property, but independent, almost without family ties. By the death of a distant relative, he had come into a few thousand roubles, and he had decided to spend this sum abroad before entering the service, before finally putting on the government yoke, without which he could not obtain a secure livelihood. Sanin had carried out this intention, and had fitted things in to such a nicety that on the day of his arrival in Frankfort he had only just enough money left to take him back to Petersburg. In the year 1840 there were few railroads in existence; tourists travelled by diligence, Sanin had taken a place in the *'bei-wagon'*; but the diligence did not start till eleven o'clock in the evening. There was a great deal of time to be got through before then. Fortunately it was lovely weather, and Sanin after dining at a hotel, famous in those days, the White Swan, set off to stroll about the town. He went in to look at Danneker's Ariadne, which he did not much care for, visited the house of Goethe, of whose works he had, however, only read *Werter*, and that in the French translation. He walked along the bank of the Maine, and was bored as a well-conducted tourist should be; at last at six o'clock in the evening, tired, and with dusty boots, he found himself in one of the least remarkable streets in Frankfort. That street he was fated not to forget long, long after. On one of its few houses he saw a signboard: 'Giovanni Roselli, Italian confectionery,' was announced upon it. Sanin went into it to get a glass of lemonade; but in the shop, where, behind the modest counter, on the shelves of a stained cupboard, recalling a chemist's shop, stood a few bottles with gold labels, and as many glass jars of biscuits, chocolate cakes, and sweetmeats—in this room, there was not a soul; only a grey cat blinked and purred, sharpening its claws on a tall wicker chair near the window and a bright patch of colour was made in the evening sunlight, by a big ball of red wool lying on the floor beside a carved wooden basket turned upside down. A confused noise was audible in the next room. Sanin stood a moment, and making the bell on the door ring its loudest, he called, raising his voice, 'Is there no one here?' At that instant the door from an inner room was thrown open, and Sanin was struck dumb with amazement.

II

A YOUNG girl of nineteen ran impetuously into the shop, her dark curls hanging in disorder on her bare shoulders, her bare arms stretched out in front of her. Seeing Sanin, she rushed up to him at once, seized him by the hand, and pulled him after her, saying in a breathless voice, 'Quick, quick, here, save him!' Not through disinclination to obey, but simply from excess of amazement, Sanin did not at once follow the girl. He stood, as it were, rooted to the spot; he had never in his life seen such a beautiful creature. She turned towards him, and with such despair in her voice, in her eyes, in the gesture of her clenched hand, which was lifted with a spasmodic movement to her pale cheek, she articulated, 'Come, come!' that he at once darted after her to the open door.

In the room, into which he ran behind the

girl, on an old-fashioned horse-hair sofa, lay a boy of fourteen, white all over—white, with a yellowish tinge like wax or old marble—he was strikingly like the girl, obviously her brother. His eyes were closed, a patch of shadow fell from his thick black hair on a forehead like stone, and delicate, motionless eyebrows; between the blue lips could be seen clenched teeth. He seemed not to be breathing; one arm hung down to the floor, the other he had tossed above his head. The boy was dressed, and his clothes were closely buttoned; a tight cravat was twisted round his neck.

The girl rushed up to him with a wail of distress. 'He is dead, he is dead!' she cried; 'he was sitting here just now, talking to me—and all of a sudden he fell down and became rigid. . . . My God! can nothing be done to help him? And mamma not here! Pantaleone, Pantaleone, the doctor!' she went on suddenly in Italian. 'Have you been for the doctor?'

'Signora, I did not go, I sent Luise,' said a hoarse voice at the door, and a little bandy-legged old man came hobbling into the room in a lavender frock coat with black buttons, a high white cravat, short nankeen trousers, and blue worsted stockings. His diminutive little face was positively lost in a mass of iron-grey hair. Standing up in all directions, and falling back in ragged tufts, it gave the old man's figure a resemblance to a crested hen—a resemblance the more striking, that under the dark-grey mass nothing could be distinguished but a beak nose and round yellow eyes.

'Luise will run fast, and I can't run,' the old man went on in Italian, dragging his flat gouty feet, shod in high slippers with knots of ribbon. I've brought some water.'

In his withered, knotted fingers, he clutched a long bottle neck.

'But meanwhile Emil will die!' cried the girl, and holding out her hand to Sanin, 'O, sir, O *mein Herr*! can't you do something for him?'

'He ought to be bled—it's an apoplectic fit,' observed the old man addressed as Pantaleone.

Though Sanin had not the slightest notion of medicine, he knew one thing for certain, that boys of fourteen do not have apoplectic fits.

'It's a swoon, not a fit,' he said, turning to Pantaleone. 'Have you got any brushes?'

The old man raised his little face. 'Eh?'

'Brushes, brushes,' repeated Sanin in German and in French. 'Brushes,' he added, making as though he would brush his clothes.

The little old man understood him at last.

'Ah, brushes! *Spazzette!* to be sure we have!'

'Bring them here; we will take off his coat and try rubbing him.'

'Good . . . *Benone!* And ought we not to sprinkle water on his head?'

'No . . . later on; get the brushes now as quick as you can.'

Pantaleone put the bottle on the floor, ran out and returned at once with two brushes, one a hair-brush, and one a clothes-brush. A curly poodle followed him in, and vigorously wagging its tail, it looked up inquisitively at the old man, the girl, and even Sanin, as though it wanted to know what was the meaning of all this fuss.

Sanin quickly took the boy's coat off, unbuttoned his collar, and pushed up his shirt-sleeves, and arming himself with a brush, he began brushing his chest and arms with all his might. Pantaleone as zealously brushed away with the other—the hair-brush—at his boots and trousers. The girl flung herself on her knees by the sofa, and, clutching her head in both hands, fastened her eyes, not an eyelash quivering, on her brother.

Sanin rubbed on, and kept stealing glances at her. Mercy! what a beautiful creature she was!

III

Her nose was rather large, but handsome, aquiline-shaped; her upper lip was shaded by a light down; but then the colour of her face, smooth, uniform, like ivory or very pale milky amber, the wavering shimmer of her hair, like that of the Judith of Allorio in the Palazzo-Pitti; and above all, her eyes, dark-grey, with a black ring round the pupils, splendid, triumphant eyes, even now, when terror and distress dimmed their lustre. . . . Sanin could not help recalling the marvellous country he had just come from. . . . But even in Italy he had never met anything like her! The girl drew slow, uneven breaths; she seemed between each breath to be waiting to see whether her brother would not begin to breathe.

Sanin went on rubbing him, but he did not only watch the girl. The original figure of Pantaleone drew his attention too. The old man was quite exhausted and panting; at every movement of the brush he hopped up and down and groaned noisily, while his immense tufts of hair, soaked with perspiration, flapped heavily from side to side, like the roots of some strong plant, torn up by the water.

'You'd better, at least, take off his boots,' Sanin was just saying to him.

The poodle, probably excited by the unusualness of all the proceedings, suddenly sank on to its front paws and began barking.

'*Tartaglia—canaglia!*' the old man hissed at it. But at that instant the girl's face was transformed. Her eyebrows rose, her eyes grew wider, and shone with joy.

Sanin looked round . . . A flush had overspread the lad's face; his eyelids stirred . . . his nostrils twitched. He drew in a breath through his still clenched teeth, sighed. . . .

'Emil!' cried the girl . . . 'Emilio mio!'

Slowly the big black eyes opened. They still had a dazed look, but already smiled faintly; the same faint smile hovered on his pale lips. Then he moved the arm that hung down, and laid it on his chest

'Emilio!' repeated the girl, and she got up. The expression on her face was so tense and vivid, that it seemed that in an instant either she would burst into tears or break into laughter.

'Emil! what is it? Emil!' was heard outside, and a neatly-dressed lady with silvery grey hair and a dark face came with rapid steps into the room.

A middle-aged man followed her; the head

of a maid-servant was visible over their shoulders,

The girl ran to meet them.

'He is saved, mother, he is alive!' she cried, impulsively embracing the lady who had just entered.

'But what is it?' she repeated. 'I come back . . . and all of a sudden I meet the doctor and Luise . . .'

The girl proceeded to explain what had happened, while the doctor went up to the invalid who was coming more and more to himself, and was still smiling: he seemed to be beginning to feel shy at the commotion he had caused.

'You've been using friction with brushes, I see,' said the doctor to Sanin and Pantaleone, 'and you did very well. . . . A very good idea . . . and now let us see what further measures . . .'

He felt the youth's pulse. 'H'm! show me your tongue!'

The lady bent anxiously over him. He smiled still more ingenuously, raised his eyes to her, and blushed a little.

It struck Sanin that he was no longer wanted; he went into the shop. But before he had time to touch the handle of the street-door, the girl was once more before him; she stopped him.

'You are going,' she began, looking warmly into his face; 'I will not keep you, but you must be sure to come to see us this evening: we are so indebted to you—you, perhaps, saved my brother's life, we want to thank you—mother wants to. You must tell us who you are, you must rejoice with us . . .'

'But I am leaving for Berlin to-day,' Sanin faltered out.

'You will have time though,' the girl rejoined eagerly. 'Come to us in an hour's time to drink a cup of chocolate with us. You promise? I must go back to him! You will come?'

What could Sanin do?

'I will come,' he replied.

The beautiful girl pressed his hand, fluttered away, and he found himself in the street

IV

WHEN Sanin, an hour and a half later, returned to the Rosellis' shop he was received there like one of the family. Emilio was sitting on the same sofa, on which he had been rubbed; the doctor had prescribed him medicine and recommended 'great discretion in avoiding strong emotions' as being a subject of nervous temperament with a tendency to weakness of the heart. He had previously been liable to fainting-fits; but never had he lost consciousness so completely and for so long. However, the doctor declared that all danger was over. Emil, as was only suitable for an invalid, was dressed in a comfortable dressing-gown; his mother wound a blue woollen wrap round his neck; but he had a cheerful, almost a festive air; indeed everything had a festive air. Before the sofa, on a round table, covered with a clean cloth, towered a huge china coffee-pot, filled with fragrant chocolate, and encircled by cups, decanters of liqueur, biscuits and rolls, and even flowers; six slender wax candles were burning in two old-fashioned silver chandeliers; on one side of the sofa, a comfortable lounge-chair offered its soft embraces, and in this chair they made Sanin sit. All the inhabitants of the confectioner's shop, with whom he had made acquaintance that day, were present, not excluding the poodle, Tartaglia, and the cat; they all seemed happy beyond expression; the poodle positively sneezed with delight, only the cat was coy and blinked sleepily as before. They made Sanin tell them who he was, where he came from, and what was his name; when he said he was a Russian, both the ladies were a little surprised, uttered ejaculations of wonder, and declared with one voice that he spoke German splendidly; but if he preferred to speak French, he might make use of that language, as they both understood it and spoke it well. Sanin at once availed himself of this suggestion. 'Sanin! Sanin!' The ladies would never have expected that a Russian surname could be so easy to pronounce. His Christian name—'Dimitri'—they liked very much too. The elder lady observed that in her youth she had heard a fine opera 'Demetrio e Polibio'—but that 'Dimitri' was much nicer than 'Demetrio.' In this way Sanin talked for about an hour. The ladies on their side initiated him into all the details of their own life. The talking was mostly done by the mother, the lady with grey hair. Sanin learnt from her that her name was Leonora Roselli; that she had lost her husband, Giovanni Battista Roselli, who had settled in Frankfort as a confectioner twenty-five years ago; that Giovanni Battista had come from Vicenza and had been a most excellent, though fiery and irascible man, and a republican withal! At those words Signora Roselli pointed to his portrait, painted in oil-colours, and hanging over the sofa. It must be presumed that the painter, 'also a republican!' as Signora Roselli observed with a sigh, had not fully succeeded in catching a likeness, for in his portrait the late Giovanni Battista appeared as a morose and gloomy brigand, after the style of Rinaldo Rinaldini! Signora Roselli herself had come from 'the ancient and splendid city of Parma where there is the wonderful cupola, painted by the immortal Correggio!' But from her long residence in Germany she had become almost completely Germanised. Then she added, mournfully shaking her head, that all she had left was *this* daughter and *this* son (pointing to each in turn with her finger); that the daughter's name was Gemma, and the son's Emilio; that they were both very good and obedient children —especially Emilio . . . ('Me not obedient!' her daughter put in at that point 'Oh, you're a republican, too!' answered her mother). That the business, of course, was not what it had been in the days of her husband, who had a great gift for the confectionery line. . . . ('*Un grand uomo!*' Pantaleone confirmed with a severe air); but that still, thank God, they managed to get along!

V

Gemma listened to her mother, and at one minute laughed, then sighed, then patted her on the shoulder, and shook her finger at her, and then looked at Sanin; at last, she got up, embraced her mother and kissed her in the hollow of her neck, which made the latter laugh extremely and shriek a little. Pantaleone too was presented to Sanin. It appeared he had once been an opera singer, a baritone, but had long ago given up the theatre, and occupied in the Roselli family a position between that of a family friend and a servant. In spite of his prolonged residence in Germany, he had learnt very little German, and only knew how to swear in it, mercilessly distorting even the terms of abuse. '*Ferroflucto spitchebubbio*' was his favourite epithet for almost every German, He spoke Italian with a perfect accent—for was he not by birth from Sinigali, where may he heard '*lingua toscana in bocca romana*'! Emilio, obviously, played the invalid and indulged himself in the pleasant sensations of one who has only just escaped a danger or is returning to health after illness; it was evident, too, that the family spoiled him. He thanked Sanin bashfully, but devoted himself chiefly to the biscuits and sweetmeats. Sanin was compelled to drink two large cups of excellent chocolate, and to eat a considerable number of biscuits; no sooner had he swallowed one than Gemma offered him another—and to refuse was impossible! He soon felt at home: the time flew by with incredible swiftness. He had to tell them a great deal—about Russia in general, the Russian climate, Russian society, the Russian peasant—and especially about the Cossacks; about the war of 1812, about Peter the Great, about the Kremlin, and the Russian songs and bells. Both ladies had a very faint conception of our vast and remote fatherland; Signora Roselli, or as she was more often called, Frau Lenore, positively dumfounded Sanin with the question, whether there was still existing at Petersburg the celebrated house of ice, built last century, about which she had lately read a very curious article in one of her husband's books, '*Bellezze delle arti*.' And in reply to Sanin's exclamation, 'Do you really suppose that there is never any summer in Russia?' Frau Lenore replied that till then she had always pictured Russia like this—eternal snow, every one going about in furs, and all military men, but the greatest hospitality, and all the peasants very submissive! Sanin tried to impart to her and her daughter some more exact information. When the conversation touched on Russian music, they begged him at once to sing some Russian air and showed him a diminutive piano with black keys instead of white and white instead of black. He obeyed without making much ado and accompanying himself with two fingers of the right hand and three of the left (the first, second, and little finger) he sang in a thin nasal tenor, first 'The Sarafan,' then 'Along a Paved Street.' The ladies praised his voice and the music, but were more struck with the softness and sonorousness of the Russian language and asked for a translation of the text. Sanin complied with their wishes—but as the words of 'The Sarafan,' and still more of 'Along a Paved Street' (*sur une rue pavée une jeune fille allait à l' eau* was how he rendered the sense of the original) were not calculated to inspire his listeners with an exalted idea of Russian poetry, he first recited, then translated, and then sang Pushkin's, 'I remember a marvellous moment,' set to music by Glinka, whose minor bars he did not render quite faithfully. Then the ladies went into ecstasies. Frau Lenore positively discovered in Russian a wonderful likeness to the Italian. Even the names Pushkin (she pronounced it Pussekin) and Glinka sounded somewhat familiar to her. Sanin on his side begged the ladies to sing something; they too did not wait to be pressed. Frau Lenore sat down to the piano and sang with Gemma some duets and 'stornelle.' The mother had once had a fine contralto; the daughter's voice was not strong, but was pleasing.

VI

BUT it was not Gemma's voice—it was herself Sanin was admiring. He was sitting a little behind and on one side of her, and kept thinking to himself that no palm-tree, even in the poems of Benediktov—the poet in fashion in those days—could rival the slender grace of her figure. When, at the most emotional passages, she raised her eyes upwards—it seemed to him no heaven could fail to open at such a look! Even the old man, Pantaleone, who with his shoulder propped against the doorpost, and his chin and mouth tucked into his capacious cravat, was listening solemnly with the air of a connoisseur—even he was admiring the girl's lovely face and marvelling at it, though one would have thought he must have been used to it! When she had finished the duet with her daughter, Frau Lenore observed that Emilio had a fine voice, like a silver bell, but that now he was at the age when the voice changes —he did, in fact, talk in a sort of bass constantly falling into falsetto—and that he was therefore forbidden to sing; but that Pantaleone now really might try his skill of old days in honour of their guest! Pantaleone promptly put on a displeased air, frowned, ruffled up his hair, and declared that he had given it all up long ago, though he could certainly in his youth hold his own, and indeed had belonged to that great period, when there were real classical singers, not to be compared to the squeaking performers of to-day! and a real school of singing; that he, Pantaleone Cippatola of Varese, had once been brought a laurel wreath from Modena, and that on that occasion some white doves had positively been let fly in the theatre; that among others a Russian prince Tarbusky—'*il principe Tarbusski*'— with whom he had been on the most friendly terms, had after supper persistently invited him to Russia, promising him mountains of gold, mountains! . . . but that he had been unwilling to leave Italy, the land of Dante—*il paese del Dante!* Afterward, to be sure, there came . . . unfortunate circumstances, he had himself been imprudent. . . . At this point the old man broke off, sighed deeply twice, looked dejected, and began again talking of the classical period of singing, of the celebrated tenor Garcia, for whom he cherished a devout, unbounded veneration. 'He was a man!' he exclaimed. 'Never had the great Garcia (*il gran Garcia*) demeaned himself by singing falsetto like the paltry tenors of to-day—*tenoracci*; always from the chest, from the chest, *voce di petto, si!*' and the old man aimed a vigorous blow with his little shrivelled fist at his own shirtfront! 'And what an actor! A volcano, *signori miei*, a volcano, *un Vesuvio*! I had the honour and the happiness of singing with him in the *opera dell' illustrissimo maestro* Rossini—in Otello! Garcia was Otello,—I was Iago—and when he rendered the phrase':—here Pantaleone threw himself into an attitude and began singing in a hoarse and shaky, but still moving voice:

> "L'i . . . ra daver . . . so daver . . . so il fato
> Io più no . . . no . . . no . . . non temerò!"

The theatre was all a-quiver, *signori miei*! though I too did not fall short, I too after him.

> "L'i ra daver . . . so . . . daver . . . so il fato
> Temèr più non davro!"

And all of a sudden, he crashed like lightning, like a tiger:*Morro!* . . . *ma vendicato* . . .

Again when he was singing . . . when he was singing that celebrated air from *"Matrimonio segreto,"* Pria che spunti . . . then he, *il gran Garcia*, after the words, *"I cavalli di galoppo"*— at the words, *"Senza posa cacciera,"*—listen, how stupendous, *come è stupendo*! At that point he made . . .' The old man began a sort of extraordinary flourish, and at the tenth note broke down, cleared his throat, and with a wave of his arm turned away, muttering, 'Why do you torment me?' Gemma jumped up at once and clapping loudly and shouting, bravo! . . . bravo! . . . she ran to the poor old super-annuated Iago and with both hands patted him affectionately on the shoulders. Only Emil laughed ruthlessly. *Cet âge est sans pitié*— that age knows no mercy—Lafontaine has said already.

Sanin tried to soothe the aged singer and began talking to him in Italian—(he had picked up a smattering during his last tour there)—began talking of *'paese del Dante, dove il si suona.'* This phrase, together with *'Lasciate ogni speranza,'* made up the whole stock of poetic Italian of the young tourist; but Pantalèone was not won over by his blandishments. Tucking his chin deeper than ever into his cravat and sullenly rolling his eyes, he was once more like a bird, an angry one too,—a crow or a kite. Then Emil, with a faint momentary blush, such as one so often sees in spoilt children, addressing his sister, said if she wanted to entertain their guest, she could do nothing better than read him one of those little comedies of Malz, that she read so nicely. Gemma laughed, slapped her brother on the arm, exclaimed that he 'always had such ideas!' She went promptly, however, to her room, and returning thence with a small book in her hand, seated herself at the table before the lamp, looked round, lifted one finger as much as to say'hush!'—a typically Italian gesture—and began reading.

VII

MALZ was a writer flourishing at Frankfort about 1830, whose short comedies, written in a light vein in the local dialect, hit off local Frankfort types with bright and amusing, though not deep, humour. It turned out that Gemma really did read excellently—quite like an actress in fact She indicated each personage, and sustained the character capitally, making full use of the talent of mimicry she had inherited with her Italian blood; she had no mercy on her soft voice or her lovely face, and when she had to represent some old crone in her dotage, or a stupid burgomaster, she made the drollest grimaces, screwing up her eyes, wrinkling up her nose, lisping, squeaking. . . . She did not herself laugh during the reading; but when her audience (with the exception of Pantaleone: he had walked off in indignation so soon as the conversation turned *o quel ferroflucto Tedesco*) interrupted her by an outburst of unanimous laughter, she dropped the book on her knee, and laughed musically too, her head thrown back, and her black hair dancing in little ringlets on her neck and her shaking shoulders. When the laughter ceased, she picked up the book at once, and again resuming a suitable expression, began the reading seriously. Sanin could not get over his admiration; he was particularly astonished at the marvellous way in which a face so ideally beautiful assumed suddenly a comic, sometimes almost a vulgar expression. Gemma was less successful in the parts of young girls—of so-called '*jeunes premières*'; in the love-scenes in particular she failed; she was conscious of this herself, and for that reason gave them a faint shade of irony as though she did not quite belieive in all these rapturous vows and elevated sentiments, of which the author, however, was himself rather sparing—so far as he could be.

Sanin did not notice how the evening was flying by, and only recollected the journey before him when the clock struck ten. He leaped up from his seat as though he had been stung.

'What is the matter?' inquired Frau Lenore.

'Why, I had to start for Berlin to-night, and I have taken a place in the diligence!'

'And when does the diligence start?'

'At half-past ten!'

'Well, then, you won't catch it now,' observed Gemma; 'you must stay . . . and I will go on reading.'

'Have you paid the whole fare or only given a deposit?' Frau Lenore queried.

'The whole fare!' Sanin said dolefully with a gloomy face.

Gemma looked at him, half closed her eyes, and laughed, while her mother scolded her: 'The young gentleman has paid away his money for nothing, and you laugh!'

'Never mind,' answered Gemma; 'it won't ruin him, and we will try and amuse him. Will you have some lemonade?'

Sanin drank a glass of lemonade, Gemma took up Malz once more; and all went merrily again.

The clock struck twelve. Sanin rose to take leave.

'You must stay some days now in Frankfort,' said Gemma: 'why should you hurry away? It would be no nicer in any other town.' She paused. 'It wouldn't, really,' she added with a smile. Sanin made no reply, and reflected that considering the emptiness of his purse, he would have no choice about remaining in Frankfort till he got an answer from a friend in Berlin, to whom he proposed writing for money.

'Yes, do stay,' urged Frau Lenore too. 'We will introduce you to Mr. Karl Klüber, who is engaged to Gemma. He could not come to-day, as he was very busy at his shop . . . you must have seen the biggest draper's and silk mercer's shop in the *Zeile*. Well, he is the manager there. But he will be delighted to call on you himself.'

Sanin—heaven knows why—was slightly disconcerted by this piece of information. 'He's a lucky fellow, that fiancé!' flashed across his mind. He looked at Gemma, and fancied he detected an ironical look in her eyes. He began saying good-bye.

'Till to-morrow? Till to-morrow, isn't it?' queried Frau Lenore.

'Till to-morrow!' Gemma declared in a tone

not of interrogation, but of affirmation, as though it could not be otherwise.

'Till to-morrow!' echoed Sanin.

Emil, Pantaleone, and the poodle Tartaglia accompanied him to the corner of the street. Pantaleone could not refrain from expressing his displeasure at Gemma's reading.

'She ought to be ashamed! She mouths and whines, *una caricatura!* She ought to represent Merope or Clytemnaestra—something grand, tragic—and she apes some wretched German woman! I can do that . . . *merz, kerz, smerz,*' he went on in a hoarse voice poking his face forward, and brandishing his fingers. Tartaglia began barking at him, while Emil burst out laughing. The old man turned sharply back.

Sanin went back to the White Swan (he had left his things there in the public hall) in a rather confused frame of mind. All the talk he had had in French, German, and Italian was ringing in his ears.

'Engaged!' he whispered as he lay in bed, in the modest apartment assigned to him. 'And what a beauty! But what did I stay For?'

Next day he sent a letter to his, friend in Berlin.

VIII

He had not finished dressing, when a waiter announced the arrival of two gentlemen. One of them turned out to be Emil; the other, a good-looking and well-grown young man, with a handsome face, was Herr Karl Klüber, the betrothed of the lovely Gemma.

One may safely assume that at that time in all Frankfort, there was not in a single shop a manager as civil, as decorous, as dignified, and as affable as Herr Klüber. The irreproachable perfection of his get-up was on a level with the dignity of his deportment, with the elegance—a little affected and stiff, it is true, in the English style (he had spent two years in England)—but still fascinating, elegance of his manners! It was clear from the first glance that this handsome, rather severe, excellently brought-up and superbly washed young man was accustomed to obey his superior and to command, his inferior, and that behind the counter of his shop he must infallibly inspire respect even in his customers! Of his supernatural honesty there could never be a particle of doubt: one had but to look at his stiffly starched collars! And his voice, it appeared.

was just what one would expect; deep, and of a self-confident richness, but not too loud, with positively a certain caressing note in its timbre. Such a voice was peculiarly fitted to give orders to assistants under his control: 'Show the crimson Lyons velvet!' or, 'Hand the lady a chair!'

Herr Klüber began with introducing himself; as he did so, he bowed with such loftiness, moved his legs with such an agreeable air, and drew his heels together with such polished courtesy that no one could fail to feel, 'that man has both linen and moral principles of the first quality!' The finish of his bare right hand —(the left, in a suède glove, held a hat shining like a looking-glass, with the right glove placed within it)—the finish of the right hand, proffered modestly but resolutely to Sanin, surpassed all belief; each finger-nail was a perfection in its own way! Then he proceeded to explain in the choicest German that he was anxious to express his respect and his indebtedness to the foreign gentleman who had performed so signal a service to his future kinsman, the brother of his betrothed; as he spoke, he waved his left hand with the hat in it in the direction of Emil, who seemed bashful and turning away to the window, put his finger in his mouth. Herr Klüber added that he should esteem himself happy should he be able in return to do anything for the foreign gentleman. Sanin, with some difficulty, replied, also in German, that he was delighted . . . that the service was not worth speaking of . . . and he begged his guests to sit down. Herr Klüber thanked him, and lifting his coat-tails, sat down on a chair; but he perched there so lightly and with such a transitory air that no one could fail to realise, 'this man is sitting down from politeness, and will fly up again in an instant.' And he did in fact fly up again quickly, and advancing with two discreet little dance-steps, he announced that to his regret he was unable to stay any longer, as he had to hasten to his shop—business before everything! but as the next day was Sunday, he had, with the consent of Frau Lenore and Fräulein Gemma, arranged a holiday excursion to Soden, to which he had the honour of inviting the foreign gentleman, and he cherished the hope that he would not refuse to grace the party with his presence. Sanin did not refuse so to grace it; and Herr Klüber repeating once more his complimentary sentiments, took leave, his pea-green trousers making a spot of cheerful colour, and his brand-new boots squeaking cheerfully as he moved.

IX

Emil, who had continued to stand with his face to the window, even after Sanin's invitation to him to sit down, turned round directly his future kinsman had gone out, and with a childish pout and blush, asked Sanin if he might remain a little while with him. 'I am much better to-day,' he added, 'but the doctor has forbidden me to do any work.'

'Stay by all means! You won't be in the least in my way,' Sanin cried at once. Like every true Russian he was glad to clutch at any excuse that saved him from the necessity of doing anything himself.

Emil thanked him, and in a very short time he was completely at home with him and with his room; he looked at all his things, asked him about almost every one of them, where he had bought it, and what was its value. He helped him to shave, observing that it was a mistake not to let his moustache grow; and finally told him a number of details about his mother, his sister, Pantaleone, the poodle Tartaglia, and all their daily life. Every semblance of timidity vanished in Emil; he suddenly felt extraordinarily attracted to Sanin—not at all because he had saved his life the day before, but because he was such a nice person! He lost no time in Confiding all his secrets to Sanin. He expatiated with special warmth on the fact that his mother was set on making him a shopkeeper, while he *knew*, knew for certain, that he was born an artist, a musician, a singer; that Pantaleone even encouraged him, but that Herr Klüber supported mamma, over whom he had great influence; that the very idea of his being a shopkeeper really originated with Herr Klüber, who considered that nothing in the world could compare with trade! To measure out cloth—and cheat the public, extorting from it *'Narren—oder Russen Preise'* (fools'—or Russian prices)—that was his ideal![1]

'Come! now you must come and see us!' he cried, directly Sanin had finished his toilet arid written his letter to Berlin.

'It's early yet,' observed Sanin.

'That's no matter,' replied Emil caressingly. 'Come along! We'll go to the post—and from there to our place. Gemma will be so glad to see you! You must have lunch with us. . . .

---

[1] In former days—and very likely it is not different now—when, from May onwards, a great number of Russians visited Frankfort, prices rose in all the shops, and were called 'Russians',' or, alas! 'fools' prices.'

You might say a word to mamma about me, my career. . . .'

'Very well, let's go,' said Sanin, and they set off.

X

Gemma certainly was delighted to see him, and Frau Lenore gave him a very friendly welcome; he had obviously made a good impression on both of them the evening before. Emil ran to see to getting lunch ready, after a preliminary whisper, 'don't forget!' in Sanin's ear.

'I won't forget,' responded Sanin.

Frau Lenore was not quite well; she had a sick headache, and, half-lying down in an easy chair, she tried to keep perfectly still. Gemma wore a full yellow blouse, with a black leather belt round the waist; she too seemed exhausted, and was rather pale; there were dark rings round her eyes, but their lustre was not the less for it; it added something of charm and mystery to the classical lines of her face. Sanin was especially struck that day by the exquisite beauty of her hands; when she smoothed and put back her dark, glossy tresses he could not take his eyes off her long supple fingers, held slightly apart from one another like the hand of Raphael's Fornarina.

It was very hot out-of-doors; after lunch Sanin was about to take leave, but they told him that on such a day the best thing was to stay where one was, and he agreed; he stayed. In the back room where he was sitting with the ladies of the household, coolness reigned supreme; the windows looked out upon a little garden overgrown with acacias. Multitudes of bees, wasps, and humming beetles kept up a steady, eager buzz in their thick branches, which were studded with golden blossoms; through the half-drawn curtains and the lowered blinds this never-ceasing hum made its way into the room, telling of the sultry heat in the air outside, and making the cool of the closed and snug abode seem the sweeter.

Sanin talked a great deal, as on the day before, but not of Russia, nor of Russian life. Being anxious to please his young friend, who had been sent off to Herr Klüber's immediately after lunch, to acquire a knowledge of bookkeeping, he turned the conversation on the Comparative advantages and disadvantages of art and commerce. He was not surprised at Frau Lenore's standing up for commerce—he had expected that; but Gemma too shared her opinion.

'If one's an artist, and especially a singer,' she declared with a vigorous downward sweep of her hand, 'one's got to be first-rate! Secondrate's worse than nothing; and who can tell if one will arrive at being first-rate?' Pantaleone, who took part too in the conversation—(as an old servant and an old man he had the privilege of sitting down in the presence of the ladies of the house; Italians are not, as a rule, strict in matters of etiquette)—Pantaleone, as a matter of course, stood like a rock for art. To tell the truth, his arguments were somewhat feeble; he kept expatiating for the most part on the necessity, before all things, of possessing *'un certo estro d'inspirazione'*—a certain force of inspiration! Frau Lenore remarked to him that he had, to be sure, possessed such an *'estro'*—and yet . . . 'I had enemies,' Pantaleone observed gloomily. 'And how do you know that Emil will not have enemies, even if this "*estro*" is found in him?' 'Very well, make a tradesman of him, then,' retorted Pantaleone in vexation; 'but Giovan' Battista would never have done it, though he was a confectioner himself!' 'Giovan' Battista, my husband, was a reasonable man, and even though he was in his youth led away . . .' But the old man would hear nothing more, and walked away, repeating reproachfully, 'Ah! Giovan'

Battista! . . .' Gemma exclaimed that if Emil felt like a patriot, and wanted to devote all his powers to the liberation of Italy, then, of course, for such a high and holy cause he might sacrifice the security of the future—but not for the theatre! Thereupon Frau Lenore became much agitated, and began to implore her daughter to refrain at least from turning her brother's head, and to content herself with being such a desperate republican herself! Frau Lenore groaned as she uttered these words, and began complaining of her head, which was 'ready to split.' (Frau Lenore, in deference to their guest, talked to her daughter in French.)

Gemma began at once to wait upon her; she moistened her forehead with eau-de-cologne, gently blew on it, gently kissed her cheek, made her lay her head on a pillow, forbade her to speak, and kissed her again. Then, turning to Sanin, she began telling him in a half-joking, half-tender tone what a splendid mother she had, and what a beauty she had been. '"Had been," did I say? she is charming now! Look, look, what eyes!'

Gemma instantly pulled a white handkerchief out of her pocket, covered her mother's face with it, and slowly drawing it downwards, gradually uncovered Frau Lenore's forehead, eyebrows, and eyes; she waited a moment and asked her to open them. Her mother obeyed; Gemma cried out in ecstasy (Frau Lenore's eyes really were very beautiful), and rapidly sliding the handkerchief over the lower, less regular part of the face, fell to kissing her again. Frau Lenore laughed, and turning a little away, with a pretence of violence, pushed her daughter away. She too pretended to struggle with her mother, and lavished caresses on her—not like a cat, in the French manner, but with that special Italian grace in which is always felt the presence of power.

At last Frau Lenore declared she was tired out . . . Then Gemma at once advised her to have a little nap, where she was, in her chair, 'and I and the Russian gentleman—"*avec le monsieur russe*"—will be as quiet, as quiet . . . as little mice . . . "*comme des petites souris*."' Frau Lenore smiled at her in reply, closed her eyes, and after a few sighs began to doze. Gemma quickly dropped down on a bench beside her and did not stir again, only from time to time she put a finger of one hand to her lips—with the other hand she was holding up a pillow behind her mother's head—and said softly, 'sh-sh!' with a sidelong look at Sanin, if he permitted himself the smallest movement In the end he too sank into a kind of dream, and sat motionless as though spell-bound while all his faculties were absorbed in admiring the picture presented him by the half-dark room, here and there spotted with patches of light crimson, where fresh, luxuriant roses stood in the old-fashioned green glasses, and the sleeping woman with demurely folded hands and kind, weary face, framed in the snowy whiteness of the pillow, and the young, keenly-alert and also kind, clever, pure, and unspeakably beautiful creature with such black, deep, overshadowed, yet shining eyes. . . . What was it? A dream? a fairy tale? And how came *he* to be in it?

XI

THE bell tinkled at the outer door. A young peasant lad in a fur cap and a red waistcoat came into the shop from the street Not one customer had looked into it since early morning . . . 'You see how much business we do!' Frau Lenore observed to Sanin at lunch-time with a sigh. She was still asleep; Gemma was afraid to take her arm from the pillow, and whispered to Sanin: 'You go, and mind the shop for me!' Sanin went on tiptoe into the shop at once. The boy wanted a quarter of a pound of peppermints. 'How much must I take?' Sanin whispered from the door to Gemma. 'Six kreutzers!' she answered in the same whisper. Sanin weighed out a quarter of a pound, found some paper, twisted it into a cone, tipped the peppermints into it, spilt them, tipped them in again, spilt them again, at last handed them to the boy, and took the money. . . . The boy gazed at him in amazement, twisting his cap in his hands on his stomach, and in the next room, Gemma was stifling with suppressed laughter. Before the first customer had walked out, a second appeared, then a third. . . . 'I bring luck, it's clear!' thought Sanin. The second customer wanted a glass of orangeade, the third, half-a-pound of sweets. Sanin satisfied their needs, zealously clattering the spoons, changing the saucers, and eagerly plunging his fingers into drawers and jars. On reckoning up, it appeared that he had charged too little for the orangeade, and taken two kreutzers too much for the sweets. Gemma did not cease laughing softly, and Sanin too was aware of an extraordinary lightness of heart, a peculiarly happy state of mind. He felt as if he had for ever been standing behind the counter and dealing in orangeade and sweetmeats, with that exquisite creature looking at him through the doorway with affectionately mocking eyes, while the summer sun, forcing its way through the sturdy leafage of the chestnuts that grew in front of the windows, filled the whole room with the greenish-gold of the midday light and shade, and the heart grew soft in the sweet languor of idleness, carelessness, and youth—first youth!

A fourth customer asked for a cup of coffee; Pantaleone had to be appealed to. (Emil had not yet come back from Herr Klüber's shop.) Sanin went and sat by Gemma again. Frau Lenore still went on sleeping, to her daughter's great delight. 'Mamma always sleeps off her sick headaches,' she observed. Sanin began talking—in a whisper, of course, as before—of his minding the shop; very seriously inquired the price of various articles of confectionery; Gemma just as seriously told him these prices, and meanwhile both of them were inwardly laughing together, as though conscious they were playing in a very amusing farce. All of a sudden, an organ-grinder in the street began playing an air from the Freischütz: '*Durch die Felder, durch die Auen* . . .' The dance tune fell shrill and quivering on the motionless air. Gemma started . . . 'He will wake mamma!' Sanin promptly darted out into the street, thrust a few kreutzers into the organ-grinder's hand, and made him cease playing and move away. When he came back, Gemma thanked him with a little nod of the head, and with a pensive smile she began herself just audibly humming the beautiful melody of Weber's, in which Max expresses all the perplexities of first love. Then she asked Sanin whether he knew 'Freischütz,' whether he was fond of Weber, and added that though she was herself an Italian, she liked *such* music best of all. From Weber the conversation glided off on to poetry and romanticism, on to Hoffmann, whom every one was still reading at that time.

And Frau Lenore still slept, and even snored just a little, and the sunbeams, piercing in narrow streaks through the shutters, were incessantly and imperceptibly shifting and travelling over the floor, the furniture, Gemma's dress, and the leaves and petals of the flowers.

XII

It appeared that Gemma was not very fond of Hoffmann, that she even thought him . . . tedious! The fantastic, misty northern element in his stories was too remote from her clear, southern nature. 'It's all fairy-tales, all written for children!' she declared with some contempt. She was vaguely conscious, too, of the lack of poetry in Hoffmann. But there was one of his stories, the title of which she had forgotten, which she greatly liked; more precisely speaking, it was only the beginning of this story that she liked; the end she had either not read or had forgotten. The story was about a young man who in some place, a sort of restaurant perhaps, meets a girl of striking beauty, a Greek; she is accompanied by a mysterious and strange, wicked old man. The young man falls in love with the girl at first sight; she looks at him so mournfully, as though beseeching him to deliver her. . . . He goes out for an instant, and, coming back into the restaurant, finds there neither the girl nor the old man; he rushes off in pursuit of her, continually comes upon fresh traces of her, follows them up, and can never by any means come upon her anywhere. The lovely girl has vanished for him for ever and ever, and he is never able to forget her imploring glance, and is tortured by the thought that all the happiness of his life, perhaps, has slipped through his fingers.

Hoffmann does not end his story quite in that way; but so it had taken shape, so it had remained, in Gemma's memory.

'fancy,' she said, 'such meetings and such partings happen oftener in the world than we suppose.'

Sanin was silent . . . and soon after he began talking . . . of Herr Klüber. It was the first time he had referred to him; he had not once remembered him till that instant.

Gemma was silent in her turn, and sank in to thought, biting the nail of her forefinger and fixing her eyes away. Then she began to speak in praise of her betrothed, alluded to the excursion he had planned for the next day, and, glancing swiftly at Sanin, was silent again.

Sanin did not know on what subject to turn the conversation.

Emil ran in noisily and waked Frau Lenore . . . Sanin was relieved by his appearance.

Frau Lenore got up from her low chair. Pantaleone came in and announced that dinner was ready. The friend of the family, ex-singer, and servant also performed the duties of cook.

XIII

Sanin stayed on after dinner too. They did not let him go, still on the same pretext of the terrible heat; and when the heat began to decrease, they proposed going out into the garden to drink coffee in the shade of the acacias.

Sanin consented. He felt very happy. In the quietly monotonous, smooth current of life lie hid great delights, and he gave himself up to these delights with zest, asking nothing much of the present day, but also thinking nothing of the morrow, nor recalling the day before. How much the mere society of such a girl as Gemma meant to him! He would shortly part from her and, most likely, for ever; but so long as they were borne, as in Uhland's song, in one skiff over the sea of life, untossed by tempest, well might the traveller rejoice and be glad. And everything seemed sweet and delightful to the happy voyager. Frau Lenore offered to play against him and Pantaleone at 'tresette,' instructed him in this not complicated Italian game, and won a few kreutzers from him, and he was well content. Pantaleone, at Emil's request, made the poodle, Tartaglia, perform all his tricks, and Tartaglia jumped over a stick 'spoke,' that is, barked, sneezed, shut the door with his nose, fetched his master's trodden-down slippers; and, finally, with an old cap on his head, he portrayed Marshal Bernadotte, subjected to the bitterest upbraidings by the Emperor Napoleon on account of his treachery. Napoleon's part was, of course, performed by Pantaleone, and very faithfully he performed it: he folded his arms across his chest, pulled a cocked hat over his eyes, and spoke very gruffly and sternly, in French—and heavens! what French! Tartaglia sat before his sovereign, all huddled up, with dejected tail, and eyes blinking and twitching in confusion, under the peak of his cap which was stuck on awry; from time to time when Napoleon raised his voice, Bernadotte rose on his hind paws. '*Fuori, traditore!*' cried Napoleon at last, forgetting in the excess of his wrath that he had to sustain his rôle as a Frenchman to the end; and Bernadotte promptly flew under the sofa, but quickly darted out again with a joyful bark, as though to announce that the performance was over. All the spectators laughed, and Sanin more than all.

Gemma had a particularly charming, continual, soft laugh, with very droll little shrieks . . . Sanin was fairly enchanted by that laugh —he could have kissed her for those shrieks!

Night came on at last. He had in decency to take leave! After saying good-bye several times over to every one, and repeating several times to all, 'till to-morrow!'—Emil he went so far as to kiss—Sanin started home, carrying with him the image of the young girl, at one time laughing, at another thoughtful, calm, and even indifferent—but always attractive! Her eyes, at one time wide open, clear and bright as day, at another time half shrouded by the lashes and deep and dark as night, seemed to float before his eyes, piercing in a strange sweet way across all other images and recollections.

Of Herr Klüber, of the causes impelling him to remain in Frankfort—in short, of everything that had disturbed his mind the evening before—he never thought once.

XIV

WE must, however, say a few words about Sanin himself.

In the first place, he was very, very goodlooking. A handsome, graceful figure, agreeable, rather unformed features, kindly bluish eyes, golden hair, a clear white and red skin, and, above all, that peculiar, naïvely-cheerful, confiding, open, at the first glance, somewhat foolish expression, by which in former days one could recognise directly the children of steady-going, noble families, 'sons of their fathers,' fine young landowners, born and reared in our open, half-wild country parts,— a hesitating gait, a voice with a lisp, a smile like a child's the minute you looked at him . . . lastly, freshness, health, softness, softness, softness,—there you have the whole of Sanin. And secondly, he was not stupid and had picked up a fair amount of knowledge. Fresh he had remained, for all his foreign tour; the disturbing emotions in which the greater part of the young people of that day were tempest-tossed were very little known to him.

Of late years, in response to the assiduous search for 'new types,' young men have begun to appear in our literature, determined at all hazards to be 'fresh' . . . as fresh as Flensburg oysters, when they reach Petersburg. . . . Sanin was not like them. Since we have had recourse already to simile, he rather recalled a young, leafy, freshly-grafted apple-tree in one of our fertile orchards—or better still, a well-groomed, sleek, sturdy-limbed, tender young 'three-year-old' in some old-fashioned seignorial stud stable, a young horse that they have hardly begun to break in to the traces. . . . Those who came across Sanin in later years, when life had knocked him about a good deal, and the sleekness and plumpness of youth had long vanished, saw in him a totally different man.

Next day Sanin was still in bed when Emil, in his best clothes, with a cane in his hand and much pomade on his head, burst into his room, announcing that Herr Klüber would be here directly with the carriage, that the weather promised to be exquisite, that they had everything ready by now, but that mamma was not going, as her head was bad again. He began to hurry Sanin, telling him that there was not a minute to lose. . . . And Herr Klüber did, in fact, find Sanin still at his toilet He knocked at the door, came in, bowed with a bend from the waist, expressed his readiness to wait as long as might be desired, and sat down, his hat balanced elegantly on his knees. The handsome shop-manager had got himself up and perfumed himself to excess: his every action was accompanied by a powerful whiff of the most refined aroma. He arrived in a comfortable open carriage—one of the kind called landau—drawn by two tall and powerful but not well-shaped horses. A quarter of an hour later Sanin, Klüber, and Emil, in this same carriage, drew up triumphantly at the steps of the confectioner's shop. Madame Roselli resolutely refused to join the party; Gemma wanted to stay with her mother; but she simply turned her out.

'I don't want any one,' she declared; 'I shall go to sleep. I would send Pantaleone with you too, only there would be no one to mind the shop.'

'May we take Tartaglia?' asked Emil.

'Of course you may.'

Tartaglia immediately scrambled, with delighted struggles, on to the box and sat there, licking himself; it was obviously a thing he was accustomed to. Gemma put on a large straw hat with brown ribbons; the hat was bent down in front, so as to shade almost the whole of her face from the sun. The line of shadow stopped just at her lips; they wore a tender maiden flush, like the petals of a centifoil rose, and her teeth gleamed stealthily —innocently too, as when children smile. Gemma sat facing the horses, with Sanin; Klüber and Emil sat opposite. The pale face of Frau Lenore appeared at the window; Gemma waved her handkerchief to her, and the horses started.

XV

SODEN is a little town half an hour's distance from Frankfort. It lies in a beautiful country among the spurs of the Taunus Mountains, and is known among us in Russia for its waters, which are supposed to be beneficial to people with weak lungs. The Frankforters visit it more for purposes of recreation, as Soden possesses a fine park and various 'wirtschaften,' where one may drink beer and coffee in the shade of the tall limes and maples. The road from Frankfort to Soden runs along the right bank of the Maine, and is planted all along with fruit trees. While the carriage was rolling slowly along an excellent road, Sanin stealthily watched how Gemma behaved to her betrothed; it was the first time he had seen them together. *She* was quiet and simple in her manner, but rather more reserved and serious than usual; *he* had the air of a condescending schoolmaster, permitting himself and those under his authority a discreet and decorous pleasure. Sanin saw no signs in him of any marked attentiveness, of what the French call *'empressement,'* in his demeanour to Gemma. It was clear that Herr Klüber considered that it was a matter settled once for all, and that therefore he saw no reason to trouble or excite himself. But his condescension never left him for an instant! Even during a long ramble before dinner about the wooded hills and valleys behind Soden, even when enjoying the beauties of nature, he treated nature itself with the same condescension, through which his habitual magisterial severity peeped out from time to time. So, for example, he observed in regard to one stream that it ran too straight through the glade, instead of making a few picturesque curves; he disapproved, too, of the conduct of a bird —a chaffinch—for singing so monotonously. Gemma was not bored, and even, apparently, was enjoying herself; but Sanin did not recognise her as the Gemma of the preceding days; it was not that she seemed under a cloud—her beauty had never been more dazzling—but her soul seemed to have withdrawn into herself. With her parasol open and her gloves still buttoned up, she walked sedately, deliberately, as well-bred young girls walk; and spoke little. Emil, too, felt stiff, and Sanin more so than all. He was somewhat embarrassed too by the fact that the conversation was all the time in German. Only Tartaglia was in high spirits! He darted, barking frantically, after blackbirds, leaped over ravines, stumps and roots, rushed headlong into the water, lapped at it in desperate haste, shook himself, whining, and was off like an arrow, his red tongue trailing after him almost to his shoulder. Herr Klüber, for his part, did everything he supposed conducive to the mirthfulness of the company; he begged them to sit down in the shade of a spreading oak-tree, and taking out of a side pocket a small booklet entitled, *'Knallerbsen; oder du sollst und wirst lachen!'*

(Squibs; or you must and shall laugh!) began reading the funny anecdotes of which the little book was full. He read them twelve specimens; he aroused very little mirth, however; only Sanin smiled, from politeness, and he himself, Herr Klüber, after each anecdote, gave vent to a brief, business-like, but still condescending laugh. At twelve o'clock the whole party returned to Soden to the best tavern there.

They had to make arrangements about dinner. Herr Klüber proposed that the dinner should be served in a summer-house closed in on all sides—'*im Gartensalon*'; but at this point Gemma rebelled and declared that she would have dinner in the open air, in the garden, at one of the little tables set before the tavern; that she was tired of being all the while with the same faces, and she wanted to see fresh ones. At some of the little tables, groups of visitors were already sitting.

While Herr Klüber, yielding condescendingly to 'the caprice of his betrothed,' went off to interview the head waiter, Gemma stood immovable, biting her lips and looking on the ground; she was conscious that Sanin was persistently and, as it were, inquiringly looking at her—it seemed to enrage her. At last Herr Klüber returned, announced that dinner would be ready in half an hour, and proposed their employing the interval in a game of skittles, adding that this was very good for the appetite, he, he, he! Skittles he played in masterly fashion; as he threw the ball, he put himselt into amazingly heroic postures, with artistic play of the muscles, with artistic flourish and shake of the leg. In his own way he was an athlete—and was superbly built! His hands, too, were so white and handsome, and he wiped them on such a sumptuous, gold-striped. Indian bandana!

The moment of dinner arrived, and the whole party seated themselves at the table.

XVI

WHO does not know what a German dinner is like? Watery soup with knobby dumplings and pieces of cinnamon, boiled beef dry as cork, with white fat attached, slimy potatoes, soft beetroot and mashed horseradish, a bluish eel with French capers and vinegar, a roast joint with jam, and the inevitable '*Mehlspeise*,' something of the nature of a pudding with sourish red sauce; but to make up, the beer and wine first-rate! With just such a dinner the tavern-keeper at Soden en regaled his customers. The dinner, itself, however, went off satisfactorily. No special liveliness was perceptible, certainly; not even when Herr Klüber proposed the toast 'What we like!' (Was wir lieben!) But at least everything was decorous and seemly. After dinner, coffee was served, thin, reddish, typically German coffee. Herr Klüber, with true gallantry, asked Gemma's permission to smoke a cigar. . . . But at this point suddenly something occurred, unexpected, and decidedly unpleasant, and even unseemly!

At one of the tables near were sitting several officers of the garrison of the Maine. From their glances and whispering together it was easy to perceive that they were struck by Gemma's beauty; one of them, who had probably stayed in Frankfort, stared at her persistently, as at a figure familiar to him; he obviously knew who she was. He suddenly got up, and glass in hand—all the officers had been drinking hard, and the cloth before them was crowded with bottles—approached the table at which Gemma was sitting. He was a very young flaxen-haired man, with a rather pleasing and even attractive face, but his features were distorted with the wine he had drunk, his cheeks were twitching, his blood-shot eyes wandered, and wore an insolent expression. His companions at first tried to hold him back, but afterwards let him go, interested apparently to see what he would do, and how it would end. Slightly unsteady on his legs, the officer stopped before Gemma, and in an unnaturally screaming voice, in which, in spite of himself, an inward struggle could be discerned, he articulated, 'I drink to the health of the prettiest confectioner in all Frankfort, in all the world (he emptied his glass), and in return I take this flower, picked by her divine little fingers!' He took from the table a rose that lay beside Gemma's plate. At first she was astonished, alarmed, and turned fearfully white . . . then alarm was replaced by indignation; she suddenly crimsoned all over, to her very hair—and her eyes, fastened directly on the offender, at the same time darkened and flamed, they were filled with black gloom, and burned with the fire of irrepressible fury. The officer must have been confused by this look; he muttered something unintelligible, bowed, and walked back to his friends. They greeted him with a laugh, and faint applause.

Herr Klüber rose spasmodically from his seat, drew himself up to his full height, and putting on his hat pronounced with dignity, but not too loud, 'Unheard of! Unheard of! Unheard of impertinence!' and at once calling up the waiter, in a severe voice asked for the bill . . . more than that, ordered the carriage to be put to, adding that it was impossible for respectable people to frequent the establishment if they were exposed to insult! At those words Gemma, who still sat in her place without stirring—her bosom was heaving violently—Gemma raised her eyes to Herr Klüber . . . and she gazed as intently, with the same expression at him as at the officer. Emil was simply shaking with rage.

'Get up, *mein Fräulein*,' Klüber admonished her with the same severity, 'it is not proper for you to remain here. We will go inside, in the tavern!'

Gemma rose in silence; he offered her his arm, she gave him hers, and he walked into the tavern with a majestic step, which became, with his whole bearing, more majestic and haughty the farther he got from the place where they had dined. Poor Emil dragged himself after them.

But while Herr Klüber was settling up with the waiter, to whom, by way of punishment, he gave not a single kreutzer for himself, Sanin with rapid steps approached the table at which the officers were sitting, and addressing Gemma's assailant, who was at that instant offering her rose to his companions in turns to smell, he uttered very distinctly in French, 'What you have just done, sir, is conduct unworthy of an honest man, unworthy of the uniform you wear, and I have come to tell you you are an ill-bred cur!' The young man leaped on to his feet, but another officer, rather older, checked him with a gesture, made him sit down, and turning to Sanin asked him also in French, 'Was he a relation, brother, or betrothed of the girl?'

'I am nothing to her at all,' cried Sanin, 'I am a Russian, but I cannot look on at such insolence with indifference; but here is my card and my address; *monsieur l'officier* can find me.'

As he uttered these words, Sanin threw his visiting-card on the table, and at the same moment hastily snatched Gemma's rose, which one of the officers sitting at the table had dropped into his plate. The young man was again on the point of jumping up from the table, but his companion again checked him, saying, 'Dönhof, be quiet! Dönhof, sit still.' Then he got up himself, and putting his hand to the peak of his cap, with a certain shade of respectfulness in his voice and manner, told Sanin that to-morrow morning an officer of the regiment would have the honour of calling upon him. Sanin replied with a short bow, and hurriedly returned to his friends.

Herr Klüber pretended he had not noticed either Sanin's absence nor his interview with the officers; he was urging on the coachman, who was putting in the horses, and was furiously angry at his deliberateness. Gemma too said nothing to Sanin, she did not even look at him; from her knitted brows, from her pale and compressed lips, from her very immobility it could be seen that she was suffering inwardly. Only Emil obviously wanted to speak to Sanin, wanted to question him; he had seen Sanin go up to the officers, he had seen him give them something white—a scrap of paper, a note, or a card. . . . The poor boy's heart was beating, his cheeks burned, he was ready to throw himself on Sanin's neck, ready to cry, or to go with him at once to crush all those accursed officers into dust and ashes! He controlled himself, however, and did no more than watch intently every movement of his noble Russian friend.

The coachman had at last harnessed the horses; the whole party seated themselves in the carriage. Emil climbed on to the box, after Tartaglia; he was more comfortable there, and had not Klüber, whom he could hardly bear the sight of, sitting opposite to him.

The whole way home Herr Klüber discoursed . . . and he discoursed alone; no one, absolutely no one, opposed him, nor did any one agree with him. He especially insisted on the point that they had been wrong in not following his advice when he suggested dining in a shut-up summer-house. There no unpleasantness could have occurred! Then he expressed a few decided and even liberal sentiments on the unpardonable way in which the government favoured the military, neglected their discipline, and did not sufficiently consider the civilian element in society (*das bürgerliche Element in der Societät!*), and foretold that in time this cause would give rise to discontent, which might well pass into revolution, of which (here he dropped a sympathetic though severe sigh) France had given them a sorrowful example! He added, however, that he personally had the greatest respect for authority, and never . . . no, never! . . . could be a revolutionist—but he could not but express his . . . disapprobation at the sight of such licence! Then he made a few general observations on morality and immorality, good-breeding, and the sense of dignity.

During all these lucubrations, Gemma, who even while they were walking before dinner had not seemed quite pleased with Herr Klüber, and had therefore held rather aloof from Sanin, and had been, as it were, embarrassed by his presence—Gemma was unmistakably ashamed of her betrothed! Towards the end of the drive she was positively wretched, and though, as before, she did not address a word to Sanin, she suddenly flung an imploring glance at him . . . . He, for his part, felt much more sorry for her than indignant with Herr Klüber; he was even secretly, half-consciously, delighted at what had happened in the course of that day, even though he had every reason to expect a challenge next morning.

This miserable *partie de plaisir* came to an end at last. As he helped Gemma out of the carriage at the confectionery shop, Sanin without a word put into her hand the rose he had recovered. She flushed crimson, pressed his hand, and instantly hid the rose. He did not want to go into the house, though the evening was only just beginning. She did not even invite him. Moreover Pantaleone, who came out on the steps, announced that Frau Lenore was asleep. Emil took a shy good-bye of Sanin; he felt as it were in awe of him; he greatly admired him. Klüber saw Sanin to his lodging, and took leave of him stiffly. The well-regulated German, for all his self-confidence, felt awkward. And indeed every one felt awkward.

But in Sanin this feeling of awkwardness soon passed off. It was replaced by a vague, but pleasant, even triumphant feeling. He walked up and down his room, whistling, and not caring to think about anything, and was very well pleased with himself.

XVII

'I WILL wait for the officer's visit till ten o'clock,' he reflected next morning, as he dressed, 'and then let him come and look for me!' But Germans rise early: it had not yet struck nine when the waiter informed Sanin that the Herr Seconde Lieutenant von Richter wished to see him. Sanin made haste to put on his coat, and told him to ask him up. Herr Richter turned out, contrary to Sanin's expectation, to be a very young man, almost a boy. He tried to give an expression of dignity to his beardless face, but did not succeed at all: he could not even conceal his embarrassment, and as he sat down on a chair, he tripped over his sword, and almost fell. Stammering and hesitating, he announced to Sanin in bad French that he had come with a message from his friend, Baron von Dönhof; that this message was to demand from Herr von Sanin an apology for the insulting expressions used by him on the previous day; and in case of refusal on the part of Herr von Sanin, Baron von Dönhof would ask for satisfaction. Sanin replied that he did not mean to apologise, but was ready to give him satisfaction. Then Herr von Richter, still with the same hesitation, asked with whom, at what time and place, should he arrange the necessary preliminaries. Sanin answered that he might come to him in two hours 'time, and that meanwhile, he, Sanin, would try and find a second. ('Who the devil is there I can have for a second?' he was thinking to himself meantime.) Herr von Richter got up and began to take leave . . . but at the doorway he stopped, as though stung by a prick of conscience, and turning to Sanin observed that his friend, Baron von Dönhof, could not but recognise. . . . that he had been . . . to a certain extent, to blame himself in the incident of the previous day, and would, therefore, be satisfied with slight apologies (*'des exghizes léchères.'*) To this Sanin replied that he did not intend to make any apology whatever, either slight or considerable, since he did not consider himself to blame. 'In that case,' answered Herr von Richter, blushing more than ever, 'you will have to exchange friendly shots —*des goups de bisdolet à l'amiaple!'*

'I don't understand that at all,' observed Sanin; 'are we to fire in the air or what?'

'Oh, not exactly that,' stammered the sub-lieutenant, utterly disconcerted, 'but I supposed since it is an affair between men of honour . . . I will talk to your second,' he broke off, and went away.

Sanin dropped into a chair directly he had gone, and stared at the floor. 'What does it all mean? How is it my life has taken such a turn all of a sudden? All the past, all the future has suddenly vanished, gone,—and all that's left is that I am going to fight some one about something in Frankfort.' He recalled a crazy aunt of his who used to dance and sing:

> 'O my lieutenant!
> My little cucumber!
> My little love!
> Dance with me, my little dove!'

And he laughed and hummed as she used to: 'O my lieutenant! Dance with me, little dove!' 'But I must act, though, I mustn't waste time,' he cried aloud—jumped up and saw Pantaleone facing him with a note in his hand.

''I knocked several times, but you did not answer; I thought you weren't at home,' said the old man, as he gave him the note. 'From Signorina Gemma.'

Sanin took the note, mechanically, as they say, tore it open, and read it. Gemma wrote to him that she was very anxious—about he knew what—and would be very glad to see him at once.

'The Signorina is anxious,' began Pantaleone, who obviously knew what was in the note, 'she told me to see what you are doing and to bring you to her.'

Sanin glanced at the old Italian, and pondered. A sudden idea flashed upon his brain. For the first instant it struck him as too absurd to be possible.

'After all . . . why not?' he asked himself.

'M. Pantaleone!' he said aloud.

The old man started, tucked his chin into his cravat and stared at Sanin.

'Do you know,' pursued Sanin, 'what happened yesterday?'

Pantaleone chewed his lips and shook his immense top-knot of hair. 'Yes.'

(Emil had told him all about it directly he got home.)

'Oh, you know! Well, an officer has just this minute left me. That scoundrel challenges me to a duel. I have accepted his challenge. But I have no second. Will *you* be my second?'

Pantaleone started and raised his eyebrows

so high that they were lost under his overhanging hair.

'You are absolutely obliged to fight?' he said at last in Italian; till that instant he had made use of French.

'Absolutely. I can't do otherwise—it would mean disgracing myself for ever.'

'H'm. If I don't consent to be your second you will find some one else.'

'Yes . . . undoubtedly.'

Pantaleone looked down. 'But allow me to ask you, Signor de Tsanin, will not your duel throw a slur on the reputation of a certain lady?'

'I don't suppose so; but in any case, there's no help for it.'

'H'm!' Pantaleone retired altogether into his cravat. 'Hey, but that *ferroflucto Klüberio*—what's he about?' he cried all of a sudden, looking up again.

'He? Nothing.'

'*Che!*' Pantaleone shrugged his shoulders contemptuously. 'I have, in any case, to thank you,' he articulated at last in an unsteady voice 'that even in my present humble condition you recognise that I am a gentleman—*un galant'uomo*! In that way you have shown yourself to be a real *galant'uomo*. But I must consider your proposal.'

'There's no time to lose, dear Signor Ci . . . cippa . . .'

'Tola,' the old man chimed in. 'I ask only for one hour for reflection. . . . The daughter of my benefactor is involved in this. . . . And, therefore, I ought, I am bound, to reflect! . . . In an hour, in three-quarters of an hour, you shall know my decision.'

'Very well; I will wait.'

'And now . . . what answer am I to give to Signorina Gemma?'

Sanin took a sheet of paper, wrote on it, 'Set your mind at rest, dear friend; in three hours' time I will come to you, and everything shall be explained. I thank you from my heart for your sympathy,' and handed this sheet to Pantaleone.

He put it carefully into his side-pocket, and once more repeating 'In an hour!' made towards the door; but turning sharply back, ran up to Sanin, seized his hand, and pressing it to his shirt-front, cried, with his eyes to the ceiling: 'Noble youth! Great heart! (*Nobil gwvanotto! Gran cuore!*) permit a weak old man (*a un vecchiotto!*) to press your valorous right hand (*la vostra valorosa destra!*)' Then he skipped back a pace or two, threw up both hands, and went away.

Sanin looked after him. took up the

news paper and tried to read. But his eyes wandered in vain over the lines: he understood nothing.

XVIII

AN hour later the waiter came in again to Sanin, and handed him an old, soiled visiting-card, on which were the following words: 'Pantaleone Cippatola of Varese, court singer (*cantante di camera*) to his Royal Highness the Duke of Modena'; and behind the waiter in walked Pantaleone himself. He had changed his clothes from top to toe. He had on a black frock coat, reddish with long wear, and a white piqué waistcoat, upon which a pinchbeck chain meandered playfully; a heavy cornelian seal hung low down on to his narrow black trousers. In his right hand he carried a black beaver hat, in his left two stout chamois gloves; he had tied his cravat in a taller and broader bow than ever, and had stuck into his starched shirt-front a pin with a stone, a so-called 'cat's eye.' On his forefinger was displayed a ring, consisting of two clasped hands with a burning heart between them. A smell of garments long laid by, a smell of camphor and of musk hung about the whole person of the old man; the anxious solemnity of his deportment must have struck the most casual spectator! Sanin rose to meet him.

'I am your second,' Pantaleone announced in French, and he bowed bending his whole body forward, and turning out his toes like a dancer. 'I have come for instructions. Do you want to fight to the death?'

'Why to the death, my dear Signor Cippatola? I will not for any consideration take back my words—but I am not a bloodthirsty person! . . . But come, wait a little, my opponent's second will be here directly. I will go into the next room, and you can make arrangements with him. Believe me I shall never forget your kindness, and I thank you from my heart'

'Honour before everything!' answered Pantaleone, and he sank into an arm-chair, without waiting for Sanin to ask him to sit down. 'If that *ferroflucto spitchebubbio*,' he said, passing from French into Italian,'if that counter-jumper Klüberio could not appreciate his obvious duty or was afraid, so much the worse for him! . . . A cheap soul, and that's all about it! . . . As for the conditions of the duel, I am your second, and your interests are sacred to me! . . . When I lived in Padua there was. a regiment of the white dragoons stationed there, and I was very intimate with many of the officers! . . . I was quite familiar with their whole code. And I used often to converse on these subjects with your principe Tarbuski too. . . . Is this second to come soon?'

'I am expecting him every minute—and here he comes,' added Sanin, looking into the street.

Pantaleone got up, looked at his watch, straightened his topknot of hair, and hurriedly stuffed into his shoe an end of tape which was sticking out below his trouser-leg, and the young sub-lieutenant came in, as red and embarrassed as ever.

Sanin presented the seconds to each other. 'M. Richter, sous-lieutenant, M. Cippatola, artiste!' The sub-lieutenant was slightly disconcerted by the old man's appearance . . . Oh, what would he have said had any one whispered to him at that instant that the 'artist' presented to him was also employed in the culinary art! But Pantaleone assumed an air as though taking part in the preliminaries of duels was for him the most everyday affair: probably he was assisted at this juncture by the recollections of his theatrical career, and he played the part of second simply as a part Both he and the sub-lieutenant were silent for a little.

'Well? Let us come to business!' Pantaleone spoke first, playing with his cornelian seal.

'By all means,' responded the sub-lieutenant, 'but . . . the presence of one of the principals . . .'

'I will leave you at once, gentlemen,' cried Sanin, and with a bow he went away into the bedroom and closed the door after him.

He flung himself on the bed and began thinking of Gemma . . . but the conversation of the seconds reached him through the shut door. It was conducted in the French language; both maltreated it mercilessly, each after his own fashion. Pantaleone again alluded to the dragoons in Padua, and Principe Tarbuski; the sub-lieutenant to *'exghizes léchères'* and *'goups de bistolet à l'amiaple.'* But the old man would not even hear of any *exghizes*! To Sanin's horror, he suddenly proceeded to talk of a certain young lady, an innocent maiden, whose little finger was worth more than all the officers in the world . . . (*oune zeune damigella innoucenta, qu'a elle sola dans soun péti doa vale piu que tout le zouffissié del mondo!*), and repeated several times with heat: 'It's shameful! it's shameful!' (*E ouna onta, ouna onta!*) The sub-lieutenant at first made him no reply, but presently an angry quiver could be heard in the young man's voice, and he observed that he had not come there to listen to sermonising.

'At your age it is always a good thing to hear the truth!' cried Pantaleone.

The debate between the seconds several times became stormy; it lasted over an hour, and was concluded at last on the following conditions: 'Baron von Dönhof and M. de Sanin to meet the next day at ten o'clock in a small wood near Hanau, at the distance of twenty paces; each to have the right to fire twice at a signal given by the seconds, The pistols to be single-triggered and not rifle-barrelled.' Herr von Richter withdrew, and Pantaleone solemnly opened the bedroom door, and after communicating the result of their deliberations, cried again: '*Bravo Russo! Bravo giovanotto!* You will be victor!'

A few minutes later they both set off to the Rosellis' Shop Sanin, as a preliminary measure, had exacted a promise from Pantaleone to keep the affair of the duel a most profound secret. In reply, the old man had merely held up his finger, and half closing his eyes, whispered twice over, *Segredezza!* He was obviously in good spirits, and even walked with a freer step. All these unusual incidents, unpleasant though they might be, carried him vividly back to the time when he himself both received and gave challenges—only, it is true, on the stage. Baritones, as we all know, have a great deal of strutting and fuming to do in their parts.

XIX

EMIL ran out to meet Sanin—he had been watching for his arrival over an hour—and hurriedly whispered into his ear that his mother knew nothing of the disagreeable incident of the day before, that he must not even hint of it to her, and that he was being sent to Klüber's shop again! . . . but that he wouldn't go there, but would hide somewhere! Communicating all this information in a few seconds, he suddenly fell on Sanin's shoulder, kissed him impulsively, and rushed away down the street. Gemma met Sanin in the shop; tried to say something and could not. Her lips were trembling a little, while her eyes were half-closed and turned away. He made haste to soothe her by the assurance that the whole affair had ended . . . in utter nonsense.

'Has no one been to see you to-day?' she asked.

'A person did come to me and we had an explanation, and we . . . we came to the most satisfactory conclusion.'

Gemma went back behind the counter.

'She does not believe me!' he thoquciklyught . . . he went into the next room, however, and there found Frau Lenore.

Her sick headache had passed off but she was in a depressed state of mind. She gave him a smlie of welcome but warned him at the same time that he would be dull with her to-day as she was not in a mood to entertain him. He sat down beside her, and noticed that her eyelids were red and swollen.

'What is wrong Frau Lenore? You've never been crying surely?

'Oh!' she whispered, nodding her head towards the romm where her daughter was 'Dont' speak of it . . . aloud.'

'But what have you been crying for?'

'Ah M'sieu Sanin I don't know myself what for!'

'No one has hurt your feelings?'

'Oh no! . . . I felt very low all of a sudden. I thought of Givovanni Battista . . . of my youth . . . Then how quickly low all passed away I have grown old my frind, and I can't reconcil myself to that anyhow . I feel I'm just the same I was . . . but old age—it's here! it is here!' Tears came into Frau Lenore's eyes. 'You look at me I see and wonder. . . . But you will get old too my friend and will find out how bitter it is!'

Sanin tried to comfort her spoke of her childern in whow her own youth lived again, even attempted to scoff at her a little declaring that she was fishing for compliments . . . but she quite seriously begged him to leave off, and for the first time he realised that for such a sorrow, the despondency of old age, there is no comfort or cure; one has to wait till it passes off of itself. He proposed a game of tresette, and he could have thought of nothing better. She agreed at once and seemed to get more cheerful.

Sanin played with her until dinner-time and after dinner Pantaleone too took a hand in the game. Never had his topknot hung so low over his forehead, never had his chin retreated so far into his cravat! Every movement was accompanied by such intense solemnity that as one looked at him the thought involuntarily arose, 'What secret is that man guarding with such determination?' But *segredezza! segredezza!*

During the whole of that day he tried in every possible way to show the profoundest respect for Sanin; at table, passing by the ladies, he solemnly and sedately handed the dishes first to him; when they were at cards he intentionally gave him the game; he announced, apropos of nothing at all, that the Russians were the most great-hearted, brave, and resolute people in the world!

'Ah, you old flatterer!' Sanin thought to himself.

And he was not so much surprised at Signora Roselli's unexpected state of mind, as at the way her daughter behaved to him. It was not that she avoided him . . . on the contrary she sat continually a little distance from him, listened to what he said, and looked at him; but she absolutely declined to get into conversation with him, and directly he began talking to her, she softly rose from her place, and went out for some instants. Then she came in again, and again seated herself in some corner, and sat without stirring, seeming meditative and perplexed . . . perplexed above all. Frau Lenore herself noticed at last, that she was not as usual, and asked her twice what was the matter.

'Nothing,' answered Gemma; 'you know I am sometimes like this,'

'That is true,' her mother assented.

So passed all that long day, neither gaily nor drearily—neither cheerfully nor sadly. Had Gemma been different—Sanin . . . who knows? . . . might not perhaps have been able to resist the temptation for a little display—or he might simply have succumbed to melancholy at the possibility of a separation for ever. . . . But as he did not once succeed in getting a word with Gemma, he was obliged to confine himself to striking minor chords on the piano for a quarter of an hour before evening coffee.

Emil came home late, and to avoid questions about Herr Klüber, beat a hasty retreat. The time came for Sanin too to retire.

He began saying good-bye to Gemma. He recollected for some reason Lensky's parting from Olga in *Oniegin*. He pressed her hand warmly, and tried to get a look at her face, but she turned a little away and released her fingers.

XX

It was bright starlight when he came out on the steps. What multitudes of stars, big and little, yellow, red, blue and white were scattered over the sky! They seemed all flashing, swarming, twinkling unceasingly. There was no moon in the sky, but without it every object could be clearly discerned in the half-clear, shadowless twilight. Sanin walked down the street to the end . . . He did not want to go home at once; he felt a desire to wander about a little in the fresh air. He turned back and had hardly got on a level with the house, where was the Rosellis' shop, when one of the windows looking out on the street, suddenly creaked and opened; in its square of blackness—there was no light in the room—appeared a woman's figure, and he heard his name—'Monsieur Dimitri!'

He rushed at once up to the window . . . Gemma! She was leaning with her elbows on the window-sill, bending forward.

'Monsieur Dimitri,' she began in a cautious voice, 'I have been wanting all day long to give you something . . . but I could not make up my mind to; and just now, seeing you, quite unexpectedly again, I thought that it seems it is fated' . . .

Gemma was forced to stop at this word. She could not go on; something extraordinary happened at that instant.

All of a sudden, in the midst of the profound stillness, over the perfectly unclouded sky, there blew such a violent blast of wind, that the very earth seemed shaking underfoot, the delicate starlight seemed quivering and trembling, the air went round in a whirlwind. The wind, not cold, but hot, almost sultry, smote against the trees, the roof of the house, its walls, and the street; it instantaneously snatched off Sanin's hat, crumpled up and tangled Gemma's curls. Sanin's head was on a level with the window-sill; he could not help clinging close to it, and Gemma clutched hold of his shoulders with both hands, and pressed her bosom against his head. The roar, the din, and the rattle lasted about a minute. . . . Like a flock of huge birds the revelling whirlwind darted reveiling away. A profound stillness reigned once more.

Sanin raised his head and saw above him such an exquisite, scared, excited face, such immense, large, magnificent eyes—it was such a beautiful creature he saw, that his heart stood still within him, he pressed his lips to the delicate tress of hair, that had fallen on his bosom, and could only murmur, 'O Gemma!'

'What was that? Lightning?' she asked, her eyes wandering afar, while she did not take her bare arms from his shoulder.

'Gemma!' repeated Sanin.

She sighed, looked around behind her into the room, and with a rapid movement pulling the now faded rose out of her bodice, she threw it to Sanin.

'I wanted to give you this flower.'

He recognised the rose, which he had won back the day before. . . .

But already the window had slammed-to, and through the dark pane nothing could be seen, no trace of white.

Sanin went home without his hat. . . . He did not even notice that he had lost it.

XXI

It was quite morning when he fell asleep. And no wonder! In the blast of that instantaneous summer hurricane, he had almost as instantaneously felt, not that Gemma was lovely, not that he liked her—that he had known before . . . but that he almost . . . loved her! As suddenly as that blast of wind, had love pounced down upon him. And then this senseless duel! He began to be tormented by mournful forebodings. And even suppose they didn't kill him. . . . What could come of his love for this girl, another man's betrothed? Even supposing this 'other man' was no danger, that Gemma herself would care for him, or even cared for him already . . . What would come of it? How ask what! Such a lovely creature! . . .

He walked about the room, sat down to the table, took a sheet of paper, traced a few lines on it, and at once blotted them out. . . . He recalled Gemma's wonderful figure in the dark window, in the starlight, set all a-fluttering by the warm hurricane; he remembered her marble arms, like the arms of the Olympian goddesses, felt their living weight on his shoulders. . . . Then he took the rose she had thrown him, and it seemed to him that its half-withered petals exhaled a fragrance of her, more delicate than the ordinary scent of the rose.

'And would they kill him straight away or maim him?'

He did not go to bed, and fell asleep in his clothes on the sofa.

Some one slapped him on the shoulder. . . . He opened his eyes, and saw Pantaleone.

'He sleeps like Alexander of Macedon on the eve of the battle of Babylon!' cried the old man.

'What o'clock is it?' inquired Sanin.

'A quarter to seven; it's a two hours' drive to Hanau, and we must be the first on the field. Russians are always beforehand with their enemies! I have engaged the best carriage in Frankfort!'

Sanin began washing. 'And where are the pistols?'

'That *ferroflucto Tedesco* will bring the pistols. He'll bring a doctor too.'

Pantaleone was obviously putting a good face on it as he had done the day before; but when he was seated in the carriage with Sanin, when the coachman had cracked his whip and the horses had started off at a gallop, a sudden change came over the old singer and friend of Paduan dragoons. He began to be confused and positively faint-hearted. Something seemed to have given way in him, like a badly built wall.

'What are we doing, my God, *Santissima Madonna!*' he cried in an unexpectedly high pipe, and he clutched at his head. 'What am I about, old fool, madman, *frenetico?*'

Sanin wondered and laughed, and putting his arm lightly round Pantaleone's waist, he reminded him of the French proverb: *'Le vin est tiré—il faut le boire.'*

'Yes, yes,' answered the old man, 'we will drain the cup together to the dregs—but still I'm a madman! I'm a madman! All was going on so quietly, so well . . . and all of a sudden: ta-ta-ta, tra-ta-ta!'

'Like the *tutti* in the orchestra,' observed Sanin with a forced smile. 'But it's not your fault.'

'I know it's not. I should think not indeed! And yet . . . such insolent conduct! *Diavolo, diavolo!*' repeated Pantaleone, sighing and shaking his topknot.

The carriage still rolled on and on.

It was an exquisite morning. The streets of Frankfort, which were just beginning to show signs of life, looked so clean and snug; the windows of the houses glittered in flashes like tinfoil; and as soon as the carriage had driven beyond the city walls, from overhead, from a blue but not yet glaring sky, the larks' loud trills showered down in floods. Suddenly at a turn in the road, a familiar figure came from behind a tall poplar, took a few steps forward and stood still. Sanin looked more closely.... Heavens! it was Emil!

'But does he know anything about it?' he demanded of Pantaleone.

'I tell you I'm a madman,' the poor Italian wailed despairingly, almost in a shriek. 'The wretched boy gave me no peace all night, and this morning at last I revealed all to him!'

'So much for your *segredezza*!' thought Sanin. The carriage had got up to Emil. Sanin told the coachman to stop the horses, and called the 'wretched boy' up to him. Emil approached with hesitating steps, pale as he had been on the day he fainted. He could scarcely stand.

'What are you doing here?' Sanin asked him sternly. 'Why aren't you at home?'

'Let . . . let me come with you,' faltered Emil in a trembling voice, and he clasped his hands. His teeth were chattering as in a fever. 'I won't get in your way—only take me.'

'If you feel the very slightest affection or respect for me,' said Sanin, 'you will go at mice home or to Herr Klüber's shop, and you won't say one word to any one, and will wait for my return!'

'Your return,' moaned Emil—and his voice quivered and broke, 'but if you're——'

'Emil!' Sanin interrupted—and he pointed to the coachman,' do control yourself! Emil, please, go home! Listen to me, my dear! You say you love me. Well, I beg you!' He held out his hand to him. Emil bent forward, sobbed, pressed it to his lips, and darting away from the road, ran back towards Frankfort across country.

'A noble heart too,' muttered Pantaleone; but Sanin glanced severely at him. . . . The old man shrank into the corner of the carriage. He was conscious of his fault; and moreover, he felt more and more bewildered every instant; could it really be he who was acting as second, who had got horses, and had made all arrangements, and had left his peaceful abode at six o'clock? Besides, his legs were stiff and aching.

Sanin thought it as well to cheer him up, and he chanced on the very thing, he hit on the right word.

'Where is your old spirit, Signor Cippatola? Where is *il antico valor*?'

SignorCippatola drew himself up and scowled '*Il antico valor?*' he boomed in a bass voice. '*Non è ancora spnfo* (it's not all lost yet), *il antico valor!*

He put himself in a dignified attitude, began talking of his. career, of the opera, of the great tenor Garcia—and arrived at Hanau a hero.

After all, if you think of it, nothing is stronger in the world . . . and weaker—than a word!

XXII

THE copse in which the duel was to take place was a quarter of a mile from Hanau. Sanin and Pantaleone arrived there first, as the latter had predicted; they gave orders for the carriage to remain outside the wood, and they plunged into the shade of the rather thick and close-growing trees. They had to wait about an hour.

The time of waiting did not seem particularly disagreeable to Sanin; he walked up and down the path, listened to the birds singing, watched the dragonflies in their flight, and like the majority of Russians in similar circumstances, tried not to think. He only once dropped into reflection; he came across a young lime-tree, broken down, in all probability by the squall of the previous night. It was unmistakably dying . . . all the leaves on it were dead. 'What is it? an omen?' was the thought that flashed across his mind; but he promptly began whistling, leaped over the very tree, and paced up and down the path. As for Pantaleone, he was grumbling, abusing the Germans, sighing and moaning, rubbing first his back and then his knees. He even yawned from agitation, which gave a very comic expression to his tiny shrivelled-up face. Sanin could scarcely help laughing when he looked at him.

They heard, at last, the rolling of wheels along the soft road. 'It's they!' said Pantaleone, and he was on the alert and drew himself up, not without a momentary nervous shiver, which he made haste, however, to cover with the ejaculation 'B-r-r!' and the remark that the morning was rather fresh. A heavy dew drenched the grass and leaves, but the sultry heat penetrated even into the wood.

Both the officers quickly made their appearance under its arched avenues; they were accompanied by a little thick-set man, with a phlegmatic, almost sleepy, expression of face—the army doctor. He carried in one hand an earthenware pitcher of water—to be ready for any emergency; a satchel with surgical instruments and bandages hung on his left shoulder. It was obvious that he was thoroughly used to such excursions; they constituted one of the sources of his income; each duel yielded him eight gold crowns—four from each of the combatants. Herr von Richter carried a case of pistols, Herr von Dönhof—probably considering it the thing—was swinging in his hand a little cane.

'Pantaleone!' San in whispered to the old man; 'if . . . if I'm killed—anything may happen—take out of my side pocket a paper—there's a flower wrapped up in it—and give the paper to Signorina Gemma. Do you hear? You promise?'

The old man looked dejectedly at him, and nodded his head affirmatively. . . . But God knows whether he understood what Sanin was asking him to do.

The combatants and the seconds exchanged the customary bows; the doctor alone did not move as much as an eyelash; he sat down yawning on the grass, as much as to say, 'I'm not here for expressions of chivalrous courtesy.' Herr von Richter proposed to Herr 'Tshibadola' that he should select the place; Herr 'Tshibadola' responded, moving his tongue with difficulty—' the wall' within him had completely given way again. 'You act, my dear sir; I will watch. . . .'

And Herr von Richter proceeded to act He picked out in the wood close by a very pretty clearing all studded with flowers; he measured out the steps, and marked the two extreme points with sticks, which he cut and pointed. He took the pistols out of the case, and squatting on his heels, he rammed in the bullets; in short, he fussed about and exerted himself to the utmost, continually mopping his perspiring brow with a white handkerchief. Pantaleone, who accompanied him, was more like a man frozen. During all these preparations, the two principals stood at a little distance, looking like two schoolboys who have been punished, and are sulky with their tutors.

The decisive moment arrived. . . . 'Each took his pistol. . . .'

But at this point Herr von Richter observed to Pantaleone that it was his duty, as the senior second, according to the rules of the duel, to address a final word of advice and exhortation to be reconciled to the combatants, before uttering the fatal 'one! two! three!'; that although this exhortation had no effect of any sort and was, as a rule, nothing but an empty formality, still, by the performance of this Formality, Herr Cippatola would be rid of a certain share of responsibility; that, properly speaking, such an admonition formed the direct duty of the so-called 'impartial witness' (*unpartheiischer Zeuge*), but since they had no such person present, he, Herr von Richter, would readily yield this privilege to his honoured colleague. Pantaleone, who had already succeeded in obliterating himself behind a bush, so as not to see the offending officer at all, at first made out nothing at all of Herr von Richter's speech, especially, as it had been delivered through the nose, but all of a sudden he started, stepped hurriedly forward, and convulsively thumping at his chest, in a hoarse voice wailed out in his mixed jargon '*A la la la . . . Che bestialita! Deux zeun ommes comme ça que si battono—perchè? Che diavolo? Andata a casa!*'

'I will not consent to a reconciliation,' Sanin intervened hurriedly.

'And I too will not,' his opponent repeated after him.

'Well, then shout one, two, three!' von Richter said, addressing the distracted Pantaleone.

The latter promptly ducked behind the bush again, and from there, all huddled together, his eyes screwed up, and his head turned away, he shouted at the top of his voice: '*Una . . . due . . . tre!*'

The first shot was Sanin's, and he missed. His bullet went ping against a tree. Baron von Dönhof shot directly after him—intentionally, to one side, into the air.

A constrained silence followed. . . . No one moved. Pantaleone uttered a faint moan.

'Is it your wish to go on?' said Dönhof.

'Why did you shoot in the air?' inquired Sanin.

'That's nothing to do with you.'

'Will you shoot in the air the second time?' Sanin asked again.

'Possibly: I don't know.'

'Excuse me, excuse me, gentlemen . . .' began von Richter; 'duellists have not the right to talk together. That's out of order.'

'I decline my shot,' said Sanin, and he threw his pistol on the ground.

'And I too do not intend to go on with the duel,' cried Dönhof, and he too threw his pistol on the ground. 'And more than that, I am prepared to own that I was in the wrong—the day before yesterday.'

He moved uneasily, and hesitatingly held out his hand. Sanin went rapidly up to him and shook it. Both the young men looked at each other with a smile, and both their faces flushed crimson.

'*Bravi! bravi!*' Pantaleone roared suddenly as if he had gone mad, and clapping his hands, he rushed like a whirlwind from behind the bush; while the doctor, who had been sitting on one side on a felled tree, promptly rose, poured the water out of the jug and walked off with a lazy, rolling step out of the wood.

'Honour is satisfied, and the duel is over!' von Richter announced.

'*Fuori!*' Pantaleone boomed once more, through old associations.

When he had exchanged bows with the officers, and taken his seat in the carriage, Sanin certainly felt all over him, if not a sense of pleasure, at least a certain lightness of heart, as after an operation is over; but there was another feeling astir within him too, a feeling akin to shame. . . . The duel, in which he had just played his part, struck him as something false, a got-up formality, a common officers' and students' farce. He recalled the phlegmatic doctor he recalled how he had grinned, that is, wrinkled up his nose, when he saw him coming out of the wood almost arm-in-arm with Baron Dönhof. And afterwards when Pantaleone had paid him the four crowns due to him . . . Ah! there was something nasty about it!

Yes, Sanin was a little conscience-smitten and ashamed . . . though, on the other hand, what was there for him to have done? Could he have left the young officer's insolence unrebuked? could he have behaved like Herr Klüber? He had stood up for Gemma, he had championed her . . . that was so; and yet, there was an uneasy pang in his heart, and he was conscience-smitten, and even ashamed.

Not so Pantaleone—he was simply in his glory! He was suddenly possessed by a feeling of pride. A victorious general, returning from the field of battle he has won, could not have looked about him with greater self-satisfaction. Sanin's demeanour during the duel filled him with enthusiasm. He called him a hero, and would not listen to his exhortations and even his entreaties. He compared him to a monument of marble or of bronze, with the statue of the commander in Don Juan! For himself he admitted he had been conscious of some perturbation of mind, 'but, of course, I am an artist,' he observed; 'I have a highly-strung nature, while you are the son of the snows and the granite rocks.'

Sanin was positively at a loss how to quiet the jubilant artist.

Almost at the same place in the road where two hours before they had come upon Emil, he again jumped out from behind a tree, and, with a cry of joy upon his lips, waving his cap and leaping into the air, he rushed straight at the carriage, almost fell under the wheel, and, without waiting for the horses to stop, clambered up over the carriage-door and fairly clung to Sanin.

'You are alive, you are not wounded!' he kept repeating. 'Forgive me, I did not obey you, I did not go back to Frankfort . . . I could not! I waited for you here . . . Tell me how was it? You . . . killed him?'

Sanin with some difficulty pacified Emil and made him sit down.

With great verbosity, with evident pleasure, Pantaleone communicated to him all the details of the duel, and, of course, did not omit to refer again to the monument of bronze and the statue of the commander. He even rose from his seat and, standing with his feet wide apart to preserve his equilibrium, folding his arm on his chest and looking contemptuously over his shoulder, gave an ocular representation of the commander—Sanin! Emil listened with awe, occasionally interrupting the narrative with an exclamation, or swiftly getting up and as swiftly kissing his heroic friend.

The carriage wheels rumbled over the paved roads of Frankfort, and stopped at last before the hotel where Sanin was living.

Escorted by his two companions, he went up the stairs, when suddenly a woman came with hurried steps out of the dark corridor; her face was hidden by a veil, she stood still, facing Sanin, wavered a little, gave a trembling sigh, at once ran down into the street and vanished, to the great astonishment of the waiter, who explained that 'that lady had been for over an hour waiting for the return of the foreign gentleman.' Momentary as was the apparition, Sanin recognised Gemma. He recognised her eyes under the thick silk of her brown veil.

'Did Fräulein Gemma know, then?' . . . he said slowly in a displeased voice in German, addressing Emil and Pantaleone, who were following close on his heels.

Emil blushed and was confused.

'I was obliged to tell her all,' he faltered; 'she guessed, and I could not help it. . . . But now that's of no consequence,' he hurried to add eagerly, 'everything has ended so splendidly, and she has seen you well and uninjured!'

Sanin turned away.

'What a couple of chatterboxes you are!' he observed in a tone of annoyance, as he went into his room and sat down on a chair.

'Don't be angry, please,' Emil implored.

'Very well, I won't be angry'—(Sanin was not, in fact, angry—and, after all, he could hardly have desired that Gemma should know nothing about it). 'Very well . . . that's enough embracing. You get along now. I want to be alone. I'm going to sleep. I'm tired.'

'An excellent idea!' cried Pantaleone. 'You need repose! You have fully earned it, noble signor! Come along, Emilio! On tip-toe! On tip-toe! Sh—sh—sh!'

When he said he wanted to go to sleep, Sanin had simply wished to get rid of his companions; but when he was left alone, he was really aware of considerable weariness in all his limbs; he had hardly closed his eyes all the preceding night, and throwing himself on his bed he fell immediately into a sound sleep.

XXIII

He slept for some hours without waking. Then he began to dream that he was once more fighting a duel, that the antagonist standing facing him was Herr Klüber, and on a fir-tree was sitting a parrot, and this parrot was Pantaleone, and he kept tapping with his beak: one, one, one!

'One . . . one . . . one!' he heard the tapping too distinctly; he opened his eyes, raised his head . . . some one was knocking at his door.

'Come in!' called Sanin.

The waiter came in and answered that a lady very particularly wished to see him.

'Gemma!' flashed into his head . . . but the lady turned out to be her mother, Frau Lenore.

Directly she came in, she dropped at once into a chair and began to cry.

'What is the matter, my dear, good Madame Roselli?' began Sanin, sitting beside her and softly touching her hand. 'What has happened? calm yourself, I entreat you.'

'Ah, Herr Dimitri, I am very . . . very miserable!'

'You are miserable?'

'Ah, very! Could I have foreseen such a thing? All of a sudden, like thunder from a clear sky . . .'

She caught her breath.

'But what is it? Explain! Would you like a glass of water?'

'No, thank you.' Frau Lenore wiped her eyes with her handkerchief and began to cry with renewed energy. 'I know all, you see! All!'

'All? that is to say?'

'Everything that took place to-day! And

the cause . . . I know that too! You acted like an honourable man; but what an unfortunate combination of circumstances! I was quite right in not liking that excursion to Soden . . . quite right!' (Frau Lenore had said nothing of the sort on the day of the excursion, but she was convinced now that she had foreseen 'all' even then.) 'I have come to you as to an honourable man, as to a friend, though I only saw you for the first time five days ago. . . . But you know I am a widow, a lonely woman . . . My daughter . . .'

Tears choked Frau Lenore's voice. Sanin did not know what to think. 'Your daughter?' he repeated.

'My daughter, Gemma,' broke almost with a groan from Frau Lenore, behind the tear-soaked handkerchief, 'informed me to-day that she would not marry Herr Klüber, and that I must refuse him!'

Sanin positively started back a little; he had not expected that.

'I won't say anything now,' Frau Lenore went on, 'of the disgrace of it, of its being something unheard of in the world for a girl to jilt her betrothed; but you see it's ruin for us, Herr Dimitri!' Frau Lenore slowly and carefully twisted up her handkerchief in a tiny, tiny little ball, as though she would enclose all her grief within it. 'We can't go on living on the takings of our shop, Herr Dimitri! and Herr Klüber is very rich, and will be richer still. And what is he to be refused for? Because he did not defend his betrothed? Allowing that was not very handsome on his part, still, he's a civilian, has not had a university education, and as a solid business man, it was for him to look with contempt on the frivolous prank of some unknown little officer. And what sort of insult was it, after all, Herr Dimitri?'

'Excuse me, Frau Lenore, you seem to be blaming me.'

'I am not blaming you in the least, not in the least! You're quite another matter; you are, like all Russians, a military man . . .'

'Excuse me, I'm not at all . . .'

'You're a foreigner, a visitor, and I'm grateful to you,' Frau Lenore went on, not heeding Sanin. She sighed, waved her hands, unwound her handkerchief again, and blew her nose. Simply from the way in which her distress expressed itself, it could be seen that she had not been born under a northern sky.

'And how is Herr Klüber to look after his shop, if he is to fight with his customers? It's utterly inconsistent! And now I am to send him away! But what are we going to live on? At one time we were the only people that made angel cakes, and nougat of pistachio nuts, and we had plenty of customers; but now all the shops make angel cakes! Only consider; even without this, they cll talk in the town about your duel . . . it's impossible to keep it secret. And all of a sudden, the marriage broken off! It will be a scandal, a scandal! Gemma is a splendid girl, she loves me; but she's an obstinate republican, she doesn't care for the opinion of others. You're the only person that can persuade her!'

Sanin was more amazed than ever. 'I, Frau Lenore?'

'Yes, you alon . . . you alone. That's why I have come to you; I could not think of anything else to do! You are so clever, so good! You have fought in her defence. She will trust you! She is bound to trust you—why, you have risked your life on her account! You will make her understand, for I can do nothing more; you make her understand that she will bring ruin on herself and all of us. You saved my son—save my daughter too! God Himself sent you here . . . I am ready on my knees to beseech you. . . .' And Frau Lenore half rose from her seat as though about to fall at Sanin's feet. . . . He restrained her.

'Frau Lenore! For mercy's sake I What are you doing?'

She clutched his hand impulsively. 'You promise . . .'

'Frau Lenore, think a moment; what right have I . . .'

'You promise? You don't want me to die here at once before your eyes?'

Sanin was utterly nonplussed. It was the first time in his life he had had to deal with any one of ardent Italian blood.

'I will do whatever you like.' he cried. 'I will talk to fräulein Gemma. . . .'

Frau Lenore uttered a cry of delight.

'Only I really can't say what result will come of it . . .'

'Ah, don't go back, don't go back from your words!' cried Frau Lenore in an imploring voice; 'you have already consented! The result is certain to be excellent. Any way, *I* can do nothing more! She won't listen to *me*!'

'Has she so positively stated her disinclination to marry Herr Klüber?' Sanin inquired after a short silence.

'As if she'd cut the knot with a knife! She's her father all over, Giovanni Battista! Wilful girl!'

'Wilful? Is she!'. . . Sanin said slowly.

'Yes . . . yes . . . but she's an angel too. She will mind you. Are you coming soon?

Oh, my dear Russian friend!' Frau Lenore rose impulsively from her chair, and as impulsively clasped the head of Sanin, who was sitting opposite her. 'Accept a mother's blessing—and give me some water!'

Sanin brought Signora Roselli a glass of water, gave her his word of honour that he would come directly, escorted her down the stairs to the street, and when he was back in his own room, positively threw up his arms and opened his eyes wide in his amazement.

'Well,' he thought, 'well, *now* life is going round in a whirl! And it's whirling so that I'm giddy.' He did not attempt to look within, to realise what was going on in himself: it was all uproar and confusion, and that was all he knew! What a day it had been! His lips murmured unconsciously: 'Wilful . . . her mother says . . . and I have got to advise her . . . her! And advise her what?'

Sanin, really, was giddy, and above all this whirl of shifting sensations and impressions and unfinished thoughts, there floated continually the image of Gemma, the image so ineffaceably impressed on his memory on that hot night, quivering with electricity, in that dark window, in the light of the swarming stars!

XXIV

With hesitating footsteps Sanin approached the house of Signora Roselli. His heart was beating violently; he distinctly felt, and even heard it thumping at his side. What should he say to Gemma, how should he begin? He went into the house, not through the shop, but by the back entrance. In the little outer room he met Frau Lenore. She was both relieved and scared at the sight of him.

'I have been expecting you,' she said in a whisper, squeezing his hand with each of hers in turn. 'Go into the garden; she is there. Mind, I rely on you!'

Sanin went into the garden.

Gemma was sitting on a garden-seat near the path, she was sorting a big basket full of cherries, picking out the ripest, and putting them on a dish. The sun was low—it was seven o'clock in the evening—and there was more purple than gold in the full slanting light with which it flooded the whole of Signora Roselli's little garden. From time to time, faintly audibly, and as it were deliberately, the leaves rustled, and belated bees buzzed abruptly as they flew from one flower to the next, and somewhere a dove was cooing a never-changing, unceasing note. Gemma had on the same round hat in which she had driven to Soden. She peeped at Sanin from under its turned-down brim, and again bent over the basket.

Sanin went up to Gemma, unconsciously making each step shorter, and . . . and . . . and nothing better could he find to say to her than to ask why was she sorting the cherries.

Gemma was in no haste to reply.

'These are riper,' she observed at last, 'they will go into jam, and those are for tarts. You know the round sweet tarts we sell?'

As she said those words, Gemma bent her head still lower, and her right hand with two cherries in her fingers was suspended in the air between the basket and the dish.

'May I sit by you?' asked Sanin.

'Yes.' Gemma moved a little along on the seat. Sanin placed himself beside her. 'How am I to begin?' was his thought. But Gemma got him out of his difficulty.

'You have fought a duel to-day,' she began eagerly, and she turned all her lovely, bashfully flushing face to him—and what depths of gratitude were shining in those eyes! 'And you are so calm! I suppose for you danger does not exist?'

'Oh, come! I have not been exposed to

any danger. Everything went off very satisfactorily and inoffensively.'

Gemma passed her finger to right and to left before her eyes. . . . Also an Italian gesture. 'No! no! don't say that! You won't deceive me! Pantaleone has told me everything!'

'He's a trustworthy witness! Did he compare me to the statue of the commander?'

'His expressions may be ridiculous, but his feeling is not ridiculous, nor is what you have done to-day. And all that on my account . . . for me . . . I shall never forget it.'

'I assure you, Fräulein Gemma . . .'

'I shall never forget it,' she said deliberately; once more she looked intently at him, and turned away.

He could now see her delicate pure profile, and it seemed to him that he had never seen anything like it, and had never known anything like what he was feeling at that instant. His soul was on fire.

'And my promise!' flashed in among his thoughts.

'Fräulein Gemma . . .' he began after a momentary hesitation.

'What?'

She did not turn to him, she went on sorting the cherries, carefully taking them by their stalks with her finger-tips, assiduously picking out the leaves . . . But what a confiding caress could be heard in that one word, 'What?'

'Has your mother said nothing to you . . . about . . .'

'About?'

'About me?'

Gemma suddenly flung back into the basket the cherries she had taken.

'Has she been talking to you?' she asked in her turn.

'Yes.'

'What has she been saying to you?'

'She told me that you . . . that you have suddenly decided to change . . . your former intention.' Gemma's head was bent again. She vanished altogether under her hat; nothing could be seen but her neck, supple and tender, as the stalk of a big flower.

'What intentions?'

'Your intentions . . . relative to . . . the future arrangement of your life.'

'That is . . . you are speaking . . . of Herr Klüber?'

'Yes.'

'Mamma told you I don't want to be Herr Klüber's wife?'

'Yes.'

Gemma moved forward on the seat. The

basket tottered, fell . . . a few cherries rolled on to the path. A minute passed by . . . another.

'Why did she tell you so?' he heard her voice saying. Sanin as before could only see Gemma's neck. Her bosom rose and fell more rapidly than before.

'Why? Your mother thought that as you and I, in a short time, have become, so to say, friends, and you have some confidence in me, I am in a position to give you good advice—and you would mind what I say.'

Gemma's hands slowly slid on to her knees. She began plucking at the folds of her dress.

'What advice will you give me, Monsieur Dimitri?' she asked, after a short pause.

Sanin saw that Gemma's fingers were trembling on her knees . . . She was only plucking at the folds of her dress to hide their trembling. He softly laid his hand on those pale, shaking fingers.

'Gemma,' he said, 'why don't you look at me?' She instantly tossed her hat back on to her shoulder, and bent her eyes upon him, confiding and grateful as before. She waited for him to speak. . . . But the sight of her face had bewildered, and, as it were, dazed him. The warm glow of the evening sun lighted up her youthful head, and the expression of that head was brighter, more radiant than its glow.

'I will mind what you say, Monsieur Dimitri,' she said, faintly smiling, and faintly arching her brows; 'but what advice do you give me?'

'What advice?' repeated Sanin. 'Well, you see, your mother considers that to dismiss Herr Klüber simply because he did not show any special courage the day before yesterday . . .'

'Simply, because?' said Gemma. She bent down, picked up the basket, and set it beside her on the garden seat.

'That . . . altogether . . . to dismiss him, would be, on your part . . . unreasonable; that it is a step, all the consequences of which ought to be thoroughly weighed; that in fact the very position of your affairs imposes certain obligations on every member of your family . . .'

'All that is mamma's opinion,' Gemma interposed; 'those are her words; but what is your opinion?'

'Mine?' Sanin was silent for a while. He felt a lump rising in his throat and catching at his breath. 'I too consider,' he began with an effort . . .

Gemma drew herself up. 'Too? You too?'

'Yes . . . that is . . .' Sanin was unable, positively unable to add a single word more.

'Very well,' said Gemma. 'If you, as a friend, advise me to change my decision—that is, not to change my former decision—I will think it over.' Not knowing what she was doing, she began to tip the cherries back from the plate into the basket. . . . 'Mamma hopes that I will mind what you say. Well . . . perhaps I really will mind what you say.'

'But excuse me, Fräulein Gemma, I should like first to know what reason impelled you . . .'

'I will mind what you say,' Gemma repeated, her face right up to her brows was working, her cheeks were white, she was biting her lower lip. 'You have done so much for me, that I am bound to do as you wish; bound to carry out your wishes. I will tell mamma . . . I will think again. Here she is, by the way, coming here.'

Frau Lenore did in fact appear in the doorway leading from the house to the garden. She was in an agony of impatience; she could not keep still. According to her calculations, Sanin must long ago have finished all he had to say to Gemma, though his conversation with her had not lasted a quarter of an hour.

'No, no, no, for God's sake, don't tell her anything yet,' Sanin articulated hurriedly, almost in alarm. 'Wait a little . . . I will tell you, I will write to you . . . and till then don't decide on anything . . . wait!'

He pressed Gemma's hand, jumped up from the seat, and to Frau Lenore's great amazement, rushed past her, and raising his hat, muttered something unintelligible—and vanished.

She went up to her daughter.

'Tell me, please, Gemma . . .'

The latter suddenly got up and hugged her. . . . 'Dear mamma, can you wait a little, a tiny bit . . . till to-morrow? Can you? And till to-morrow not a word? . . . Ah! . . .'

She burst into sudden happy tears, incomprehensible to herself. This surprised Frau Lenore, the more as the expression of Gemma's face was far from sorrowful,—rather joyful in fact.

'What is it?' she asked. 'You never cry . . . and here, all at once . . .'

'Nothing, mamma, never mind! you only wait We must both wait a little. Don't ask me anything till to-morrow—and let us sort the cherries before the sun has set.'

'But you will be reasonable?'

'Oh, I'm very reasonable!' Gemma shook her head significantly. She began to make up little bunches of cherries, holding them high above her flushed face. She did not wipe away her tears; they had dried of themselves

XXV

Almost running, Sanin returned to his hotel room. He felt, he knew that only there, only by himself, would it be clear to him at last what was the matter, what was happening to him. And so it was; directly he had got inside his room, directly he had sat down to the writing-table, with both elbows on the table and both hands pressed to his face, he cried in a sad and choked voice, 'I love her, love her madly!' and he was all aglow within, like a fire when a thick layer of dead ash has been suddenly blown off. An instant more . . . and he was utterly unable to understand how he could have sat beside her . . . her!— and talked to her and not have felt that he worshipped the very hem of her garment, that he was ready as young people express it 'to die at her feet.' The last interview in the garden had decided everything. Now when he thought of her, she did not appear to him with blazing curls in the shining starlight; he saw her sitting on the garden-seat, saw her all at once tossing back her hat, and gazing at him so confidingly . . . and the tremor and hunger of love ran through all his veins. He remembered the rose which he had been carrying about in his pocket for three days: he snatched it out, and pressed it with such feverish violence to his lips, that he could not help frowning with the pain. Now he considered nothing, reflected on nothing, did not deliberate, and did not look forward; he had done with all his past, he leaped forward into the future; from the dreary bank of his lonely bachelor life he plunged headlong into that glad, seething, mighty torrent—and little he cared, little he wished to know, where it would carry him, or whether it would dash him against a rock! No more the soft-flowing currents of the Uhland song, which had lulled him not long ago. . . . These were mighty, irresistible torrents! They rush flying onwards—and he flies with them. . . .

He took a sheet of paper, and without blotting out a word, almost with one sweep of the pen, wrote as follows:—

'DEAR GEMMA,—You know what advice I undertook to give you, what your mother desired, and what she asked of me; but what you don't know and what I must tell you now is, that I love you, love you with all the ardour of a heart that loves for the first time! This passion has flamed up in me suddenly, but with such force that I can find no words for it! When your mother came to me and asked me, it was still only smouldering in me, or else I should certainly, as an honest man, have refused to carry out her request. . . . The confession I make you now is the confession of an honest man. You ought to know whom you have to do with—between us there should exist no misunderstandings. You see that I cannot give you any advice. . . . I love you, love you, love you—and I have nothing else—either in my head or in my heart!!

'DM. SANIN.'

When he had folded and sealed this note, Sanin was on the point of ringing for the waiter and sending it by him . . . 'No!' he thought, 'it would be awkward. . . . By Emil? But to go to the shop, and seek him out there among the other employés, would be awkward too. Besides, it's dark by now, and he has probably left the shop.' Reflecting after this fashion, Sanin put on his hat, however, and went into the street; he turned a corner, another, and to his unspeakable delight, saw Emil before him. With a satchel under his arm, and a roll of papers in his hand, the young enthusiast was hurrying home.

'They may well say every lover has a lucky star,' thought Sanin, and he called to Emil.

The latter turned and at once rushed to him.

Sanin cut short his transports, handed him the note, and explained to whom and how he was to deliver it. . . . Emil listened attentively.

'So that no one sees? 'he inquired, assuming an important and mysterious air, that said, 'We understand the inner meaning of it all!'

'Yes, my friend,' said Sanin and he was a little disconcerted; however, he patted Emil on the cheek. . . . 'And if there should be an answer. . . . You will bring me the answer, won't you? I will stay at home.'

'Don't worry yourself about that!' Emil whispered gaily; he ran off, and as he ran nodded once more to him.

Sanin went back home, and without lighting a candle, flung himself on the sofa, put his hands behind his head, and abandoned himself to those sensations of newly conscious love, which it is no good even to describe. One who has felt them knows their languor and sweetness; to one who has felt them not, one could never make them known.

The door opened—Emil's head appeared.

'I have brought it,' he said in a whisper: here it is—the answer!'

He showed and waved above his head a folded sheet of paper.

Sanin leaped up from the sofa and snatched it out of Emil's hand. Passion was working too powerfully within him: he had no thought of reserve now, nor of the observance of a suitable demeanour—even before this boy, her brother. He would have been scrupulous, he would have controlled himself—if he could!

He went to the window, and by the light of a street lamp which stood just opposite the house, he read the following lines:—

'I beg you, I beseech you—*don't come to see us, don't show yourself all day to-morrow.* It's necessary, absolutely necessary for me, and then everything shall be settled. I know you will not say no, because . . .

'Gemma.'

Sanin read this note twice through. Oh, how touchingly sweet and beautiful her handwriting seemed to him! He thought a little, and turning to Emil, who, wishing to give him to understand what a discreet young person he was, was standing with his face to the wall, and scratching on it with his finger-nails, he called him aloud by name.

Emin ran at once to Sanin. 'What do you want me to do?'

'Listen, my young friend . . .'

'Monsieur Dimitri,' Emil interrupted in a plaintive voice, 'why do you address me so formally?'

Sanin laughed. 'Oh, very well. Listen, my dearest boy—(Emil gave a little skip of delight)—listen; *there* you understand, there, you will say, that everything shall be done exactly as is wished—(Emil compressed his lips and nodded solemnly)—and as for me . . . what are you doing to-morrow, my dear boy?'

'I? what am I doing? What would you like me to do?'

'If you can, come to me early in the morning—and we will walk about the country round Frankfort till evening. . . . Would you like to?'

Emil gave another little skip. 'I say, what in the world could be jollier? Go a walk with you—why, it's simply glorious! I'll be sure to come!'

'And if they won't let you?'

'They will let me!'

'Listen . . . Don't say *there* that I asked you to come for the whole day.'

'Why should I? But I'll get away all the same! What does it matter?'

Emil warmly kissed Sanin, and ran away.

Sanin walked up and down the room a long

while, and went late to bed. He gave himself up to the same delicate and sweet sensations, the same joyous thrill at facing a new life. Sanin was very glad that the idea had occurred to him to invite Emil to spend the next day with him; he was like his sister. 'He will recall her,' was his thought.

But most of all, he marvelled how he could have been yesterday other than he was to-day. It seemed to him that he had loved Gemma for all time; and that he had loved her just as he loved her to-day.

XXVI

At eight o'clock next morning, Emil arrived at Sanin's hotel leading Tartaglia by a string. Had he sprung of German parentage, he could not have shown greater practicality. He had told a lie at home; he had said he was going for a walk with Sanin till lunch-time, and then going to the shop. While Sanin was dressing, Emil began to talk to him, rather hesitatingly, it is true, about Gemma, about her rupture with Herr Klüber; but Sanin preserved an austere silence in reply, and Emil, looking as though he understood why so serious a matter should not be touched on lightly, did not return to the subject, and only assumed from time to time an intense and even severe expression.

After drinking coffee, the two friends set off together—on foot, of course—to Hausen, a little village lying a short distance from Frankfort, and surrounded by woods. The whole chain of the Taunus mountains could be seen clearly from there. The weather was lovely; the sunshine was bright and warm, but not blazing hot; a fresh wind rustled briskly among the green leaves; the shadows of high, round clouds glided swiftly and smoothly in small patches over the earth. The two young people soon got out of the town, and stepped out boldly and gaily along the well-kept road. They reached the woods, and wandered about there a long time; then they lunched very heartily at a country inn; then climbed on to the mountains, admired the views, rolled stones down and clapped their hands, watching the queer droll way in which the stones hopped along like rabbits, till a man passing below, unseen by them, began abusing them in a loud ringing voice. Then they lay full length on the short dry moss of yellowish-violet colour; then they drank beer at another inn; ran races, and tried for a wager which could jump farthest They discovered an echo, and began to call to it; sang songs, hallooed, wrestled, broke up dry twigs, decked their hats with fern, and even danced. Tartaglia, as far as he could, shared in all these pastimes; he did not throw stones, it is true, but he rolled head over heels after them; he howled when they were singing, and even drank beer, though with evident aversion; he had been trained in this art by a student to whom he had once belonged. But he was not prompt in obeying Emil—not as he was with his master Pantaleone—and when Emil ordered him to 'speak,' or to 'sneeze,' he only wagged his tail and thrust out his tongue like a pipe.

The young people talked, too. At the beginning of the walk, Sanin, as the elder, and so more reflective, turned the conversation on fate and predestination, and the nature and meaning of man's destiny; but the conversation quickly took a less serious turn. Emil began to question his friend and patron about Russia, how duels were fought there, and whether the women there were beautiful, and whether one could learn Russian quickly, and what he had felt when the officer took aim at him. Sanin, on his side, questioned Emil about his father, his mother, and in general about their family affairs, trying every time not to mention Gemma's name—and thinking only of her. To speak more precisely, it was not of her he was thinking, but of the morrow, the mysterious morrow which was to bring him new, unknown happiness! It was as though a veil, a delicate, bright veil, hung faintly fluttering before his mental vision; and behind this veil he felt . . . felt the presence of a youthful, motionless, divine image, with a tender smile on its lips, and eyelids severely—with affected severity—downcast. And this image was not the face of Gemma, it was the face of happiness itself! For, behold, at last *his* hour had come, the veil had vanished, the lips were parting, the eyelashes are raised—his divinity has looked upon him—and at once light as from the sun, and joy and bliss unending! He dreamed of this morrow—and his soul thrilled with joy again in the melting torture of ever-growing expectation!

And this expectation, this torture, hindered nothing. It accompanied every action, and did not prevent anything. It did not prevent him from dining capitally at a third inn with Emil; and only occasionally, like a brief flash of lightning, the thought shot across him, What if any one in the world knew? This suspense did not prevent him from playing leap-frog with Emil after dinner. The game took place on an open green lawn. And the confusion, the stupefaction of Sanin may be imagined! At the very moment when, accompanied by a sharp bark from Tartaglia, he was flying like a bird, with his legs outspread over Emil, who was bent double, he suddenly saw on the farthest border of the lawn two officers, in whom he recognised at once his adversary and his second, Herr von Dönhof and Herr von Richter! Each of them had stuck an eyeglass in his eye, and was staring at him, chuckling! . . . Sanin got on his feet, turned away hurriedly, put on the coat he had flung down, jerked out a word to Emil; the latter, too, put on his jacket, and they both immediately made off.

It was late when they got back to Frankfort. 'They'll scold me,' Emil said to Sanin as he said good-bye to him. 'Well, what does it matter? I've had such a splendid, splendid day!'

When he got home to his hotel, Sanin found a note there from Gemma. She fixed a meeting with him for next day, at seven o'clock in the morning, in one of the public gardens which surround Frankfort on all sides.

How his heart throbbed! How glad he was that he had obeyed her so unconditionally! And, my God, what was promised . . . what was not promised, by that unknown, unique, impossible, and undubitably certain morrow!

He feasted his eyes on Gemma's note. The

long, elegant tail of the letter G, the first letter of her name, which stood at the bottom of the sheet, reminded him of her lovly fingers, her hand. . . . He thought thathe had not once touched that hand with his lips. . . . 'Italian women,' he mused, 'in spite of what's said of them, are modest and severe.. . . And Gemma above all! Queen . . . godess . . . pure, virginal marble. . . .'

'But the time will come; and it is not far off. . . .' There was that night in Frankfort one happy man. . . . He slept; but he might have said of himself in the words of the poet:

> 'I sleep . . . but my watchful heart sleeps not.'

And it fluttered as lightly as a butterfly flutters his wings, as he stoops over the flowers in the summer sunshine.

XXVII

At five o'clock Sanin woke up, at six he was dressed, at half-past six he was walking up and down the public garden within sight of the little arbour which Gemma had mentioned in her note. It was a still, warm, grey morning. It sometimes seemed as though it were beginning to rain; but the outstretched hand felt nothing, and only looking at one's coat-sleeve, one could see traces of tiny drops like diminutive beads, but even these were soon gone. It seemed there had never been a breath of wind in the world. Every sound moved not, but was shed around in the stillness. In the distance was a faint thickening of whitish mist; in the air there was a scent of mignonette and white acacia flowers.

In the streets the shops were not open yet, but there were already some people walking about; occasionally a solitary carriage rumbled along . . . there was no one walking in the garden. A gardener was in a leisurely way scraping the path with a spade, and a decrepit old woman in a black woollen cloak was hobbling across the garden walk. Sanin could not for one instant mistake this poor old creature for Gemma; and yet his heart leaped, and he watched attentively the retreating patch of black.

Seven! chimed the clock on the tower. Sanin stood still. Was it possible she would not come? A shiver of cold suddenly ran through his limbs. The same shiver came again an instant later, but from a different cause. Sanin heard behind him light footsteps, the light rustle of a woman's dress. . . . He turned round: she!

Gemma was coming up behind him along

the path. She was wearing a grey cape and a small dark hat. She glanced at Sanin, turned her head away, and catching him up, passed rapidly by him.

'Gemma,' he articulated, hardly audibly.

She gave him a little nod, and continued to walk on in front. He followed her.

He breathed in broken gasps. His legs shook under him.

Gemma passed by the arbour, turned to the right, passed by a small flat fountain, in which the sparrows were splashing busily, and, going behind a clump of high lilacs, sank down on a bench. The place was snug and hidden. Sanin sat down beside her.

A minute passed, and neither he nor she uttered a word. She did not even look at him; and he gazed not at her face, but at her clasped hands, in which she held a small parasol. What was there to tell, what was there to say, which could compare, in importance, with the simple fact of their presence there, together, alone, so early, so close to each other.

'You . . . are not angry with me?' Sanin articulated at last.

It would have been difficult for Sanin to have said anything more foolish than these words . . . he was conscious of it himself. . . . But, at any rate, the silence was broken.

'Angry?' she answered. 'What for? No.'
'And you believe me?' he went on.
'In what you wrote?'
'Yes.'

Gemma's head sank, and she said nothing. The parasol slipped out of her hands. She hastily caught it before it dropped on the path.

'Ah, believe me! believe what I wrote to you!' cried Sanin; all his timidity suddenly vanished, he spoke with heat; 'if there is truth on earth—sacred, absolute truth—it's that I love, love you passionately, Gemma,'

She flung him a sideway, momentary glance, and again almost dropped the parasol.

'Believe me! believe me!' he repeated. He besought her, held out his hands to her, and did not dare to touch her. 'What do you want me to do . . . to convince you?'

She glanced at him again.

'Tell me, Monsieur Dimitri,' she began; 'the day before yesterday, when you came to talk to me, you did not, I imagine, know then . . . did not feel . . .'

'I felt it,' Sanin broke in; 'but I did not know it. I have loved you from the very instant I saw you; but I did not realise at once what you had become to me! And besides, I heard that you were solemnly betrothed. . . . As far as your mother's request is concerned—in the first place, how could I refuse?—and secondly, I think I carried out her request in such a way that you could guess . . .'

They heard a heavy tread, and a rather stout gentleman with a knapsack over his shoulder, apparently a foreigner, emerged from behind the clump, and staring, with the unceremoniousness of a tourist, at the couple sitting on the garden-seat, gave a loud cough and went on.

'Your mother,' Sanin began, as soon as the sound of the heavy footsteps had ceased, 'told me your breaking off your engagement would cause a scandal'—Gemma frowned a little—'that I was myself in part responsible for unpleasant gossip, and that . . . consequently . . . I was, to some extent, under an obligation to advise you not to break with your betrothed, Herr Klüber. . . .'

'Monsieur Dimitri,' said Gemma, and she passed her hand over her hair on the side turned towards Sanin, 'don't, please, call Herr Klüber my betrothed. I shall never be his wife. I have broken with him.'

'You have broken with him? when?'
'Yesterday.'
'You saw him?'
'Yes. At our house. He came to see us.'
'Gemma? Then you love me?'

She turned to him.

'Should . . . I have come here, if not?' she whispered, and both her hands fell on the seat.

Sanin snatched those powerless, upturned palms, and pressed them to his eyes, to his lips. . . . Now the veil was lifted of which he had dreamed the night before! Here was happiness, here was its radiant form!

He raised his head, and looked at Gemma, boldly and directly. She, too, looked at him, a little downwards. Her half-shut eyes faintly glistened, dim with light, blissful tears. Her face was not smiling . . . no! it laughed, with a blissful, noiseless laugh.

He tried to draw her to him, but she drew back, and never ceasing to laugh the same noiseless laugh, shook her head. 'Wait a little,' her happy eyes seemed to say.

'O Gemma!' cried Sanin: 'I never dreamed that you would love me!'

'I did not expect this myself,' Gemma said softly.

'How could I ever have dreamed,' Sanin went on, 'when I came to Frankfort, where I only expected to remain a few hours, that I should find here the happiness of all my life!'

'All your life? Really?' queried Gemma.

'All my life, for ever and ever!' cried Sanin with fresh ardour.

The gardener's spade suddenly scraped two paces from where they were sitting.

'Let's go home,' whispered Gemma: 'we'll go together—will you?'

If she had said to him at that instant 'Throw yourself in the sea, will you?' he would have been flying headlong into the ocean before she had uttered the last word.

They went together out of the garden and turned homewards, not by the streets of the town, but through the outskirts.

XXVIII

SANIN walked along, at one time by Gemma's side, at another time a little behind her. He never took his eyes off her and never ceased smiling. She seemed to hasten . . . seemed to linger. As a matter of fact, they both—he all pale, and she all flushed with emotion—were moving along as in a dream. What they had done together a few instants before—that surrender of each soul to another soul—was so intense, so new, and so moving; so suddenly everything in their lives had been changed and displaced that they could not recover themselves, and were only aware of a whirlwind carrying them along, like the whirlwind on that night, which had almost flung them into each other's arms. Sanin walked along, and felt that he even looked at Gemma with other eyes; he instantly noted some peculiarities in her walk, in her movements,—and heavens! how infinitely sweet and precious they were to him! And she felt that that was how he was looking at her.

Sanin and she were in love for the first time; all the miracles of first love were working in them. First love is like a revolution; the uniformly regular routine of ordered life is broken down and shattered in one instant; youth mounts the barricade, waves high its bright flag, and whatever awaits it in the future —death or a new life—all alike it goes to meet with ecstatic welcome.

'What's this? Isn't that our old friend?' said Sanin, pointing to a muffled-up figure, which hurriedly slipped a little aside as though trying to remain unobserved. In the midst of his abundant happiness he felt a need to talk to Gemma, not of love—that was a settled thing and holy—but of something else.

'Yes, it's Pantaleone,' Gemma answered gaily and happily. 'Most likely he has been following me ever since I left home; all day yesterday he kept watching every movement I made . . . He guesses!'

'He guesses!' Sanin repeated in ecstasy. What could Gemma have said at which he would not have been in ecstasy?

Then he asked her to tell him in detail all that had passed the day before.

And she began at once telling him, with haste, and confusion, and smiles, and brief sighs, and brief bright looks exchanged with Sanin. She said that after their conversation the day before yesterday, mamma had kept trying to get out of her something positive; but that she had put off Frau Lenore with a promise to tell her her decision within twenty-four hours; how she had demanded this limit of time for herself, and how difficult it had been to get it; how utterly unexpectedly Herr Klüber had made his appearance more starched and affected than ever; how he had given vent to his indignation at the childish, unpardonable action of the Russian stranger—'he meant your duel, Dimitri,'—which he described as deeply insulting to him, Klüber, and how he had demanded that 'you should be at once refused admittance to the house, Dimitri,' 'For,' he had added—and here Gemma slightly mimicked his voice and manner—'"it casts a slur on my honour; as though I were not able to defend my betrothed, had I thought it necessary or advisable! All Frankfort will know by to-morrow that an outsider has fought a duel with an officer on account of my betrothed—did any one ever hear of such a thing! It tarnishes my honour!" Mamma agreed with him—fancy!—but then I suddenly told him that he was troubling himself unnecessarily about his honour and his character, and was unnecessarily annoyed at the gossip about his betrothed, for I was no longer betrothed to him and would never be his wife! I must own, I had meant to talk to you first. . . . before breaking with him finally; but he came . . . and I could not restrain myself. Mamma positively screamed with horror, but I went into the next room and got his ring—you didn't notice, I took it off two days ago—and gave it to him. He was fearfully offended, but as he is fearfully self-conscious and conceited, he did not say much, and went away. Of course I had to go through a great deal with mamma, and it made me very wretched to see how distressed she was, and I thought I had been a little hasty; but you see I had your note, and even apart from it I knew . . .'

'That I love you,' put in Sanin.

'Yes . . . that you were in love with me.'

So Gemma talked, hesitating and smiling and dropping her voice or stopping altogether every time any one met them or passed by.

And Sanin listened ecstatically, enjoying the very sound of her voice, as the day before he had gloated over her handwriting.

'Mamma is very much distressed,' Gemma began again, and her words flew very rapidly one after another; 'she refuses to take into consideration that I dislike Herr Klüber, that I never was betrothed to him from love, but only because of her urgent entreaties. . . . She suspects—you, Dimitri; that's to say, to speak plainly, she's convinced I'm in love with you, and she is more unhappy about it because only the day before yesterday nothing of the sort had occurred to her, and she even begged you to advise me. . . . It was a strange request, wasn't it? Now she calls you . . . Dimitri, a hypocrite and a cunning fellow, says that you have betrayed her confidence, and predicts that you will deceive me. . . .'

'But, Gemma,' cried Sanin, 'do you mean to say you didn't tell her? . .'

'I told her nothing! What right had I without consulting you?'

Sanin threw up his arms. 'Gemma, I hope that now, at least, you will tell all to her and take me to her. . . . I want to convince your mother that I am not a base deceiver!'

Sanin's bosom fairly heaved with the flood of generous and ardent emotions.

Gemma looked him full in the face. 'You really want to go with me now to mamma? to mamma, who maintains that . . . all this between us is impossible—and can never come to pass?' There was one word Gemma could not bring herself to utter. . . . It burnt her lips; but all the more eagerly Sanin pronounced it.

'Marry you, Gemma, be your husband—I can imagine no bliss greater!'

To his love, his magnanimity, his determination—he was aware of no limits now.

When she heard those words, Gemma, who had stopped still for an instant, went on faster than ever. . . . She seemed trying to run away from this too great and unexpected happiness!

But suddenly her steps faltered. Round the corner of a turning, a few paces from her, in a new hat and coat, straight as an arrow and curled like a poodle—emerged Herr Klüber. He caught sight of Gemma, caught sight of Sanin, and with a sort of inward snort and a backward bend of his supple figure, he advanced with a dashing swing to meet them. Sanin felt a pang; but glancing at Klüber's face, to which its owner endeavoured, as far as in him lay, to give an expression of scornful amazement, and even commiseration, glancing at that red-cheeked, vulgar face, he felt a sudden rush of anger, and took a step forward.

Gemma seized his arm, and with quiet decision, giving him hers, she looked her former betrothed full in the face. . . . The latter screwed up his face, shrugged his shoulders, shuffled to one side, and muttering between his teeth, 'The usual end to the song!' (Das alte Ende vom Liede!)—walked away with the same dashing, slightly skipping gait.

'What did he say, the wretched creature?' asked Sanin, and would have rushed after Klüber; but Gemma held him back and walked on with him, not taking away the arm she had slipped into his.

The Rosellis' shop came into sight Gemma stopped once more.

'Dimitri, Monsieur Dimitri,' she said, 'we are not there yet, we have not seen mamma yet. . . . If you would rather think a little, if . . . you are still free, Dimitri!'

In reply Sanin pressed her hand tightly to his bosom, and drew her on.

'Mamma,' said Gemma, going with Sanin to the room where Frau Lenore was sitting, 'I have brought the real one!'

XXIX

IF Gemma had announced that she had brought with her cholera or death itself, one can hardly imagine that Frau Lenore could have received the news with greater despair. She immediately sat down in a corner, with her face to the wall, and burst into floods of tears, positively wailed, for all the world like a Russian peasant woman on the grave of her husband or her son. For the first minute Gemma was so taken aback that she did not even go up to her mother but stood still like a statue in the middle of the room; while Sanin was utterly stupefied, to the point of almost bursting into tears himself! For a whole hour that inconsolable wail went on—a whole hour! Pantaleone thought it better to shut the outer door of the shop, so that no stranger should come; luckily, it was still early. The old man himself did not know what to think, and in any case, did not approve of the haste with which Gemma and Sanin had acted; he could not bring himself to blame them, and was prepared to give them his support in case of need: he greatly disliked Klüber! Emil regarded himself as the medium of communication between his friend and his sister, and almost prided himself on its all having turned out so splendidly! He was positively unable to conceive why Frau Lenore was so upset, and in his heart he decided on the spot that women, even the best of them, suffer from a lack of reasoning power! Sanin fared worst of all. Frau Lenore rose to a howl and waved him off with her hands, directly he approached her; and it was in vain that he attempted once or twice to shout aloud, standing at a distance, 'I ask you for your daughter's hand!' Frau Lenore was particularly angry with herself. 'How could she have been so blind—have seen nothing? Had my Giovann' Battista been alive,' she persisted through her tears, 'nothing of this sort would have happened!' 'Heavens, what's it all about?' thought Sanin; 'why, it's positively senseless!' He did not dare to look at Gemma, nor could she pluck up courage to lift her eyes to him. She restricted herself to waiting patiently on her mother, who at first repelled even her. . . .

At last, by degrees, the storm abated. Frau Lenore gave over weeping, permitted Gemma to bring her out of the corner, where she sat huddled up, to put her into an arm-chair near the window, and to give her some orange-flower water to drink. She permitted Sanin—not to approach . . . oh, no!—but, at any rate, to remain in the room—she had kept clamouring for him to go away—and did not interrupt him when he spoke. Sanin immediately availed himself of the calm as it set in, and displayed an astounding eloquence. He could hardly have explained his intentions and emotions with more fire and persuasive force even to Gemma herself. Those emotions were of the sincerest, those intentions were of the purest, like Almaviva's in the *Barber of Seville*. He did not conceal from Frau Lenore nor from himself the disadvantageous side of those intentions; but the disadvantages were only apparent! It is true he was a foreigner; they had not known him long, they knew nothing positive about himself or his means; but he was prepared to bring forward all the necessary evidence that he was a respectable person and not poor; he would refer them to the most unimpeachable testimony of his fellow-countrymen! He hoped Gemma would be happy with him, and that he would be able to make up to her for the separation from her own people! . . . The allusion to 'separation'—the mere word 'separation'—almost spoiled the whole business. . . . Frau Lenore began to tremble all over and move about uneasily. . . . Sanin hastened to observe that the separation would only be temporary, and that, in fact, possibly it would not take place at all!

Sanin's eloquence was not thrown away. Frau Lenore began to glance at him, though still with bitterness and reproach, no longer with the same aversion and fury; then she suffered him to come near her, and even to sit down beside her (Gemma was sitting on the other side); then she fell to reproaching him,—not in looks only, but in words, which already indicated a certain softening of heart; she fell to complaining, and her complaints became quieter and gentler; they were interspersed with questions addressed at one time to her daughter, and at another to Sanin; then she suffered him to take her hand and did not at once pull it away . . . then she wept again, but her tears were now quite of another kind. . . . Then she smiled mournfully, and lamented the absence of Giovanni Battista, but quite on different grounds from before. . . . An instant more and the two criminals, Sanin and Gemma, were on their knees at her feet, and she was laying her hands on their heads in turn; another instant and they were embracing and kissing her, and Emil, his face beaming rapturously, ran into the room and added himself to the group so warmly united.

Pantaleone peeped into the room, smiled and frowned at the same time, and going into the shop, opened the front door.

XXX

The transition from despair to sadness, and from that to 'gentle resignation,' was accomplished fairly quickly in Frau Lenore; but that gentle resignation, too, was not slow in changing into a secret satisfaction, which was, however, concealed in every way and suppressed for the sake of appearances. Sanin had won Frau Lenore's heart from the first day of their acquaintance; as she got used to the idea of his being her son-in-law, she found nothing particularly distasteful in it, though she thought it her duty to preserve a somewhat hurt, or rather careworn, expression on her face. Besides, everything that had happened the last few days had been so extraordinary. . . . One thing upon the top of another. As a practical woman and a mother, Frau Lenore considered it her duty also to put Sanin through various questions; and Sanin, who, on setting out that morning to meet Gemma, had not a notion that he should marry her—it is true he did not think of anything at all at that time, but simply gave himself up to the current of his passion—Sanin entered, with perfect readiness, one might even say with zeal, into his part—the part of the betrothed lover, and answered all her inquiries circumstantially, exactly, with alacrity. When she had satisfied herself that he was a real nobleman by birth, and had even expressed some surprise that he was not a prince, Frau Lenore assumed a serious air and 'warned him betimes' that she should be quite unceremoniously frank with him, as she was forced to be so by her sacred duty as a mother! To which Sanin replied that he expected nothing else from her, and that he earnestly begged her not to spare him!

Then Frau Lenore observed that Herr Klüber —as she uttered the name, she sighed faintly, tightened her lips, and hesitated—Herr Klüber, Gemma's former betrothed, already possessed an income of eight thousand guldens, and that with every year this sum would rapidly be increased; and what was his, Herr Sanin's income? 'Eight thousand guldens,' Sanin repeated deliberately. . . . 'That's in our money . . . about fifteen thousand roubles. . . . My income is much smaller. I have a small estate in the province of Tula. . . . With good management, it might yield—and, in fact, it could not fail to yield—five or six thousand . . . and if I go into the government service, I can easily get a salary of two thousand a year.'

'Into the service in Russia?' cried Frau Lenore. 'Then I must part with Gemma!'

'One might be able to enter in the diplomatic service,' Sanin put in; 'I have some connections. . . . There one's duties lie abroad. Or else, this is what one might do, and that's much the best of all: sell my estate and employ the sum received for it in some profitable undertaking; for instance, the improvement of your shop.' Sanin was aware that he was saying something absurd, but he was possessed by an incomprehensible recklessness! He looked at Gemma, who, ever since the 'practical 'conversation began, kept getting up, walking about the room, and sitting down again—he looked at her—and no obstacle existed for him, and he was ready to arrange everything at once in the best way, if only she were not troubled!

'Herr Klüber, too, had intended to give me a small sum for the improvement of the shop,' Lenore observed after a slight hesitation.

'Mother! for mercy's sake, mother!' cried Gemma in Italian.

'These things must be discussed in good time, my daughter,' Frau Lenore replied in the same language. She addressed herself again to Sanin, and began questioning him as to the laws existing in Russia as to marriage, and whether there were no obstacles to contracting marriages with Catholics as in Prussia. (At that time, in 1840, all Germany still remembered the controversy between the Prussian Government and the Archbishop of Cologne upon mixed marriages.) When Frau Lenore heard that by marrying a Russian nobleman, her daughter would herself become of noble rank, she evinced a certain satisfaction. 'But, of course, you will first have to go to Russia?'

'Why?'

'Why? Why, to obtain the permission of your Tsar.'

Sanin explained to her that that was not at all necessary . . . but that he might certainly have to go to Russia for a very short time before his marriage—(he said these words, and his heart ached painfully, Gemma watching him, knew it was aching, and blushed and grew dreamy)—and that he would try to take advantage of being in his own country to sell his estate . . . in any case he would bring back the money needed.

'I would ask you to bring me back some good Astrakhan lambskin for a cape,' said Frau Lenore. 'They're wonderfully good, I hear, and wonderfully cheap!'

'Certainly, with the greatest pleasure, I will bring some for you and for Gemma!' cried Sanin.

'And for me a morocco cap worked in silver,' Emil interposed, putting his head in from the next room.

'Very well, I will bring it you . . . and some slippers for Pantaleone.'

'Come, that's nonsense, nonsense,' observed Frau Lenore. 'We are talking now of serious matters. But there's another point,' added the practical lady. 'You talk of selling your estate. But how will you do that? Will you sell your peasants then, too?'

Sanin felt something like a stab at his heart. He remembered that in a conversation with Signora Roselli and her daughter about serfdom, which, in his own words, aroused his deepest indignation, he had repeatedly assured them that never on any account would he sell his peasants, as he regarded such a sale as an immoral act.

'I will try and sell my estate to some man I know something of,' he articulated, not without faltering, 'or perhaps the peasants themselves will want to buy their freedom.'

'That would be best of all,' Frau Lenore agreed. 'Though indeed selling live people . . .'

'*Barbari!*' grumbled Pantaleone, who showed himself behind Emil in the doorway, shook his topknot, and vanished.

'It's a bad business!' Sanin thought to himself, and stole a look at Gemma. She seemed not to have heard his last words. 'Well, never mind!' he thought again. In this way the practical talk continued almost uninterruptedly till dinner-time. Frau Lenore was completely softened at last, and already called Sanin 'Dimitri,' shook her finger affectionately at him, and promised she would punish him for his treachery. She asked many and minute questions about his relations, because 'that too is very important'; asked him to describe the ceremony of marriage as performed by the ritual of the Russian Church, and was in raptures already at Gemma in a white dress, with a gold crown on her head.

'She's as lovely as a queen,' she murmured with motherly pride, 'indeed there's no queen like her in the world!'

'There is no one like Gemma in the world!' Sanin chimed in.

'Yes; that's why she is Gemma!' (Gemma, as everyone knows, means in Italian a precious stone.)

Gemma flew to kiss her mother. . . . It seemed as if only then she breathed freely again, and the load that had been oppressing her dropped from off her soul.

Sanin felt all at once so happy, his heart was filled with such childish gaiety at the thought, that here, after all, the dreams had come true to which he had abandoned himself not long ago in these very rooms, his whole being was in such a turmoil that he went quickly out into the shop. He felt a great desire, come what might, to sell something in the shop, as he had done a few days before. . . . 'I have a full right to do so now!' he felt. 'Why, I am one of the family now!' And he actually stood behind the counter, and actually kept shop, that is, sold two little girls, who came in, a pound of sweets, giving them fully two pounds, and only taking half the price from them.

At dinner he received an official position, as betrothed, beside Gemma. Frau Lenore pursued her practical investigations. Emil kept laughing and urging Sanin to take him with him to Russia. It was decided that Sanin should set off in a fortnight. Only Pantaleone showed a somewhat sullen face, so much so that Frau Lenore reproached him. 'And he was his second!' Pantaleone gave her a glance from under his brows.

Gemma was silent almost all the time, but her face had never been lovelier or brighter. After dinner she called Sanin out a minute into the garden, and stopping beside the very garden-seat where she had been sorting the cherries two days before, she said to him. 'Dimitri, don't be angry with me; but I must remind you once more that you are not to consider yourself. bound . . .'

He did not let her go on ...

Gemma turned away her face. 'And as for what mamma spoke of, do you remember, the difference of our religion—see here! ...'

She snatched the garnet cross that hung round her neck on a thin cord, gave it a violent tug, snapped the cord, and handed him the cross.

'If I am yours, your faith is my faith!' Sanin's eyes were still wet when he went back with Gemma into the house.

By the evening everything went on in its accustomed way. They even played a game of *tresette*.

XXXI

SANIN woke up very early. He found himself at the highest pinnacle of human happiness; but it was not that prevented him from sleeping; the question, the vital, fateful question—how he could dispose of his estate as quickly and as advantageously as possible—disturbed his rest. The most diverse plans were mixed up in his head, but nothing had as yet come out clearly. He went out of the house to get air and freshen himself. He wanted to present himself to Gemma with a project ready prepared and not without.

What was the figure, somewhat ponderous and thick in the legs, but well-dressed, walking in front of him, with a slight roll and waddle in his gait? Where? had he seen that head, covered with tufts of flaxen hair, and as it were set right into the shoulders, that soft cushiony back, those plump arms hanging straight down at his sides? Could it be Polozov, his old schoolfellow, whom he had lost sight of for the last five years? Sanin overtook the figure walking in front of him, turned round. . . . A broad, yellowish face, little pig's eyes, with white lashes and eyebrows, a short flat nose, thick lips that looked glued together, a round smooth chin, and that expression, sour, sluggish, and mistrustful—yes; it was he, it was Ippolit Polozov!

'Isn't my lucky star working for me again?' flashed through Sanin's mind.

'Polozov! Ippolit Sidorovitch! Is it you?'

The figure stopped, raised his diminutive eyes, waited a little, and ungluing his lips at last, brought out in a rather hoarse falsetto, 'Dimitri Sanin?'

'That's me!' cried Sanin, and he shook one of Polozov's hands; arrayed in tight kid-gloves of an ashen-grey colour, they hung as lifeless as before beside his barrel-shaped legs. 'Have you been here long? Where have you come from? Where are you stopping?'

'I came yesterday from Wiesbaden,' Polozov replied in deliberate tones, 'to do some shopping for my wife, and I'm going back to Wiesbaden to-day.'

'Oh, yes! You're married, to be sure, and they say, to such a beauty!'

Polozov turned his eyes away. 'Yes, they say so.'

Sanin laughed. 'I see you're just the same . . . as phlegmatic as you were at school.'

'Why should I be different?'

'And they do say,' Sanin added with special emphasis on the word 'do,' 'that your wife is very rich.'

'They say that too.'

'Do you mean to say, Ippolit Sidorovitch, you are not certain on that point?'

'I don't meddle, my dear Dimitri . . . Pavlovitch? Yes, Pavlovitch!—in my wife's affairs.'

'You don't meddle? Not in any of her affairs?'

Polozov again shifted his eyes. 'Not in any, my boy. She does as she likes, and so do I.'

'Where are you going now?' Sanin inquired.

'I'm not going anywhere just now; I'm standing in the street and talking to you; but when we've finished talking, I'm going back to my hotel, and am going to have lunch.'

'Would you care for my company?'

'You mean at lunch?'

'Yes.'

'Delighted, it's much pleasanter to eat in company. You're not a great talker, are you?'

'I think not.'

'So much the better.'

Polozov went on. Sanin walked beside him. And Sanin speculated—Polozov's lips were glued together, again he snorted heavily, and waddled along in silence—Sanin speculated in what way had this booby succeeded in catching a rich and beautiful wife. He was not rich himself, nor distinguished, nor clever; at school he had passed for a dull, slow-witted boy, sleepy, and greedy, and had borne the nickname 'driveller.' It was marvellous!

'But if his wife is very rich, they say she's the daughter of some sort of a contractor, won't she buy my estate? Though he does say he doesn't interfere in any of his wife's affairs, that passes belief, really! Besides, I will name a moderate, reasonable price! Why not try? Perhaps, it's all my lucky star. . . . Resolved! I'll have a try!'

Polozov led Sanin to one of the best hotels in Frankfort, in which he was, of course, occupying the best apartments. On the tables and chairs lay piles of packages, cardboard boxes, and parcels. 'All purchases, my boy, for Maria

Nikolaevna!' that was the name of the wife of Ippolit Sidorovitch). Polozov dropped into an arm-chair, groaned,' Oh, the heat!' and loosened his cravat. Then he rang up the head-waiter, and ordered with intense care a very lavish luncheon. 'And at one, the carriage is to be ready! Do you hear, at one o'clock sharp!'

The head-waiter obsequiously bowed, and cringingly withdrew.

Polozov unbuttoned his waistcoat. From the very way in which he raised his eyebrows, gasped, and wrinkled up his nose, one could see that talking would be a great labour to him, and that he was waiting in some trepidation to see whether Sanin was going to oblige him to use his tongue, or whether he would take the task of keeping up the conversation on himself.

Sanin understood his companion's disposition of mind, and so he did not burden him with questions; he restricted himself to the most essential. He learnt that he had been for two years in the service (in the Uhlans! how nice he must have looked in the short uniform jacket!) that he had married three years before, and had now been for two years abroad with his wife, 'who is now undergoing some sort of cure at Wiesbaden,' and was then going to Paris. On his side too, Sanin did not enlarge much on his past life and his plans; he went straight to the principal point—that is, he began talking of his intention of selling his estate.

Polozov listened to him in silence, his eyes straying from time to time to the door, by which the luncheon was to appear. The luncheon did appear at last. The head-waiter, accompanied by two other attendants, brought in several dishes under silver covers.

'Is the property in the Tula province?' said Polozov, seating himself at the table, and tucking a napkin into his shirt collar.

'Yes.'

'In the Efremovsky district . . . I know it.'

'Do you know my place, Aleksyevka?' Sanin asked, sitting down too at the table.

'Yes, I know it.' Polozov thrust in his mouth a piece of omelette with truffles. 'Maria Nikolaevna, my wife, has an estate in that neighbourhood. . . . Uncork that bottle, waiter! You We a good piece of land, only your peasants have cut down the timber . . . Why are you selling it?'

'I want the money, my friend. I would sell it cheap. Come, you might as well buy it . . . by the way.'

Polozov gulped down a glass of wine, wiped his lips with the napkin, and again set to work chewing slowly and noisily.

'Oh,' he enunciated at last. . . . 'I don't go

in for buying estates; I've no capital. Pass the butter. Perhaps my wife now would buy it. You talk to her about it. If you don't ask too much, she's not above thinking of that. . . . What asses these Germans are, really! They can't cook fish. What could be simpler, one wonders? And yet they go on about "uniting the Fatherland." Waiter, take away that beastly stuff!'

'Does your wife really manage . . . business matters herself?' Sanin inquired.

'Yes. Try the cutlets—they're good. I can recommend them. I've told you already, Dimitri Pavlovitch, I don't interfere in any of my wife's concerns, and I tell you so again.'

Polozov went on munching.

'H'm. . . . But how can I have a talk with her, Ippolit Sidoritch?'

'It's very simple, Dimitri Pavlovitch. Go to Wiesbaden. It's not far from here. Waiter, haven't you any English mustard? No? Brutes! Only don't lose any time. We're starting the day after to-morrow. Let me pour you out a glass of wine; it's wine with a bouquet—no vinegary stuff.'

Polozov's face was flushed and animated; it was never animated but when he was eating —or drinking.

'Really, I don't know, how that could be managed,' Sanin muttered.

'But what makes you in such a hurry about it all of a sudden?'

'There is a reason for being in a hurry, brother.'

'And do you need a lot of money?'

'Yes, a lot. I . . . how can I tell you? I propose . . . getting married.'

Polozov set the glass he had been lifting to his lips on the table.

'Getting married!' he articulated in a voice thick with astonishment, and he folded his podgy hands on his stomach. 'So suddenly?'

'Yes . . . soon.'

'Your intended is in Russia, of course?'

'No, not in Russia.'

'Where then?'

'Here in Frankfort.'

'And who is she?'

A German; that is, no—an Italian. A resident here.'

'With a fortune?'

'No, without a fortune.'

'Then I suppose your love is very ardent?'

'How absurd you are! Yes, very ardent.'

'And it's for that you must have money?'

'Well, yes . . . yes, yes.'

Polozov gulped down his wine, rinsed his mouth, and washed his hands, carefully wiped them on the napkin, took out and lighted a cigar. Sanin watched him in silence.

'There's one means,' Polozov grunted at last, throwing his head back, and blowing out the smoke in a thin ring. 'Go to my wife. If she likes, she can take all the bother off your hands.'

'But how can I see your wife? You say you are starting the day after to-morrow?'

Polozov closed his eyes.

'I'll tell you what,' he said at last, rolling the cigar in his lips, and sighing. 'Go home, get ready as quick as you can, and come here. At one o'clock I am going, there's plenty of room in my carriage. I'll take you with me. That's the best plan. And now I'm going to have a nap. I must always have a nap, brother, after a meal. Nature demands it, and I won't go against it And don't you disturb me.'

Sanin thought and thought, and suddenly raised his head; he had made up his mind.

'Very well, agreed, and thank you. At half-past twelve I'll be here, and we'll go together to Wiesbaden. I hope your wife won't be angry. . . .'

But Polozov was already snoring. He muttered, 'Don't disturb me!' gave a kick, and fell asleep, like a baby.

Sanin once more scanned his clumsy figure,

his head, his neck, his upturned chin, round as an apple, and going out of the hotel, set off with rapid strides to the Rosellis' shop. He had to let Gemma know.

XXXII

HE found her in the shop with her mother. Frau Lenore was stooping down, measuring with a big folding foot-rule the space between the windows. On seeing Sanin, she stood up, and greeted him cheerfully, though with a shade of embarrassment

'What you said yesterday,' she began, 'has set my head in a whirl with ideas as to how we could improve our shop. Here, I fancy we might put a couple of cupboards with shelves of looking-glass. You know, that's the fashion nowadays. And then . . .'

'Excellent, excellent,' Sanin broke in, 'we must think it all over. . . . But come here, I want to tell you something.' He took Frau Lenore and Gemma by the arm, and led them into the next room. Frau Lenore was alarmed, and the foot-rule slipped out of her hands. Gemma too was almost frightened, but she took an intent look at Sanin, and was reassured. His face, though preoccupied, expressed at the same time keen self-confidence and determination.

He asked both the women to sit down, while he remained standing before them, and gesticulating with his hands and ruffling up his hair, he told them all his story; his meeting with Polozov, his proposed expedition to Wiesbaden, the chance of selling the estate. 'Imagine my happiness,' he cried in conclusion: 'things have taken such a turn that I may even, perhaps, not have to go to Russia! And we can have our wedding much sooner than I had anticipated!'

'When must you go?' asked Gemma.

'To-day, in an hour's time; my friend has ordered a carriage—he will take me.'

'You will write to us?'

'At once! directly I have had a talk with this lady, I will write.'

'This lady, you say, is very rich?' queried the practical Frau Lenore.

'Exceedingly rich! her father was a millionaire, and he left everything to her.'

'Everything—to her alone? Well, that's so much the better for you. Only mind, don't let your property go too cheap! Be sensible and firm. Don't let yourself be carried away! I understand your wishing to be Gemma's husband as soon as possible . . . but prudence before everything! Don't forget: the better price you get for your estate, the more there will be for you two, and for your children.'

Gemma turned away, and Sanin gave another wave of his hand. 'You can rely on my prudence, Frau Lenore! Indeed, I shan't do any bargaining with her. I shall tell her the fair price; if she'll give it—good; if not, let her go.'

'Do you know her—this lady?' asked Gemma.

'I have never seen her.'

'And when will you come back?'

'If our negotiations come to nothing—the day after to-morrow; if they turn out favourably, perhaps I may have to stay a day or two longer. In any case I shall not linger a minute beyond what's necessary. I am leaving my heart here, you know! But I have said what I had to say to you, and I must run home before setting off too. . . . Give me your hand for luck, Frau Lenore—that's what we always do in Russia.'

'The right or the left?'

'The left, it's nearer the heart. I shall reappear the day after to-morrow with my shield or on it! Something tells me I shall come back in triumph! Good-bye, my good dear ones . . .'

He embraced and kissed Frau Lenore, but he asked Gemma to follow him into her room—for just a minute—as he must tell her something of great importance. He simply wanted to say good-bye to her alone. Frau Lenore saw that, and felt no curiosity as to the matter of such great importance.

Sanin had never been in Gemma's room before. All the magic of love, all its fire and rapture and sweet terror, seemed to flame up and burst into his soul, directly he crossed its sacred threshold. . . . He cast a look of tenderness about him, fell at the sweet girl's feet and pressed his face against her waist. . . .

'You are mine,' she whispered: 'you will be back soon?'

'I am yours. I will come back,' he declared, catching his breath.

'I shall be longing for you back, my dear one!'

A few instants later Sanin was running along the street to his lodging. He did not even notice that Pantaleone, all dishevelled, had darted out of the shop-door after him, and was shouting something to him and was shaking, as though in menace, his lifted hand.

Exactly at a quarter to one Sanin presented himself before Polozov. The carriage with four horses was already standing at the hotel gates. On seeing Sanin, Polozov merely commented, 'Oh! you've made up your mind?' and putting on his hat, cloak, and over-shoes, and stuffing cotton-wool into his ears, though it was summer-time, went out on to the steps. The waiters, by his directions, disposed all his numerous purchases in the inside of the carriage, lined the place where he was to sit with silk cushions, bags, and bundles, put a hamper of provisions for his feet to rest on, and tied a trunk on to the box. Polozov paid with a liberal hand, and supported by the deferential door-keeper, whose face was still respectful, though he was unseen behind him, he climbed gasping into the carriage, sat down, disarranged everything about him thoroughly, took out and lighted a cigar, and only then extended a finger to Sanin, as though to say, 'Get in, you too!' Sanin placed himself beside him. Polozov sent orders by the door-keeper to the postillion to drive carefully—if he wanted drinks; the carriage steps grated, the doors slammed, and the carriage rolled off.

XXXIII

It takes less than an hour in these days by rail from Frankfort to Wiesbaden; at that time the extra post did it in three hours. They changed horses five times. Part of the time Polozov dozed and part of the time he simply shook from side to side, holding a cigar in his teeth; he talked very little; he did not once look out of the window; picturesque views did not interest them; he even announced that 'nature was the death of him!' Sanin did not speak either, nor did-he admire the scenery; he had no thought for it. He was all absorbed in reflections and memories. At the stations Polozov paid with exactness, took the time by his watch, and tipped the postillions—more or less—according to their zeal. When they had gone half way, he took two oranges out of the hamper of edibles, and choosing out the better, offered the other to Sanin. Sanin looked steadily at his companion, and suddenly burst out laughing.

'What are you laughing at?' the latter inquired, very carefully peeling his orange with his short white nails.

'What at?' repeated Sanin. 'Why, at our journey together.'

'What about it?' Polozov inquired again, dropping into his mouth one of the longitudinal sections into which an orange parts.

'It's so very strange Yesterday I must confess I thought no more of you than of the

Emperor of China, and to-day I'm driving with you to sell my estate to your wife, of whom, too, I have not the slightest idea.'

'Anything may happen,' responded Polozov. 'When you've lived a bit longer, you won't be surprised at anything. For instance, can you fancy me riding as an orderly officer? But I did, and the Grand Duke Mihail Pavlovitch gave the order, 'Trot! let him trot, that fat cornet! Trot now! Look sharp!'

Sanin scratched behind his ear.

'Tell me, please, Ippolit Sidorovitch, what is your wife like? What is her character? It's very necessary for me to know that, you see.'

'It was very well for him to shout, "Trot!"' Polozov went on with sudden vehemence, 'But me! how about me? I thought to myself "You can take your honours and epaulettes—and leave me in peace!" But . . . you asked about my wife? What my wife is? A person like any one else. Don't wear your heart upon your sleeve with her—she doesn't like that. The great thing is to talk a lot to her . . . something for her to laugh at. Tell her about your love, or something . . . but make it more amusing, you know.'

'How more amusing?'

'Oh, you told me, you know, that you were

in love, wanting to get married. Well, then, describe that.'

Sanin was offended. 'What do you find laughable in that?'

Polozov only rolled his eyes. The juice from the orange was trickling down his chin.

'Was it your wife sent you to Frankfort to shop for her?' asked Sanin after a short time.

'Yes, it was she.'

'What are the purchases?'

'Toys, of course.'

'Toys? have you any children?'

Polozov positively moved away from Sanin. 'That's likely! What do I want with children? Feminine fallals . . . finery. For the toilet.'

'Do you mean to say you understand such things?'

'To be sure I do.'

'But didn't you tell me you didn't interfere in any of your wife's affairs?'

'I don't in any other. But this . . . is no consequence. To pass the time—one may do it. And my wife has confidence in my taste. And I'm a first-rate hand at bargaining.'

Polozov began to speak by jerks; he was exhausted already.

'And is your wife very rich?'

'Rich; yes, rather! Only she keeps the most of it for herself.'

'But I expect you can't complain either?'

'Well, I'm her husband. I'm hardly likely not to get some benefit from it! And I'm of use to her. With me she can do just as she likes! I'm easy-going!'

Polozov wiped his face with a silk handkerchief and puffed painfully, as though to say, 'Have mercy on me; don't force me to utter another word. You see how hard it is for me.'

Sanin left him in peace, and again sank into meditation.

The hotel in Wiesbaden, before which the carriage stopped, was exactly like a palace. Bells were promptly set ringing in its inmost recesses; a fuss and bustle arose; men of good appearance in black frock-coats skipped out at the principal entrance; a door-keeper who was a blaze of gold opened the carriage doors with a flourish.

Like some triumphant general Polozov alighted and began to ascend a staircase strewn with rugs and smelling of agreeable perfumes. To him flew up another man, also very well dressed but with a Russian face—his valet. Polozov observed to him that for the future he should always take him everywhere with him, for the night before at Frankfort, he, Polozov, had been left for the night without hot water! The valet portrayed his horror on his face, and bending down quickly, took off his master's goloshes.

'Is Maria Nikolaevna at home?' inquired Polozov.

'Yes, sir. Madam is pleased to be dressing. Madam is pleased to be dining to-night at the Countess Lasunsky's.'

'Ah! there? . . . Stay! There are things there in the carriage; get them all yourself and bring them up. And you, Dmitri Pavlovitch,' added Polozov, 'take a room for yourself and come in in three-quarters of an hour. We will dine together.'

Polozov waddled off, while Sanin asked for an inexpensive room for himself; and after setting his attire to rights, and resting a little, he repaired to the immense apartment occupied by his Serenity (Durchlaucht) Prince von Polozov.

He found this 'prince' enthroned in a luxurious velvet arm-chair in the middle of a most magnificent drawing-room. Sanin's phlegmatic friend had already had time to have a bath and to array himself in a most sumptuous satin dressing-gown; he had put a crimson fez on his head. Sanin approached him and scrutinised him for some time. Polozov was sitting rigid as an idol; he did not even turn his face in his direction, did not even move an eyebrow, did not utter a sound. It was truly a sublime spectacle! After having admired him for a couple of minutes, Sanin was on the point of speaking, of breaking this hallowed silence, when suddenly the door from the next room was thrown open, and in the doorway appeared a young and beautiful lady in a white silk dress trimmed with black lace, and with diamonds on her arms and neck—Maria Nikolaevna Polozov. Her thick fair hair fell on both sides of her head, braided, but not fastened up into a knot.

XXXIV

'Ah, I beg your pardon!' she said with a smile half-embarrassed, half-ironical, instantly taking hold of one end of a plait of her hair and fastening on Sanin her large, grey, clear eyes. 'I did not think you had come yet.'

'Sanin, Dmitri Pavlovitch—known him from a boy,' observed Polozov, as before not turning towards him and not getting up, but pointing at him with one finger.

'Yes. . . . I know. . . . You told me before. Very glad to make your acquaintance. But I wanted to ask you, Ippolit Sidorovitch. . . .

My maid seems to have lost her senses to-day . . .'

'To do your hair up?'

'Yes, yes, please. I beg your pardon,' Maria Nikolaevna repeated with the same smile. She nodded to Sanin, and turning swiftly, vanished through the doorway, leaving behind her a fleeting but graceful impression of a charming neck, exquisite shoulders, an exquisite figure.

Polozov got up, and rolling ponderously, went out by the same door.

Sanin did not doubt for a single second that his presence in 'Prince Polozov's' drawing-room was a fact perfectly well known to its mistress; the whole point of her entry had been the display of her hair, which was certainly beautiful. Sanin was inwardly delighted indeed at this freak on the part of Madame Polozov; if, he thought, she is anxious to impress me, to dazzle me, perhaps, who knows, she will be accommodating about the price of the estate. His heart was so full of Gemma that all other women had absolutely no significance for him; he hardly noticed them; and this time he went no further than thinking, 'Yes, it was the truth they told me; that lady's really magnificent to look at!'

But had he not been in such an exceptional state of mind he would most likely have expressed himself differently; Maria Nikolaevna Polozov, by birth Kolishkin, was a very striking personality. And not that she was of a beauty to which no exception could be taken; traces of her plebeian origin were rather clearly apparent in her. Her forehead was low, her nose rather fleshy and turned up; she could boast neither of the delicacy of her skin nor of the elegance of her hands and feet—but what did all that matter? Any one meeting her would not, to use Pushkin's words, have stood still before 'the holy shrine of beauty,' but before the sorcery of a half-Russian, half-Gipsy woman's body in its full flower and full power . . . and he would have been nothing loath to stand still!

But Gemma's image preserved Sanin like the three-fold armour of which the poets sing.

Ten minutes later Maria Nikolaevna appeared again, escorted by her husband. She went up to Sanin . . . and her walk was such that some eccentrics of that—alas!—already distant day, were simply crazy over her walk alone. 'That woman, when she comes towards one, seems as though she is bringing all the happiness of one's life to meet one,' one of them used to say. She went up to Sanin, and holding out her hand to him, said in her caressing and, as it were, subdued voice in Russian,

'You will wait for me, won't you? I'll be back soon.'

Sanin bowed respectfully, while Maria Nikolaevna vanished behind the curtain over the outside door; and as she vanished turned her head back over her shoulder, and smiled again, and again left behind her the same impression of grace.

When she smiled, not one and not two, but three dimples came out on each cheek, and her eyes smiled more than her lips—long, crimson, juicy lips with two tiny moles on the left side of them.

Polozov waddled into the room and again established himself in the arm-chair. He was speechless as before; but from time to time a queer smile puffed out his colourless and already wrinkled cheeks. He looked like an old man, though he was only three years older than Sanin.

The dinner with which he regaled his guest would of course have satisfied the most exacting gourmand, but to Sanin it seemed endless, insupportable! Polozov ate slowly, 'with feeling, with judgment, with deliberation,' bending attentively over his plate, and sniffing at almost every morsel. First he rinsed his mouth with wine, then swallowed it and smacked his lips. . . . Over the roast meat he suddenly began to talk—but of what? Of merino sheep, of which he was intending to order a whole flock, and in such detail, with such tenderness, using all the while endearing pet names for them. After drinking a cup of coffee, hot to boiling point (he had several times in a voice of tearful irritation mentioned to the waiter that he had been served the evening before with coffee, cold—cold as ice!) and bitten off the end of a Havannah cigar with his crooked yellow teeth, he dropped off, as his habit was, into a nap, to the intense delight of Sanin, who began walking up and down with noiseless steps on the soft carpet, and dreaming of his life with Gemma and of what news he would bring back to her. Polozov, however, awoke, as he remarked himself, earlier than usual—he had slept only an hour and a half—and after drinking a glass of iced seltzer water, and swallowing eight spoonfuls of jam, Russian jam, which his valet brought him in a dark-green genuine 'Kiev' jar, and without which, in his own words, he could not live, he stared with his swollen eyes at Sanin and asked him wouldn't he like to play a game of 'fools' with him. Sanin agreed readily; he was afraid that Polozov would begin talking again about lambs and ewes and fat tails. The host and the visitor both adjourned to the drawing-room, the waiter brought in the cards, and the game began, not,—of course, for money.

At this innocent diversion Maria Nikolaevna found them on her return from the Countess Lasunsky's. She laughed aloud directly she came into the room and saw the cards and the open card-table. Sanin jumped up, but she cried, 'Sit still; go on with the game. I'll change my dress directly and come back to you,' and vanished again with a swish of her dress, pulling off her gloves as she went.

She did in fact return very soon. Her evening dress she had exchanged for a full lilac silk tea-gown, with open hanging sleeves; a thick twisted cord was fastened round her waist. She sat down by her husband, and, waiting till he was left 'fool,' said to him, 'Come, dumpling, that's enough!' (At the word 'dumpling' Sanin glanced at her in surprise, and she smiled gaily, answering his look with a look, and displaying all the dimples on her cheeks.) 'I see you are sleepy; kiss my hand and get along; and Monsieur Sanin and I will have a chat together alone.'

'I'm not sleepy,' observed Polozov, getting up ponderously from his easy-chair; 'but as for getting along, I'm ready to get along and to kiss your hand.' She gave him the palm of her hand, still smiling and looking at Sanin.

Polozov, too, looked at him, and went away without taking leave of him.

'Well, tell me, tell me,' said Maria Nikolaevna eagerly, setting both her bare elbows on the table and impatiently tapping the nails of one hand against the nails of the other, 'Is it true, they say, you are going to be married?'

As she said these words, Maria Nikolaevna positively bent her head a little on one side so as to look more intently and piercingly into Sanin's eyes.

XXXV

The free and easy deportment of Madame Polozov would probably for the first moment have disconcerted Sanin-—though he was not quite a novice and had knocked about the world a little—if he had not again seen in this very freedom and familiarity a good omen for his undertaking. 'We must humour this rich lady's caprices,' he decided inwardly; and as unconstrainedly as she had questioned him he answered, 'Yes; I am going to be married.'

'To whom? To a foreigner?'

'Yes.'

'Did you get acquainted with her lately? In Frankfort?'

'Yes.'

'And what is she? May I know?'

'Certainly. She is a confectioner's daughter.'

Maria Nikolaevna opened her eyes wide and lifted her eyebrows.

'Why, this is delightful,' she commented in a drawling voice; 'this is exquisite! I imagined that young men like you were not to be met with anywhere in these days. A confectioner's daughter!'

'I see that surprises you,' observed Sanin with some dignity; 'but in the first place, I have none of these prejudices . . .'

'In the first place, it doesn't surprise me in the least,' Maria Nikolaevna interrupted; 'I have no prejudices either. I'm the daughter of a peasant myself. There! what can you say to that? What does surprise and delight me is to have come across a man who's not afraid to love. You do love her, I suppose?'

'Yes.'

'Is she very pretty?'

Sanin was slightly stung by this last question. . . . However, there was no drawing back.

'You know, Maria Nikolaevna,' he began, 'every man thinks the face of his beloved better than all others; but my betrothed is really beautiful.'

'Really? In what style? Italian? antique?'

'Yes; she has very regular features.'

'You have not got her portrait with you?'

'No.' (At that time photography was not yet talked off. Daguerrotypes had hardly begun to be common.)

'What's her name?'

'Her name is Gemma.'

'And yours?'

'Dimitri,'

'And your father's?'

'Pavlovitch.'

'Do you know,' Maria Nikolaevna said, still in the same drawling voice, 'I like you very much, Dimitri Pavlovitch. You must be an excellent fellow. Give me your hand. Let us be friends.'

She pressed his hand tightly in her beautiful, white, strong fingers. Her hand was a little smaller than his hand, but much warmer and smoother and whiter and more full of life.

'Only, do you know what strikes me?'

'What?'

'You won't be angry? No? You say she is betrothed to you. But was that . . . was that quite necessary?'

Sanin frowned. 'I don't understand you, Maria Nikolaevna.'

Maria Nikolaevna gave a soft low laugh, and shaking her head tossed back the hair that was falling on her cheeks. 'Decidedly—he's delightful,' she commented half pensively, half carelessly. 'A perfect knight! After that, there's no believing in the people who maintain that the race of idealists is extinct!'

Maria Nikolaevna talked Russian all the time, an astonishingly pure true Moscow Russian, such as the people, not the nobles speak.

'You've been brought up at home, I expect, in a God-fearing, old orthodox family?' she queried. 'You're from what province?'

'Tula.'

'Oh! so we're from the same part. My father . . . I daresay you know who my father was?'

'Yes, I know,'

'He was born in Tula. . . . He was a Tula man. Well . . . well. Come, let us get to business now.'

'That is . . . how come to business? What do you mean to say by that?'

Maria Nikolaevna half-closed her eyes. 'Why, what did you come here for?' (when she screwed up her eyes, their expression became very kindly and a little bantering, when she opened them wide, into their clear, almost cold brilliancy, there came something ill-natured . . . something menacing. Her eyes gained a peculiar beauty from her eyebrows, which were thick, and met in the centre, and had the smoothness of sable fur). 'Don't you want me to buy your estate? You want money for your nuptials? Don't you?'

'Yes.'

'And do you want much?'

'I should be satisfied with a few thousand francs at first. Your husband knows my estate. You can consult him—I would take a very moderate price.'

Maria Nikolaevna tossed her head from left to right. '*In the first place*,' she began in deliberate tones, drumming with the tips of her fingers on the cuff of Sanin's coat, 'I am not in the habit of consulting my husband, except about matters of dress—he's my right hand in that; *and in the second place*, why do you say that you will fix a low price? I don't want to take advantage of your being very much in love at the moment, and ready to make any sacrifices. . . . I won't accept sacrifices of any kind from you. What? Instead of encouraging you . . . come, how is one to express it properly?—in your noble sentiments, eh? am I to fleece you? that's not my way. I can be hard on people, on occasion—only not in that way.'

Sanin was utterly unable to make out

whether she was laughing at him or speaking seriously, and only said to himself: 'Oh, I can see one has to mind what one's about with you!'

A man-servant came in with a Russian samovar, tea-things, cream, biscuits, etc., on a big tray; he set all these good things on the table between Sanin and Madame Polozov, and retired.

She poured him out a cup of tea. 'You don't object?' she queried, as she put sugar in his cup with her fingers . . . though sugar-tongs were lying close by.

'Oh, please! . . . From such a lovely hand . . .'

He did not finish his phrase, and almost choked over a sip of tea, while she watched him attentively and brightly.

'I spoke of a moderate price for my land,' he went on, 'because as you are abroad just now, I can hardly suppose you have a great deal of cash available, and in fact, I feel myself that the sale . . . the purchase of my land, under such conditions is something exceptional, and I ought to take that into consideration.'

Sanin got confused, and lost the thread of what he was saying, while Maria Nikolaevna softly leaned back in her easy-chair, folded her arms, and watched him with the same attentive bright look. He was silent at last.

'Never mind, go on, go on,' she said, as it were coming to his aid; 'I'm listening to you. I like to hear you; go on talking.'

Sanin fell to describing his estate, how many acres it contained, and where it was situated, and what were its agricultural advantages, and what profit could be made from it . . . he even referred to the picturesque situation of the house; while Maria Nikolaevna still watched him, and watched more and more intently and radiantly, and her lips faintly stirred, without smiling: she bit them. He felt awkward at last; he was silent a second time.

'Dimitri Pavlovitch,' began Maria Nikolaevna, and sank into thought again. . . . 'Dimitri Pavlovitch,' she repeated. . . . 'Do you know what: I am sure the purchase of your estate will be a very profitable transaction for me, and that we shall come to terms; but you must give me two days. . . . Yes, two days' grace. You are able to endure two days' separation from your betrothed, aren't you? Longer I won't keep you against your will—I give you my word of honour. But if you want five or six thousand francs at once, I am ready with great pleasure to let you have it as a loan, and then we'll settle later.'

Sanin got up. 'I must thank you, Maria Nikolaevna, for your kindhearted and friendly readiness to do a service to a man almost unknown to you. But if that is your decided wish, then I prefer to await your decision about my estate—I will stay here two days.'

'Yes; that is my wish, Dimitri Pavlovitch. And will it be very hard for you? Very? Tell me.'

'I love my betrothed, Maria Nikolaevna, and to be separated from her is hard for me.'

'Ah! you're a heart of gold!' Maria Nikolaevna commented with a sigh. 'I promise not to torment you too much. Are you going?'

'It is late,' observed Sanin.

'And you want to rest after your journey, and your game of "fools" with my husband. Tell me, were you a great friend of Ippolit Sidoritch, my husband?'

'We were educated at the same school.'

'And was he the same then?'

'The same as what?' inquired Sanin.

Maria Nikolaevna burst out laughing, and laughed till she was red in the face; she put her handkerchief to her lips, rose from her chair, and swaying as though she were tired, went up to Sanin, and held out her hand to him.

He bowed over it, and went towards the door.

'Come early to-morrow—do you hear?'

she called after him. He looked back as he went out of the room, and saw that she had again dropped into an easy-chair, and flung both arms behind her head. The loose sleeves of her tea-gown fell open almost to her shoulders, and it was impossible not to admit that the pose of the arms, that the whole figure, was enchantingly beautiful.

XXXVI

Long after midnight the lamp was burning in Sanin's room. He sat down to the table and wrote to 'his Gemma.' He told her everything; he described the Polozovs—husband and wife—but, more than all, enlarged on his own feelings, and ended by appointing a meeting with her in three days ! ! ! (with three marks of exclamation). Early in the morning he took this letter to the post, and went for a walk in the garden of the Kurhaus, where music was already being played. There were few people in it as yet; he stood before the arbour in which the orchestra was placed, listened to an adaptation of airs from 'Robert le Diable,' and after drinking some coffee, turned into a solitary side walk, sat down on a bench, and fell into a reverie. The handle of a parasol gave him a rapid, and rather vigorous, thump on the shoulder. He. . . . Before him in a light, grey-green barége dress, in a white tulle hat, and *suède* gloves, stood Maria Nikolaevna, fresh and rosy as a summer morning, though the languor of sound unbroken sleep had not yet quite vanished from her movements and her eyes.

'Good-morning,' she said. 'I sent after you to-day, but you'd already gone out. I've only just drunk my second glass—they're making me drink the water here, you know—whatever for, there's no telling . . . am I not healthy enough? And now I have to walk for a whole hour. Will you be my companion? And then we'll have some coffee.'

'I've had some already,' Sanin observed, getting up; 'but I shall be very glad to have a walk with you.'

'Very well, give me your arm then; don't be afraid: your betrothed is not here—she won't see you.'

Sanin gave a constrained smile. He experienced a disagreeable sensation every time Maria Nikolaevna referred to Gemma. However, he made haste to bend towards her obediently. . . . Maria Nikolaevna's arm slipped slowly and softly into his arm, and glided over it, and seemed to cling tight to it.

'Come—this way,' she said to him, putting up her open parasol over her shoulder. 'I'm quite at home in this park; I will take you to the best places. And do you know what? (she very often made use of this expression), we won't talk just now about that sale, we'll have a thorough discussion of that after lunch; but you must tell me now about yourself . . . so that I may know whom I have to do with. And afterwards, if you like, I will tell you about myself. Do you agree?'

'But, Maria Nikolaevna, what interest can there be for you . . .'

'Stop, stop. You don't understand me. I don't want to flirt with you.' Maria Nikolaevna shrugged her shoulders. 'He's got a betrothed like an antique statue, is it likely I am going to flirt with him? But you've something to sell, and I'm the purchaser. I want to know what your goods are like. Well, of course, you must show what they are like. I don't only want to know what I'm buying, but whom I'm buying from. That was my father's rule. Come, begin . . . come, if not from childhood —come now, have you been long abroad? And where have you been up till now? Only don't walk so fast, we're in no hurry.'

'I came here from Italy, where I spent several months.'

'Ah, you feel, it seems, a special attraction towards everything Italian. It's strange you didn't find your lady-love there. Are you fond of art? of pictures? or more of music?'

'I am fond of art. . . . I like everything beautiful.'

'And music?'

'I like music too.'

'Well, I don't at all. I don't care for anything but Russian songs—and that in the country and in the spring—with dancing, you know . . . red shirts, wreaths of beads, the young grass in the meadows, the smell of smoke . . . delicious! But we weren't talking of me. Go on, tell me.'

Maria Nikolaevna walked on, and kept looking at Sanin. She was tall—her face was almost on a level with his face.

He began to talk—at first reluctantly, unskilfully—but afterwards he talked more freely, chattered away in fact. Maria Nikolaevna was a very good listener; and moreover she seemed herself so frank, that she led others unconsciously on to frankness. She possessed that great gift of 'intimateness'—*le terrible don de la familiarité*—to which Cardinal Retz refers. Sanin talked of his travels, of his life in Petersburg, of his youth. . . . Had Maria Nikolaevna been a lady of fashion, with refined manners, he would never have opened out so; but she herself spoke of herself as a 'good fellow,' who had no patience with ceremony of any sort; it was in those words that she characterised herself to Sanin. And at the same time this 'good fellow' walked by his side with feline grace, slightly bending towards him, and peeping into his face; and this 'good fellow' walked in the form of a young feminine creature, full of the tormenting, fiery, soft and seductive charm, of which—for the undoing of us poor weak sinful men—only Slav natures are possessed, and but few of them, and those never of pure Slav blood, with no foreign alloy. Sanin's walk with Maria Nikolaevna, Sanin's talk with Maria Nikolaevna lasted over an hour. And they did not stop once; they kept walking about the endless avenues of the park, now mounting a hill and admiring the view as they went, and now going down into the valley, and getting hidden in the thick shadows, —and all the while arm-in-arm. At times Sanin felt positively irritated; he had never walked so long with Gemma, his darling Gemma . . . but this lady had simply taken possession of him, and there was no escape! 'Aren't you tired?' he said to her more than once. 'I never get tired,' she answered. Now and then they met other people walking in the park; almost all of them bowed—some respectfully, others even cringingly. To one of them, a very handsome, fashionably dressed dark man, she called from a distance with the best Parisian accent, '*Comte, vous savez, il ne faut pas venir me voir—ni aujourd' hui ni demain.*' The man took off his hat, without speaking, and dropped a low bow.

'Who's that?' asked Sanin with the bad habit of asking questions characteristic of all Russians.

'Oh, a Frenchman, there are lots of them here . . . He's dancing attendance on me too. It's time for our coffee, though. Let's go home; you must be hungry by this time, I should say. My better half must have got his eye-peeps open by now.'

'Better half! Eye-peeps!' Sanin repeated to himself . . . 'And speaks French so well . . . what a strange creature!'

Maria Nikolaevna was not mistaken. When she went back into the hotel with Sanin, her 'better half' or 'dumpling' was already seated, the invariable fez on his head, before a table laid for breakfast.

'I've been waiting for you!' he cried, making a sour face. 'I was on the point of having coffee without you.'

'Never mind, never mind,' Maria Nikolaevna responded cheerfully. 'Are you angry? That's good for you; without that you 'd turn into a mummy altogether. Here I've brought a visitor. Make haste and ring! Let us have coffee—the best coffee—in Saxony cups on a snow-white cloth!'

She threw off her hat and gloves, and clapped her hands.

Polozov looked at her from under his brows.

'What makes you so skittish to-day, Maria Nikolaevna?' he said in an undertone.

'That's no business of yours, Ippolit Sidoritch! Dimitri Pavlovitch, sit down and have some coffee for the second time. Ah, how nice it is to give orders! There's no pleasure on earth like it!'

'When you're obeyed,' grumbled her husband again.

'Just so, when one's obeyed! That's why I'm so happy! Especially with you. Isn't it so, dumpling? Ah, here's the coffee.'

On the immense tray, which the waiter brought in, there lay also a playbill. Maria Nikolaevna snatched it up at once.

'A drama!' she pronounced with indignation, 'a German drama. No matter; it's better than a German comedy. Order a box for me—*baignoire*—or no . . . better the

Fremden-Loge,' she turned to the waiter. 'Do you hear: the *Fremden-Loge* it must be!'

'But if the *Fremden-Loge* has been already taken by his excellency, the director of the town (*seine Excellenz der Herr Stadt-Director*),' the waiter ventured to demur.

'Give his excellency ten *thalers*, and let the box be mine! Do you hear!'

The waiter bent his head humbly and mournfully.

'Dimitri Pavlovitch, you will go with me to the theatre? the German actors are awful, but you will go . . . Yes? Yes? How obliging you are! Dumpling, are you not coming?

'You settle it,' Polozov observed into the cup he had lifted to his lips.

'Do you know what, you stay at home. You always go to sleep at the theatre, and you don't understand much German. I'll tell you what you'd better do, write an answer to the overseer—you remember, about our mill . . . about the peasants' grinding. Tell him that I won't have it, and I won't and that's all about it! There's occupation for you for the whole evening.'

'All right,' answered Polozov.

'Well then, that's first-rate. You're a darling. And now, gentlemen, as we have just been speaking of my overseer, let's talk about our great business. Come, directly the waiter has cleared the table, you shall tell me all, Dimitri Pavlovitch, about your estate, what price you will sell it for, how much you want paid down in advance, everything, in fact! (At last, thought Sanin, thank God!) You have told me something about it already, you remember, you described your garden delightfully, but dumpling wasn't here. . . . Let him hear, he may pick a hole somewhere! I'm delighted to think that I can help you to get married, besides, I promised you that I would go into your business after lunch, and I always keep my promises, isn't that the truth, Ippolit Sidoritch?'

Polozov rubbed his face with his open hand. 'The truth's the truth. You don't deceive any one.'

'Never! and I never will deceive any one. Well, Dimitri Pavlovitch, expound the case as we express it in the senate.'

XXXVII

Sanin proceeded to expound his case, that is to say, again, a second time, to describe his property, not touching this time on the beauties of nature, and now and then appealing to Polozov for confirmation of his 'facts and figures.' But Polozov simply gasped and shook his head, whether in approval or disapproval, it would have puzzled the devil, one might fancy, to decide. However, Maria Nikolaevna stood in no need of his aid. She exhibited commercial and administrative abilities that were really astonishing! She was familiar with all the ins-and-outs of farming; she asked questions about everything with great exactitude, went into every point; every word of hers went straight to the root of the matter, and hit the nail on the head. Sanin had not expected such a close inquiry, he had not prepared himself for it. And this inquiry lasted for fully an hour and a half. Sanin experienced all the sensations of the criminal on his trial, sitting on a narrow bench confronted by a stern and penetrating judge. 'Why, it's a cross-examination!' he murmured to himself dejectedly. Maria Nikolaevna kept laughing all the while, as though it were a joke; but Sanin felt none the more at ease for that; and when in the course of the 'cross-examination' it turned out that he had not clearly realised the exact meaning of the words 'repartition' and 'tilth,' he was in a cold perspiration all over.

'Well, that's all right!' Maria Nikolaevna decided at last. 'I know your estate now . . . as well as you do. What price do you suggest per soul?' (At that time, as every one knows, the prices of estates were reckoned by the souls living as serfs on them.)

'Well . . . I imagine . . . I could not take less than five hundred roubles for each,' Sanin articulated with difficulty. O Pantaleone, Pantaleone, where were you! This was when you ought to have cried again, 'Barbari!'

Maria Nikolaevna turned her eyes upwards as though she were calculating.

'Well?' she said at last. 'I think there's no harm in that price. But I reserved for myself two days' grace, and you must wait till to-morrow. I imagine we shall come to an arrangement, and then you will tell me how much you want paid down. And now, *basta cosi*!' she cried, noticing Sanin was about to make some reply. 'We've spent enough time over filthy lucre . . . *à demain les affaires*. Do you know what, I'll let you go now . . . (she glanced at a little enamelled watch, stuck in her belt) . . . till three o'clock . . . I must let you rest. Go and play roulette.'

'I never play games of chance,' observed Sanin.

'Really? Why, you're a paragon. Though I don't either. It's stupid throwing away one's money when one's no chance. But go into the gambling saloon, and look at the faces. Very comic ones there are there. There's one old woman with a rustic headband and a moustache, simply delicious! Our prince there's another, a good one too. A majestic figure with a nose like an eagle's, and when he puts down a *thaler*, he crosses himself under his waistcoat. Read the papers, go a walk, do what you like, in fact. But at three o'clock I expect you . . . *de pied ferme*. We shall have to dine a little earlier. The theatre among these absurd Germans begins at half-past six. She held out her hand. '*Sans rancune*, n'est-ce pas?'

'Really, Maria Nikolaevna, what reason have I to be annoyed?'

'Why, because I've been tormenting you. Wait a little, you'll see. There's worse to come,' she added, fluttering her eyelids, and all her dimples suddenly came out on her flushing cheeks. 'Till we meet!'

Sanin bowed and went out. A merry laugh rang out after him, and in the looking-glass which he was passing at that instant, the following scene was reflected: Maria Nikolaevna had pulled her husband's fez over his eyes, and he was helplessly struggling with both hands.

XXXVIII

Oh, what a deep sigh of delight Sanin heaved, when he found himself in his room! Indeed, Maria Nikolaevna had spoken the truth, he needed rest, rest from all these new acquaintances, collisions, conversations, from this suffocating atmosphere which was affecting his head and his heart, from this enigmatical, uninvited intimacy with a woman, so alien to him! And when was all this taking place? Almost the day after he had learnt that Gemma loved him, after he had become betrothed to her. Why, it was sacrilege! A thousand times he mentally asked forgiveness of his pure chaste dove, though he could not really blame himself for anything; a thousand times over he kissed the cross she had given him. Had he not the hope of bringing the business, for which he had come to Wiesbaden, to a speedy and successful conclusion, he would have rushed off headlong, back again, to sweet Frankfort, to that dear house, now his own home, to her, to throw himself at her loved feet. . . . But there was no help for it! The cup must be drunk to the dregs, he must dress, go to dinner, and from there to the theatre. . . . If only she would let him go to-morrow!

One other thing confounded him, angered him; with love, with tenderness, with grateful transport he dreamed of Gemma, of their life together, of the happiness awaiting him in the future, and yet this strange woman, this Madame Polozov persistently floated—no! not floated, poked herself, so Sanin with special vindictiveness expressed it—*poked herself* in and faced his eyes, and he could not rid himself of her image, could not help hearing her voice, recalling her words, could not help being aware even of the special scent, delicate, fresh and penetrating, like the scent of yellow lilies, that was wafted from her garments. This lady was obviously fooling him, and trying in every way to get over him . . . what for? what did she want? Could it be merely the caprice of a spoiled, rich, and most likely unprincipled woman? And that husband! What a creature he was! What were his relations with her? And why would these questions keep coming into his head, when he, Sanin, had really no interest whatever in either Polozov or his wife? Why could he not drive away that intrusive image, even when he turned with his whole soul to another image, clear and bright as God's sunshine? How, through those almost divine features, dare *those others* force themselves upon him? And not only that; those other features smiled insolently at him. Those grey, rapacious eyes, those dimples, those snake-like tresses, how was it all that seemed to cleave to him, and to shake it all off, and fling it away, he was unable, had not the power?

Nonsense! nonsense! to-morrow it would all vanish and leave no trace. . . . But would she let him go to-morrow?

Yes. . . All these question he put to himself, but the time was moving on to three o'clock, and he put on a black frockcoat and after a turn in the park, went in to the Polozovs!

He found in their drawing-room a secretary of the legation, a very tall light-haired German, with the profile of a horse, and his hair parted down the back of his head (at that time a new fashion), and . . . oh, wonder! whom besides? Von Dönhof, the very officer with whom he had fought a few days before! He had not the slightest expectation of meeting him there and could not help being taken aback. He greeted him, however.

'Are you acquainted?' asked Maria Nikolaevna who had not failed to notice Sanin's embarrassment.

'Yes . . . I have already had the honour,'

said Dönhof, and bending a little aside, in an undertone he added to Maria Nikolaevna, with a smile, 'The very man . . . your compatriot . . . the Russian . . .'

'Impossible!' she exclaimed also in an undertone; she shook her finger at him, and at once began to bid good-bye both to him and the long secretary, who was, to judge by every symptom, head over ears in love with her; he positively gaped every time he looked at her. Dönhof promptly took leave with amiable docility, like a friend of the family who understands at half a word what is expected of him; the secretary showed signs of restiveness, but Maria Nikolaevna turned him out without any kind of ceremony.

'Get along to your sovereign mistress,' she said to him (there was at that time in Wiesbaden a certain princess di Monaco, who looked surprisingly like a *cocotte* of the poorer sort); 'what do you want to stay with a plebeian like me for?'

'Really, dear madam,' protested the luckless secretary, 'all the princesses in the world. . . .'

But Maria Nikolaevna was remorseless, and the secretary went away, parting and all.

Maria Nikolaevna was dressed that day very much 'to her advantage,' as our grandmothers used to say. She wore a pink glacé silk dress, with sleeves *à la Fontange,* and a big diamond in each ear. Her eyes sparkled as much as her diamonds; she seemed in a good humour and in high spirits.

She made Sanin sit beside her, and began talking to him about Paris, where she was intending to go in a few days, of how sick she was of Germans, how stupid they were when they tried to be clever, and how inappropriately clever sometimes when they were stupid; and suddenly, point-blank, as they say—*à brûle pourpoint*—asked him, was it true that he had fought a duel with the very officer who had been there just now, only a few days ago, on account of a lady?

'How did you know that?' muttered Sanin, dumfoundered.

'The earth is full of rumours, Dimitri Pavlovitch; but anyway, I know you were quite right, perfectly right, and behaved like a knight. Tell me, was that lady your betrothed?'

Sanin slightly frowned . . .

'There, I won't, I won't,' Maria Nikolaevna hastened to say. 'You don't like it, forgive me, I won't do it, don't be angry!' Polozov came in from the next room with a newspaper in his hand. 'What do you want? Or is dinner ready?'

'Dinner'll be ready directly, but just sec what I've read in the *Northern Bee* . . . Prince Gromoboy is dead.'

Maria Nikolaevna raised her head.

'Ah! I wish him the joys of Paradise! He used,' she turned to Sanin, 'to fill all my rooms with camellias every February on my birthday. But it wasn't worth spending the winter in Petersburg for that. He must have been over seventy, I should say?' she said to her husband.

'Yes, he was. They describe his funeral in the paper. All the court were present. And here's a poem too, of Prince Kovrizhkin's on the occasion.'

'That's nice!'

'Shall I read them? The prince calls him the good man of wise counsel.'

'No, don't. The good man of wise counsel? He was simply the goodman of Tatiana Yurevna. Come to dinner. Life is for the living. Dimitri Pavlovitch, your arm.'

The dinner was, as on the day before, superb, and the meal was a very lively one. Maria Nikolaevna knew how to tell a story . . . a rare gift in a woman, and especially in a Russian one! She did not restrict herself in her expressions; her countrywomen received particularly severe treatment at her hands.

Sanin was more than once set laughing by some bold and well-directed word. Above all, Maria Nikolaevna had no patience with hypocrisy, cant, and humbug. She discovered it almost everywhere. She, as it were, plumed herself on and boasted of the humble surroundings in which she had begun life. She told rather queer anecdotes of her relations in the days of her childhood, spoke of herself as quite as much of a clodhopper as Natalya Kirilovna Narishkin. It became apparent to Sanin that she had been through a great deal more in her time than the majority of women of her age.

Polozov ate meditatively, drank attentively, and only occasionally cast first on his wife, then on Sanin, his lightish, dim-looking, but, in reality, very keen eyes.

'What a clever darling you are!' cried Maria Nikolaevna, turning to him; 'how well you carried out all my commissions in Frankfort! I could give you a kiss on your forehead for it, but you're not very keen after kisses.'

'I'm not,' responded Polozov, and he cut a pine-apple with a silver knife.

Maria Nikolaevna looked at him and drummed with her fingers on the table.

'So our bet's on, isn't it?' she said significantly.

'Yes, it's on.'

'All right. You'll lose it.'

Polozov stuck out his chin. 'Well, this time you mustn't be too sanguine, Maria Nikolaevna, maybe you will lose.'

'What is the bet? May I know?' asked Sanin.

'No . . . not now,' answered Maria Nikolaevna, and she laughed.

It struck seven. The waiter announced that the carriage was ready. Polozov saw his wife out, and at once waddled back to his easy-chair.

'Mind now! Don't forget the letter to the overseer,' Maria Nikolaevna shouted to him from the hall.

'I'll write, don't worry yourself. I'm a business-like person.'

XXXIX

IN the year 1840, the theatre at Wiesbaden was a poor affair even externally, and its company, for affected and pitiful mediocrity, for studious and vulgar commonplaceness, not one hair's-breadth above the level, which might be regarded up to now as the normal one in all German theatres, and which has been displayed in perfection lately by the company in

Carlsruhe, under the 'illustrious' direction of Herr Devrient. At the back of the box taken for her 'Serenity Madame von Polozov' (how the waiter devised the means of getting it, God knows, he can hardly have really bribed the stadt-director!) was a little room, with sofas all round it; before she went into the box, Maria Nikolaevna asked Sanin to draw up the screen that shut the box off from the theatre.

'I don't want to be seen,' she said, 'or else they'll be swarming round directly, you know,' She made him sit down beside her with his back to the house so that the box seemed to be empty. The orchestra played the overture from the *Marriage of Figaro*. The curtain rose, the play began.

It was one of those numerous home-raised products in which well-read but talentless authors, in choice, but dead language, studiously and cautiously enunciated some 'proFound' or 'vital a nd palpitating' idea, portrayed a so-called tragic conflict, and produced dulness . . . an Asiatic dulness, like Asiatic cholera. Maria Nikolaevna listened patiently to half an act, but when the first lover, discovering the treachery of his mistress (he was dressed in a cinnamon-coloured coat with 'puffs' and a plush collar, a striped waistcoat with mother-of-pearl buttons, green trousers with straps of varnished leather, and white chamois leather gloves), when this lover pressed both fists to his bosom, and poking his two elbows out at an acute angle, howled like a dog, Maria Nikolaevna could not stand it.

'The humblest French actor in the humblest little provincial town acts better and more naturally than the highest German celebrity,' she cried in indignation; and she moved away and sat down in the little room at the back. 'Come here,' she said to Sanin, patting the sofa beside her. 'Let's talk.'

Sanin obeyed.

Maria Nikolaevna glanced at him. 'Ah, I see you're as soft as silk! Your wife will have an easy time of it with you. That buffoon,' she went on, pointing with her fan towards the howling actor (he was acting the part of a tutor), 'reminded me of my young days; I, too, was in love with a teacher. It was my first . . . no, my second passion. The first time I fell in love with a young monk of the Don monastery. I was twelve years old. I only saw him on Sundays. He used to wear a short velvet cassock, smelt of lavender water, and as he made his way through the crowd with the censer, used to say to the ladies in French, "*Pardon, excusez*," but never lifted his eyes, and he had eyelashes like that!' Maria

Nikolaevna marked off with the nail of her middle finger quite half the length of the little finger and showed Sanin. 'My tutor was called—Monsieur Gaston! I must tell you he was an awfully learned and very severe person, a Swiss,—and with such an energetic face! Whiskers black as pitch, a Greek profile, and, lips that looked like cast iron! I was afraid of him! He was the only man I have ever been afraid of in my life. He was tutor to my brother, who died . . . was drowned. A gipsy. woman has foretold a violent death for me too, but that's all moonshine. I don't believe in it. Only fancy Ippolit Sidoritch with a dagger!'

'One may die from something else than a dagger,' observed Sanin.

'All that's moonshine! Are you superstitious? I'm not a bit. What is to be, will be. Monsieur Gaston used to live in our house, in the room over my head. Sometimes I'd wake up at night and hear his footstep—he used to go to bed very late—and my heart would stand still with veneration, or some other feeling. My father could hardly read and write himself, but he gave us an excellent education. Do you know, I learnt Latin!'

'You? learnt Latin?'

'Yes; I did. Monsieur Gaston taught me.

I read the *Æneid* with him. It's a dull thing, but there are fine passages. Do you remember when Dido and Æneas are in the forest? . . .'

'Yes, yes, I remember,' Sanin answered hurriedly. He had long ago forgotten all his Latin, and had only very faint notions about the *Æneid*.

Maria Nikolaevna glanced at him, as her way was, a little from one side and looking upwards. 'Don't imagine, though, that I am very learned. Mercy on us! no; I'm not learned, and I've no talents of any sort. I scarcely know how to write . . . really; I can't read aloud; nor play the piano, nor draw, nor sew—nothing! That's what I am—there you have me!'

She threw out her hands. 'I tell you all this,' she said, 'first, so as not to hear those fools (she pointed to the stage where at that instant the actor's place was being filled by an actress, also howling, and also with her elbows projecting before her) and secondly, because I'm in your debt; you told me all about yourself yesterday.'

'It was your pleasure to question me,' observed Sanin.

Maria Nikolaevna suddenly turned to him. 'And it's not your pleasure to know just what sort of woman I am? I can't wonder at it, though,' she went on, leaning back again on the sofa cushions. 'A man just going to be married, and for love, and after a duel. . . . What thoughts could he have for anything else?'

Maria Nikolaevna relapsed into dreamy silence, and began biting the handle of her fan with her big, but even, milkwhite teeth.

And Sanin felt mounting to his head again that intoxication which he had not been able to get rid of for the last two days.

The conversation between him and Maria Nikolaevna was carried on in an undertone, almost in a whisper, and this irritated and disturbed him the more. . . .

When would it all end?

Weak people never put an end to things themselves—they always wait for the end.

Some one sneezed on the stage; this sneeze had been put into the play by the author as the 'comic relief or 'element'; there was certainly no other comic element in it; and the audience made the most of it; they laughed.

This laugh, too, jarred upon Sanin.

There were moments when he actually did not know whether he was furious or delighted, bored or amused. Oh, if Gemma could have seen him!

'It's really curious,' Maria Nikolaevna began all at once. 'A man informs one and in such a calm voice, "I am going to get married"; but no one calmly says to one, "I'm going to throw myself in the water." And yet what difference is there? It's curious, really.'

Annoyance got the upper hand of Sanin. 'There's a great difference, Maria Nikolaevna! It's not dreadful at all to throw oneself in the water if one can swim; and besides . . . as to the strangeness of marriages, if you come to that . . .'

He stopped short abruptly and bit his tongue.

Maria Nikolaevna slapped her open hand with her fan.

'Go on, Dimitri Pavlovitch, go on—I know what you were going to say. "If it comes to that, my dear madam, Maria Nikolaevna Polozov," you were going to say, "anything more curious than *your* marriage it would be impossible to conceive. . . . I know your husband well, from a child!" That's what you were going to say, you who can swim!'

'Excuse me,' Sanin was beginning. . . .

'Isn't it the truth? Isn't it the truth?' Maria Nikolaevna pronounced insistently. 'Come, look me in the face and tell me I was wrong!'

Sanin did not know what to do with his eyes.

'Well, if you like; it's the truth, if you absolutely insist upon it,' he said at last.

Maria Nikolaevna shook her head. 'Quite so, quite so. Well, and did you ask yourself, you who can swim, what could be the reason of such a strange . . . step on the part of a woman, not poor . . . and not a fool . . . and not ugly? All that does not interest you, perhaps, but no matter. I'll tell you the reason not this minute, but directly the *entr' acte* is over. I am in continual uneasiness for fear some one should come in. . .'

Maria Nikolaevna had hardly uttered this last word when the outer door actually was half opened, and into the box was thrust a head—red, oily, perspiring, still young, but toothless; with sleek long hair, a pendent nose, huge ears like a bat's, with gold spectacles on inquisitive dull eyes, and a *pince-nez* over the spectacles. The head looked round, saw Maria Nikolaevna, gave a nasty grin, nodded. . . . A scraggy neck craned in after it. . . .

Maria Nikolaevna shook her handkerchief at it 'I'm not at home! *Ich bin nicht zu Hause, Herr P. . . .! Ich bin nicht zu Hause. . . . Ksh-sh! ksh-sh-sh!*'

The head was disconcerted, gave a forced laugh, said with a sort of sob, in imitation of Liszt, at whose feet he had once reverently grovelled, '*Sehr gut, sehr gut!*' and vanished.

'What is that object? 'inquired Sanin.

'Oh, a Wiesbaden critic. A literary man or a flunkey, as you like. He is in the pay of a local speculator here, and so is bound to praise everything and be ecstatic over every one, though for his part he is soaked through and through with the nastiest venom, to which he does not dare to give vent. I am afraid he's an awful scandalmonger; he'll run at once to tell every one I'm in the theatre. Well, what does it matter?'

The orchestra played through a waltz, the curtain floated up again. . . . The grimacing and whimpering began again on the stage.

'Well,' began Maria Nikolaevna, sinking again on to the sofa. 'Since you are here and obliged to sit with me, instead of enjoying the society of your betrothed—don't turn away your eyes and get cross—I understand you, and have promised already to let you go to the other end of the earth—but now hear my confession. Do you care to know what I like more than anything?'

'Freedom,' hazarded Sanin.

Maria Nikolaevna laid her hand on his hand.

'Yes, Dimitri Pavlovitch,' she said, and in her voice there was a note of something special, a sort of unmistakable sincerity and gravity, 'freedom, more than all and before all. And don't imagine I am boasting of this—there is nothing praiseworthy in it; only it's *so* and always will be *so* with me to the day of my death. I suppose it must have been that I saw a great deal of slavery in my childhood and suffered enough from it. Yes, and Monsieur Gaston, my tutor, opened my eyes too. Now you can, perhaps, understand why I married Ippolit Sidoritch: with him I'm free, perfectly free as air, as the wind. . . . And I knew that before marriage; I knew that with him I should be a free Cossack!'

Maria Nikolaevna paused and flung her fan aside.

'I will tell you one thing more; I have no distaste for reflection . . . it's amusing, and indeed our brains are given us for that; but on the consequences of what I do I never reflect, and if I suffer I don't pity myself—not a little bit; it's not worth it. I have a favourite saying: *Cela ne tire pas à conséquence*,—I don't know how to say that in Russian. And after all, what does *tire à conséquence*? I shan't be asked to give an account of myself here, you see—in this world; and up there (she pointed upwards with her finger), well, up there—let them manage as best they can. When they come to judge me up there, *I* shall not be *I*! Are you listening to me? Aren't you bored?'

Sanin was sitting bent up. He raised his head. 'I'm not at all bored, Maria Nikolaevna, and I am listening to you with curiosity. Only I . . . confess . . . I wonder why you say all this to me?'

Maria Nikolaevna edged a little away on the sofa.

'You wonder? . . . Are you slow to guess? Or so modest?'

Sanin lifted his head higher than before.

'I tell you all this,' Maria Nikolaevna continued in an unmoved tone, which did not, however, at all correspond with the expression of her face, 'because I like you very much; yes, don't be surprised, I'm not joking; because since I have met you, it would be painful to me that you had a disagreeable recollection of me . . . not disagreeable even, that I shouldn't mind, but untrue. That's why I have made you come here, and am staying alone with you and talking to you so openly. . . . Yes, yes, openly. I'm not telling a lie. And observe, Dimitri Pavlovitch, I know you're in love with another woman, that you're going to be married to her. . . . Do justice to my disinterestedness! Though indeed it's a good opportunity for you to say in your turn: *Cela ne tire pas à conséquence!*'

She laughed, but her laugh suddenly broke off, and she stayed motionless, as though her own words had suddenly struck her, and in her eyes, usually so gay and bold, there was a gleam of something like timidity, even like sadness.

'Snake! ah, she's a snake!' Sanin was thinking meanwhile; 'but what a lovely snake!'

'Give me my opera-glass,' Maria Nikolaevna said suddenly. 'I want to see whether this *jeune première* really is so ugly. Upon my word, one might fancy the government appointed her in the interests of morality, so that the young men might not lose their heads over her.'

Sanin handed her the opera-glass, and as she took it from him, swiftly, but hardly audibly, she snatched his hand in both of hers.

'Please don't be serious,' she whispered with a smile. 'Do you know what, no one can put fetters on me, but then you see I put no fetters on others. I love freedom, and I don't acknowledge duties—not only for myself. Now move to one side a little, and let us listen to the play.'

Maria Nikolaevna turned her opera-glass upon the stage, and Sanin proceeded to look in the same direction, sitting beside her in the half dark of the box, and involuntarily drinking in the warmth and fragrance of her luxurious body, and as involuntarily turning over and over in his head all she had said during the evening—especially during the last minutes.

XL

THE play lasted over an hour longer, but Maria Nikolaevna and Sanin soon gave up looking at the stage. A conversation sprang up between them again, and went on the same lines as before; only this time Sanin was less silent. Inwardly he was angry with himself and with Maria Nikolaevna; he tried to prove to her all the inconsistency of her 'theory,' as though she cared for theories! He began arguing with her, at which she was secretly rejoiced; if a man argues, it means that he is giving in or will give in. He had taken the bait, was giving way, had left off keeping shyly aloof! She retorted, laughed, agreed, mused dreamily, attacked him . . . and meanwhile his face and her face were close together, his eyes no longer avoided her eyes. . . . Those eyes of hers seemed to ramble, seemed to hover over his features, and he smiled in response to them

—a smile of civility, but still a smile. It was so much gained for her that he had gone off into abstractions, that he was discoursing upon truth in personal relations, upon duty, the sacredness of love and marriage. . . . It is well known that these abstract propositions serve admirably as a beginning . . . as a starting-point. . . .

People who knew Maria Nikolaevna well used to maintain that when her strong and vigorous personality showed signs of something soft and modest, something almost of maidenly shamefacedness, though one wondered where she could have got it from . . . then . . . then, things were taking a dangerous turn.

Things had apparently taken such a turn for Sanin. . . . He would have felt contempt for himself, if he could have succeeded in concentrating his attention for one instant; but he had not time to concentrate his mind nor to despise himself.

She wasted no time. And it all came from his being so very good-looking! One can but exclaim, No man knows what may be his making or his undoing!

The play was over. Maria Nikolaevna asked Sanin to put on her shawl and did not stir, while he wrapped the soft fabric round her really queenly shoulders. Then she took his arm, went out into the corridor, and almost cried out aloud. At the very door of the box Dönhof sprang up like some apparition; while behind his back she got a glimpse of the figure of the Wiesbaden critic. The 'literary man's' oily face was positively radiant with malignancy.

'Is it your wish, madam, that I find you your carriage?' said the young officer addressing Maria Nikolaevna with a quiver of ill-disguised fury in his voice.

'No, thank you,' she answered . . . 'my man will find it. Stop! 'she added in an imperious whisper, and rapidly withdrew drawing Sanin along with her.

'Go to the devil! Why are you staring at me?' Dönhof roared suddenly at the literary man. He had to vent his feelings upon some one!

'*Sehr gut! sehr gut!*' muttered the literary man, and shuffled off.

Maria Nikolaevna's footman, waiting for her in the entrance, found her carriage in no time. She quickly took her seat in it; Sanin leapt in after her. The doors were slammed to, and Maria Nikolaevna exploded in a burst of laughter.

'What are you laughing at?' Sanin inquired.

'Oh, excuse me, please . . . but it struck me: what if Dönhof were to have another duel with you . . . on my account. . . . wouldn't that be wonderful?'

'Are you very great friends with him?' Sanin asked.

'With him? that boy? He's one of my followers. You needn't trouble yourself about him!'

'Oh, I'm not troubling myself at all.'

Maria Nikolaevna sighed. 'Ah, I know you're not. But listen, do you know what, you're such a darling, you mustn't refuse me one last request. Remember in three days' time I am going to Paris, and you are returning to Frankfort. . . . Shall we ever meet again?'

'What is this request?'

'You can ride, of course?'

'Yes.'

'Well, then, to-morrow morning I'll take you with me, and we'll go a ride together out of the town. We'll have splendid horses. Then we'll come home, wind up our business, and amen! Don't be surprised, don't tell me it's a caprice, and I'm a madcap—all that's very likely—but simply say, I consent.'

Maria Nikolaevna turned her face towards him. It was dark in the carriage, but her eyes glittered even in the darkness.

'Very well, I consent,' said Sanin with a sigh.

'Ah! You sighed!' Maria Nikolaevna mimicked him. 'That means to say, as you've begun, you must go on to the bitter end. But no, no. . . . You're charming, you're good, and I'll keep my promise. Here's my hand, without a glove on it, the right one, for business. Take it, and have faith in its pressure. What sort of a woman I am, I don't know; but I'm an honest fellow, and one can do business with me.'

Sanin, without knowing very well what he was doing, lifted the hand to his lips. Maria Nikolaevna softly took it, and was suddenly still, and did not speak again till the carriage stopped.

She began getting out. . . . What was it? Sanin's fancy? or did he really feel on his cheek a swift burning kiss?

'Till to-morrow!' whispered Maria Nikolaevna on the steps, in the light of the four tapers of a candelabrum, held up on her appearance by the gold-laced door-keeper. She kept her eyes cast down. 'Till to-morrow!'

When he got back to his room, Sanin found on the table a letter from Gemma. He felt a momentary dismay, and at once made haste to rejoice over it to disguise his dismay from himself. It consisted of a few lines. She was delighted at the 'successful opening of negotiations,' advised him to be patient, and added that all at home were well, and were already rejoicing at the prospect of seeing him back again. Sanin felt the letter rather stiff, he took pen and paper, however . . . and threw it all aside again. 'Why write? I shall be back myself to-morrow . . . it's high time!'

He went to bed immediately, and tried to get to sleep as quickly as possible. If he had stayed up and remained on his legs, he would certainly have begun thinking about Gemma, and he was for some reason . . . ashamed to think of her. His conscience was stirring within him. But he consoled himself with the reflection that to-morrow it would all be over for ever, and he would take leave for good of this feather-brained lady, and would forget all this rotten idiocy! . . .

Weak people in their mental colloquies, eagerly make use of strong expressions.

Et puts . . . cela ne tire pas à conséquence!

XLI

SUCH were Sanin's thoughts, as he went to bed; but what he thought next morning when Maria Nikolaevna knocked impatiently at his door with the coral handle of her riding-whip, when he saw her in the doorway, with the train of a dark-blue riding habit over her arm, with a man's small hat on her thickly coiled curls, with a veil thrown back over her shoulder, with a smile of invitation on her lips, in her eyes, over all her face—what he thought then —history does not record.

'Well? are you ready?' rang out a joyous voice.

Sanin buttoned his coat, and took his hat in silence. Maria Nikolaevna flung him a bright look, nodded to him, and ran swiftly down the staircase. And he ran after her.

The horses were already waiting in the street at the steps. There were three of them, a golden chestnut thorough-bred mare, with a thin-lipped mouth, that showed the teeth, with black prominent eyes, and legs like a stag's, rather thin but beautifully shaped, and full of fire and spirit, for Maria Nikolaevna; a big, powerful, rather thick-set horse, raven black all over, for Sanin; the third horse was destined for the groom. Maria Nikolaevna leaped adroitly on to her mare, who stamped and wheeled round, lifting her tail, and sinking on to her haunches. But Maria Nikolaevna, who was a first-rate horse-woman, reined her in; they had to take leave of Polozov, who in his inevitable fez and in an open dressing-gown, came out on to the balcony, and from there waved a *batiste* handkerchief, without the faintest smile, rather a frown, in fact, on his face. Sanin too mounted his horse; Maria Nikolaevna saluted Polozov with her whip, then gave her mare a lash with it on her arched and flat neck. The mare reared on her hind legs, made a dash forward, moving with a smart and shortened step, quivering in every sinew, biting the air and snorting abruptly. Sanin rode behind, and looked at Maria Nikolaevna; her slender supple figure, moulded by close-fitting but easy stays, swayed to and fro with self-confident grace and skill. She turned her head and beckoned him with her eyes alone. He came alongside of her.

'See now, how delightful it is,' she said. 'I tell you at the last, before parting, you are charming, and you shan't regret it.'

As she uttered those last words, she nodded her head several times as if to confirm them and make him feel their full weight.

She seemed so happy that Sanin was simply astonished; her face even wore at times that sedate expression which children sometimes have when they are very . . . very much pleased.

They rode at a walking pace for the short distance to the city walls, but then started off at a vigorous gallop along the high road. It was magnificent, real summer weather; the wind blew in their faces, and sang and whistled sweetly in their ears. They felt very happy; the sense of youth, health and life, of free eager onward motion, gained possession of both; it grew stronger every instant.

Maria Nikolaevna reined in her mare, and again went at a walking pace; Sanin followed her example.

'This,' she began with a deep blissful sigh, 'this now is the only thing worth living for. When you succeed in doing what you want to, what seemed impossible—come, enjoy it, heart and soul, to the last drop!' She passed her hand across her throat 'And how good and kind one feels oneself then! I now, at this moment . . . how good I feel! I feel as if I could embrace the whole world! No, not the whole world. . . . That man now I couldn't.' She pointed with her whip at a poorly dressed old man who was stealing along on one side. 'But I am ready to make him happy. Here, take this,' she shouted loudly in German, and she flung a net purse at his feet. The heavy little bag (leather purses were not thought of at that time) fell with a ring on to the road. The old man was astounded, stood still, while Maria Nikolaevna chuckled, and put her mare into a gallop.

'Do you enjoy riding so much?' Sanin asked, as he overtook her.

Maria Nikolaevna reined her mare in once more: only in this way could she bring her to a stop.

'I only wanted to get away from thanks. If any one thanks me, he spoils my pleasure. You see I didn't do that for his sake, but for my own. How dare he thank me? I didn't hear what you asked me.'

'I asked . . . I wanted to know what makes you so happy to-day.'

'Do you know what,' said Maria Nikolaevna; either she had again not heard Sanin's question, or she did not consider it necessary to answer it. 'I'm awfully sick of that groom, who sticks up there behind us, and most likely does nothing but wonder when we gentlefolks are going home again. How shall we get rid of him?' She hastily pulled a little pocket-book out of her pocket. 'Send him back to the town with a note? No . . . that won't do. Ah! I have it! What's that in front of us? Isn't it an inn?'

Sanin looked in the direction she pointed. 'Yes, I believe it is an inn.'

'Well, that's first-rate. I'll tell him to stop at that inn and drink beer till we come back.'

'But what will he think?'

'What does it matter to us? Besides, he won't think at all; he'll drink beer—that's all. Come, Sanin (it was the first time she had used his surname alone), on, gallop!'

When they reached the inn, Maria Nikolaevna called the groom up and told him what she wished of him. The groom, a man of English extraction and English temperament, raised his hand to the beak of his cap without a word, jumped off his horse, and took him by the bridle.

'Well, now we are free as the birds of the air!' cried Maria Nikolaevna. 'Where shall we go. North, south, east, or west? Look— I'm like the Hungarian king at his coronation (she pointed her whip in each direction in turn). All is ours! No, do you know what: see, those glorious mountains—and that forest! Let's go there, to the mountains, to the mountains!'

'In die Berge wo die Freiheit thront!'

She turned off the high-road and galloped along a narrow untrodden track, which certainly seemed to lead straight to the hills. Sanin galloped after her.

XLII

THIS track soon changed into a tiny footpath, and at last disappeared altogether, and was crossed by a stream. Sanin counselled turning back, but Maria Nikolaevna said, 'No! I want to get to the mountains! Let's go straight, as the birds fly,' and she made her mare leap the stream. Sanin leaped it too. Beyond the stream began a wide meadow, at first dry, then wet, and at last quite boggy; the water oozed up everywhere, and stood in pools in some places. Maria Nikolaevna rode her mare straight through these pools on purpose, laughed, and said, 'Let's be naughty children.'

'Do you know,' she asked Sanin, 'what is meant by pool-hunting?'

'Yes,' answered Sanin.

'I had an uncle a huntsman,' she went on. 'I used to go out hunting with him—in the spring. It was delicious! Here we are now, on the pools with you. Only, I see, you're a Russian, and yet mean to marry an Italian. Well, that's your sorrow. What's that? A stream again! Gee up!'

The horse took the leap, but Maria Nikolaevna's hat fell off her head, and her curls tumbled loose over her shoulders. Sanin was just going to get off his horse to pick up the hat, but she shouted to him, 'Don't touch it, I'll get it myself,' bent low down from the saddle, hooked the handle of her whip into the veil, and actually did get the hat. She put it on her head, but did not fasten up her hair, and again darted off, positively holloaing. Sanin dashed along beside her, by her side leaped trenches, fences, brooks, fell in and scrambled out, flew down hill, flew up hill, and kept watching her face. What a face it was! It was all, as it were, wide open: wide-open eyes, eager, bright, and wild; lips, nostrils, open too, and breathing eagerly; she looked straight before her, and it seemed as though that soul longed to master everything it saw, the earth, the sky, the sun, the air itself; and would complain of one thing only—that dangers were so few, and all she could overcome. 'Sanin!' she cried, 'why, this is like Bürger's Lenore! Only you're not dead—eh? Not dead . . . I am alive!' She let her force and daring have full fling. It seemed not an Amazon on a galloping horse, but a young female centaur at full speed, half-beast and half-god, and the sober, well-bred country seemed astounded, as it was trampled underfoot in her wild riot!

Maria Nikolaevna at last drew up her foaming and bespattered mare; she was staggering under her, and Sanin's powerful but heavy horse was gasping for breath.

'Well, do you like it?' Maria Nikolaevna asked in a sort of exquisite whisper.

'I like it!' Sanin echoed back ecstatically. And his blood was on fire.

'This isn't all, wait a bit.' She held out her hand. Her glove was torn across.

'I told you I would lead you to the forest, to the mountains. . . . Here they are, the mountains!' The mountains, covered with tall forest, rose about two hundred feet from the place they had reached in their wild ride. 'Look, here is the road; let us turn into it—and forwards. Only at a walk. We must let our horses get their breath.'

They rode on. With one vigorous sweep of her arm Maria Nikolaevna flung back her hair. Then she looked at her gloves and took them off. 'My hands will smell of leather,' she said, 'you won't mind that, eh?'. . . Maria Nikolaevna smiled, and Sanin smiled too. Their mad gallop together seemed to have finally brought them together and made them friends.

'How old are you?' she asked suddenly.

'Twenty-two.'

'Really? I'm twenty-two too. A nice age. Add both together and you're still far off old age. It's hot, though. Am I very red, eh?'

'Like a poppy!'

Maria Nikolaevna rubbed her face with her handkerchief. 'We've only to get to the forest and there it will be cool. Such an old forest is like an old friend. Have you any friends?'

Sanin thought a little. 'Yes . . . only few. No real ones.'

'I have; real ones—but not old ones. This is a friend too—a horse. How carefully it carries one! Ah, but it's splendid here! Is it possible I am going to Paris the day after to-morrow?'

'Yes . . . is it possible?' Sanin chimed in.

'And you to Frankfort?'

'I am certainly going to Frankfort.'

'Well, what of it? Good luck go with you! Anyway, to-day's ours . . . ours . . . ours!'

The horses reached the forest's edge and pushed on into the forest The broad soft shade of the forest wrapt them round on all sides.

'Oh, but this is paradise!' cried Maria Nikolaevna. 'Further, deeper into the shade, Sanin!'

The horses moved slowly on, 'deeper into the shade,' slightly swaying and snorting. The path, by which they had come in, suddenly turned off and plunged into a rather narrow gorge. The smell of heather and bracken, of the resin of the pines, and the decaying leaves of last year, seemed to hang, close and drowsy, about it. Through the clefts of the big brown rocks came strong currents of fresh air. On both sides of the path rose round hillocks covered with green moss.

'Stop!' cried Maria Nikolaevna, 'I want to sit down and rest on this velvet. Help me to get off.'

Sanin leaped off his horse and ran up to her. She leaned on both his shoulders, sprang instantly to the ground, and seated herself on one of the mossy mounds. He stood before her, holding both the horses' bridles in his hand.

She lifted her eyes to him . . . 'Sanin, are you able to forget?'

Sanin recollected what had happened yesterday . . . in the carriage. 'What is that—a question . . . or a reproach?'

'I have never in my life reproached any one for anything. Do you believe in magic?'

'What?'

'In magic?—you know what is sung of in our ballads—our Russian peasant ballads?'

'Ah! That's what you're speaking of,' Sanin said slowly.

'Yes, that's it. I believe in it . . . and you will believe in it.'

'Magic is sorcery . . .' Sanin repeated.

Anything in the world is possible. I used not to believe in it—but I do now. I don't know myself.'

Maria Nikolaevna thought a moment and looked about her. 'I fancy this place seems familiar to me. Look, Sanin, behind that bushy oak—is there a red wooden cross, or not?'

Sanin moved a few steps to one side. 'Yes, there is.' Maria Nikolaevna smiled. 'Ah, that's good! I know where we are. We haven't got lost as yet. What's that tapping? A woodcutter?'

Sanin looked into the thicket. 'Yes . . . there's a man there chopping up dry branches.'

'I must put my hair to rights,' said Maria Nikolaevna. 'Else he'll see me and be shocked.' She took off her hat and began plaiting up her long hair, silently and seriously. Sanin stood facing her . . . All the lines of her graceful limbs could be clearly seen through the dark folds of her habit, dotted here and there with tufts of moss.

One of the horses suddenly shook itself behind Sanin's back; he himself started and trembled from head to foot. Everything was in confusion within him, his nerves were strung up like harpstrings. He might well say he did not know himself. . . . He really was bewitched. His whole being was filled full of one thing . . . one idea, one desire. Maria Nikolaevna turned a keen look upon him.

'Come, now everything's as it should be,' she observed, putting on her hat. 'Won't you sit down? Here! No, wait a minute . . . don't sit down! What's that?'

Over the tree-tops, over the air of the forest, rolled a dull rumbling.

'Can it be thunder?'

'I think it really is thunder,' answered Sanin.

'Oh, this is a treat, a real treat! That was the only thing wanting!' The dull rumble was heard a second time, rose, and fell in a crash. 'Bravo! Bis! Do you remember I spoke of the *Æneid* yesterday? *They* too were overtaken by a storm in the forest, you know. We must be off, though.' She rose swiftly to her feet. 'Bring me my horse. . . . Give me your hand. There, so. I'm not heavy.'

She hopped like a bird into the saddle. Sanin too mounted his horse.

'Are you going home?' he asked in an unsteady voice.

'Home indeed!' she answered deliberately and picked up the reins. 'Follow me,' she commanded almost roughly. She came out on to the road and passing the red cross, rode down into a hollow, clambered up again to a cross road, turned to the right and again up the mountainside. . . . She obviously knew where the path led, and the path led farther and farther into the heart of the forest. She said nothing and did not look round; she moved imperiously in front and humbly and submissively he followed without a spark of will in his sinking heart. Rain began to fall in spots. She quickened her horse's pace, and he did not linger behind her. At last through the dark green of the young firs under an overhanging grey rock, a tumbledown little hut peeped out at him, with a low door in its wattle wall. . . . Maria Nikolaevna made her mare push through the fir bushes, leaped off her, and appearing suddenly at the entrance to the hut, turned to Sanin, and whispered 'Æneas.'

Four hours later, Maria Nikolaevna and Sanin, accompanied by the groom, who was nodding in the saddle, returned to Wiesbaden, to the hotel. Polozov met his wife with the letter to the overseer in his hand. After staring rather intently at her, he showed signs of some displeasure on his face, and even muttered, 'You don't mean to say you've won your bet?'

Maria Nikolaevna simply shrugged her shoulders.

The same day, two hours later, Sanin was standing in his own room before her, like one distraught, ruined. . . .

'Where are you going, dear?' she asked him. 'To Paris, or to Frankfort?'

'I am going where you will be, and will be with you till you drive me away,' he answered with despair and pressed close to him the hands of his sovereign. She freed her hands, laid them on his head, and clutched at his hair with her fingers. She slowly turned over and twisted the unresisting hair, drew herself up, her lips curled with triumph, while her eyes, wide and clear, almost white, expressed nothing but the ruthlessness and glutted joy of conquest The hawk, as it clutches a captured bird, has eyes like that.

XLIII

This was what Dimitri Sanin remembered when in the stillness of his room turning over his old papers he found among them a garnet cross. The events we have described rose clearly and consecutively before his mental vision. . . . But when he reached the moment when he addressed that humiliating prayer to Madame Polozov, when he grovelled at her feet, when his slavery began, he averted his gaze from the images he had evoked, he tried to recall no more, And not that his memory failed him, oh no! he knew only too well what followed upon that moment, but he was stifled by shame, even now, so many years after; he dreaded that feeling of self-contempt, which he knew for certain would overwhelm him, and like a torrent, flood all other feelings if he did not bid his memory be still. But try as he would to turn away from these memories, he could not stifle them entirely. He remembered the scoundrelly, tearful, lying, pitiful letter he had sent to Gemma, that never received an answer. . . . See her again, go back to her, after such falsehood, such treachery, no! no! he could not, so much conscience and honesty was left in him. Moreover, he had lost every trace of confidence in himself, every atom of self-respect; he dared not rely on himself for anything. Sanin recollected too how he had later on—oh, ignominy!—sent the Polozovs' footman to Frankfort for his things, what cowardly terror he had felt, how he had had one thought only, to get away as soon as might be to Paris—to Paris; how in obedience to Maria Nikolaevna, he had humoured and tried to please Ippolit Sidoritch and been amiable to Dönhof, on whose finger he noticed just such an iron ring as Maria Nikolaevna had given him! ! ! Then followed memories still worse, more ignominious . . . the waiter hands him a visiting card, and on it is the name, 'Pantaleone Cippatola, court singer to His Highness the Duke of Modena!' He hides from the old man, but cannot escape meeting him in the corridor, and a face of exasperation rises before him under an upstanding topknot of grey hair; the old eyes blaze like red-hot coals, and he hears menacing cries and curses: '*Maledizione!*' hears even the terrible words: '*Codardo! Infame traditore!*' Sanin closes his eyes, shakes his head, turns away again and again, but still he sees himself sitting in a travelling carriage on the narrow front seat . . . In the comfortable places facing the horses sit Maria Nikolaevna and Ippolit Sidoritch, the four horses trotting all together fly along the paved roads of Wiesbaden to Paris! to Paris! Ippolit Sidoritch is eating a pear which Sanin has peeled for him, while Maria Nikolaevna watches him and smiles at him, her bondslave, that smile he knows already, the smile of the proprietor, the slave-owner. . . . But, good God, out there at the corner of the street not far from the city walls, wasn't it Pantaleone again, and who with him? Can it be Emilio? Yes, it was he, the enthusiastic devoted boy! Not long since his young face had been full of reverence before his hero, his ideal, but now his pale handsome face, so handsome that Maria Nikolaevna noticed him and poked her head out of the carriage window, that noble face is glowing with anger and contempt; his eyes, so like *her* eyes! are fastened upon Sanin, and the tightly compressed lips part to revile him. . . .

And Pantaleone stretches out his hand and points Sanin out to Tartaglia standing near, and Tartaglia barks at Sanin, and the very bark of the faithful dog sounds like an unbearable reproach. . . . Hideous!

And then, the life in Paris, and all the humiliations, all the loathsome tortures of the slave, who dare not be jealous or complain, and who is cast aside at last, like a worn-out garment. . . .

Then the going home to his own country, the poisoned, the devastated life, the petty interests and petty cares, bitter and fruitless regret, and as bitter and fruitless apathy, a punishment not apparent, but of every minute, continuous, like some trivial but incurable disease, the payment farthing by farthing of the debt, which can never be settled. . . .

The cup was full enough.

How had the garnet cross given Sanin by Gemma existed till now, why had he not sent it back, how had it happened that he had never come across it till that day? A long, long while he sat deep in thought, and taught as he was by the experience of so many years, he still could not comprehend how he could have deserted Gemma, so tenderly and passionately loved, for a woman he did not love at all. . . . Next day he surprised all his friends and acquaintances by announcing that he was going abroad.

The surprise was general in society. Sanin was leaving Petersburg, in the middle of the winter, after having only just taken and furnished a capital flat, and having even secured seats for all the performances of the Italian Opera, in which Madame Patti . . . Patti, herself, herself, was to take part! His friends and acquaintances wondered; but it is not human nature as a rule to be interested long in other people's affairs, and when Sanin set off for abroad, none came to the railway station to see him off but a French tailor, and he only in the hope of securing an unpaid account '*pour un saute-en-barque en velours noir tout à fait chic.*'

XLIV

Sanin told his friends he was going abroad, but he did not say where exactly: the reader will readily conjecture that he made straight for Frankfort. Thanks to the general extension of railways, on the fourth day after leaving Petersburg he was there. He had not visited the place since 1840. The hotel, the White Swan, was standing in its old place and still flourishing, though no longer regarded as first class. The *Zeile*, the principal street of Frankfort was little changed, but there was not only no trace of Signora Roselli's house, the very street in which it stood had disappeared. Sanin wandered like a man in a dream about the places once so familiar, and recognised nothing; the old buildings had vanished; they were replaced by new streets of huge continuous houses and fine villas; even the public garden, where that last interview with Gemma had taken place, had so grown up and altered that Sanin wondered if it really were the same garden. What was he to do? How and where could he get information? Thirty years, no little thing! had passed since those days. No one to whom he applied had even heard of the name Roselli; the hotel-keeper advised him to have recourse to the public library, there, he told him, he would find all the old newspapers, but what good he would get from that, the hotel-keeper owned he didn't see. Sanin in despair made inquiries about Herr Klüber. That name the hotel-keeper knew well, but there too no success awaited him. The elegant shop-manager, after making much noise in the world and rising to the position of a capitalist, had speculated, was made bankrupt, and died in prison. . . . This piece of news did not, however, occasion Sanin the slightest regret. He was beginning to feel that his journey had been rather precipitate. . . . But, behold, one day, as he was turning over a Frankfort directory, he came on the name: Von Dönhof, retired major. He promptly took a carriage and drove to the address, though why was this Von Dönhof certain to be that Dönhof, and why even was the right Dönhof likely to be able to tell him any news of the Roselli family? No matter, a drowning man catches at straws.

Sanin found the retired major von Dönhof at home, and in the grey-haired gentleman who received him he recognised at once his adversary of bygone days. Dönhof knew him too, and was positively delighted to see him; he recalled to him his young days, the escapades of his youth. Sanin heard from him that the Roselli family had long, long ago emigrated to America, to New York; that Gemma had married a merchant; that he, Dönhof, had an acquaintance also a merchant, who would probably know her husband's address, as he did a great deal of business with America. Sanin begged Dönhof to consult this friend, and, to his delight, Dönhof brought him the address of Gemma's husband, Mr. Jeremy Slocum, New York, Broadway, No. 501. Only this address dated from the year 1863.

'Let us hope,' cried Dönhof, 'that our Frankfort belle is still alive and has not left New York! By the way,' he added, dropping his voice, 'what about that Russian lady, who was staying, do you remember, about that time at Wiesbaden—Madame von Bo . . . von Bolozov, is she still living?'

'No,' answered Sanin, 'she died long ago.'

Dönhof looked up, but observing that Sanin had turned away and was frowning, he did not say another word, but took his leave.

That same day Sanin sent a letter to Madame Gemma Slocum, at New York. In the letter he told her he was writing to her from Frankfort, where he had come solely with the object of finding traces of her, that he was very well aware that he was absolutely without a right to expect that she would answer his appeal; that he had not deserved her forgiveness, and could only hope that among happy surroundings she had long ago forgotten his existence. He added that he had made up his mind to recall himself to her memory in consequence of a chance circumstance which had too vividly brought back to him the images of the past; he described his life, solitary, childless, joyless; he implored her to understand the grounds that had induced him to address her, not to let him carry to the grave the bitter sense of his own wrongdoing, expiated long since by suffering, but never forgiven, and to make him happy with even the briefest news of her life in the new world to which she had gone away. 'In writing one word to me,' so Sanin ended his letter, 'you will be doing a good action worthy of your noble soul, and I shall thank you to my last breath. I am stopping here at the *White Swan* (he underlined those words) and shall wait, wait till spring, for your answer.'

He despatched this letter, and proceeded to wait. For six whole weeks he lived in the hotel, scarcely leaving his room, and resolutely seeing no one. No one could write to him from Russia nor from anywhere; and that just suited his mood; if a letter came addressed to him he would know at once that it was the one he was waiting for. He read from morning till evening, and not journals, but serious books —historical works. These prolonged studies, this stillness, this hidden life, like a snail in its shell, suited his spiritual condition to perfection; and for this, if nothing more, thanks to Gemma! But was she alive? Would she answer?

At last a letter came, with an American postmark, from New York, addressed to him. The handwriting of the address on the envelope was English. . . . He did not recognise it, and there was a pang at his heart. He could not at once bring himself to break open the envelope. He glanced at the signature—Gemma! The tears positively gushed from his eyes: the mere fact that she signed her name, without a surname, was a pledge to him of reconciliation, of forgiveness! He unfolded the thin sheet of blue notepaper: a photograph slipped out. He made haste to pick it up—and was struck dumb with amazement: Gemma, Gemma living, young as he had known her thirty years ago! The same eyes, the same lips, the same form of the whole face! On the back of the photograph was written, 'My daughter Mariana.' The whole letter was very kind and simple. Gemma thanked Sanin for not having hesitated to write to her, for having confidence in her; she did not conceal from him that she had passed some painful moments after his disappearance, but she added at once that for all that she considered—and had always considered—her meeting him as a happy thing, seeing that it was that meeting which had prevented her from becoming the wife of Mr. Klüber, and in that way, though indirectly, had led to her marriage with her husband, with whom she had now lived twenty-eight years, in perfect happiness, comfort, and prosperity; their house was known to every one in New York. Gemma informed Sanin that she was the mother of five children, four sons and one daughter, a girl of eighteen, engaged to be married, and her photograph she enclosed as she was generally considered very like her mother. The sorrowful news Gemma kept for the end of the letter. Frau Lenore had died in New York, where she had followed her daughter and son-in-law, but she had lived long enough to rejoice in her children's happiness and to nurse her grandchildren. Pantaleone, too, had meant to come out to America, but he had died on the very eve of leaving Frankfort. 'Emilio, our beloved, incomparable Emilio, died a glorious death for the freedom of his country in Sicily, where he was one of the "Thousand" under the leadership of the great Garibaldi; we all bitterly lamented the loss of our priceless brother, but, even in the midst of our tears, we were proud of him—and shall always be proud of him—and hold his memory sacred! His lofty, disinterested soul was worthy of a martyr's crown!' Then Gemma expressed her regret that Sanin's life had apparently been so unsuccessful, wished him before everything peace and a tranquil spirit, and said that she would be very glad to see him again, though she realised how unlikely such a meeting was. . . .

We will not attempt to describe the feelings Sanin experienced as he read this letter. For such feelings there is no satisfactory expression; they are too deep and too strong and too vague for any word. Only music could reproduce them.

Sanin answered at once; and as a wedding gift to the young girl, sent to 'Mariana Slocum, from an unknown friend,' a garnet cross, set in a magnificent pearl necklace. This present, costly as it was, did not ruin him; during the thirty years that had elapsed since his first visit to Frankfort, he had succeeded in accumulating a considerable fortune. Early in May he went back to Petersburg, but hardly for long. It is rumoured that he is selling all his lands and preparing to go to America.

FIRST LOVE

The party had long ago broken up. The clock struck half-past twelve. There was left in the room only the master of the house and Sergei Nikolaevitch and Vladimir Petrovitch.

The master of the house rang and ordered the remains of the supper to be cleared away. 'And so it's settled,' he observed, sitting back farther in his easy-chair and lighting a cigar; 'each of us is to tell the story of his first love. It's your turn, Sergei Nikolaevitch.'

Sergei Nikolaevitch, a round little man with a plump, light-complexioned face, gazed first at the master of the house, then raised his eyes to the ceiling. 'I had no first love,' he said at last; 'I began with the second.'

'How was that?'

'It's very simple. I was eighteen when I had my first flirtation with a charming young lady, but I courted her just as though it were nothing new to me; just as I courted others later on. To speak accurately, the first and last time I was in love was with my nurse when I was six years old; but that's in the remote past. The details of our relations have slipped out of my memory, and even if I remembered them, whom could they interest?'

FIRST LOVE

'Then how's it to be?' began the master of the house. 'There was nothing much of interest about my first love either; I never fell in love with any one till I met Anna Nikolaevna, now my wife,—and everything went as smoothly as possible with us; our parents arranged the match, we were very soon in love with each other, and got married without loss of time. My story can be told in a couple of words. I must confess, gentlemen, in bringing up the subject of first love, I reckoned upon you, I won't say old, but no longer young, bachelors. Can't you enliven us with something, Vladimir Petrovitch?'

'My first love, certainly, was not quite an ordinary one,' responded, with some reluctance, Vladimir Petrovitch, a man of forty, with black hair turning grey.

'Ah!' said the master of the house and Sergei Nikolaevitch with one voice: 'So much the better. . . . Tell us about it.'

'If you wish it . . . or no; I won't tell the story; I'm no hand at telling a story; I make it dry and brief, or spun out and affected. If you'll allow me, I'll write out all I remember and read it you.'

His friends at first would not agree, but Vladimir Petrovitch insisted on his own way. A fortnight later they were together again, and Vladimir Petrovitch kept his word.

His manuscript contained the following story:—

FIRST LOVE

I

I was sixteen then. It happened in the summer of 1833.

I lived in Moscow with my parents. They had taken a country house for the summer near the Kalouga gate, facing the Neskutchny gardens. I was preparing for the university, but did not work much and was in no hurry.

No one interfered with my freedom. I did what I liked, especially after parting with my last tutor, a Frenchman who had never been able to get used to the idea that he had fallen 'like a bomb' (*comme une bombe*) into Russia, and would lie sluggishly in bed with an expression of exasperation on his face for days together. My father treated me with careless kindness; my mother scarcely noticed me, though she had no children except me; other cares completely absorbed her. My father, a man still young and very handsome, had married her from mercenary considerations; she was ten years older than he. My mother led a melancholy life; she was for ever agitated, jealous and angry, but not in my father's presence; she was very much afraid of him, and he was severe, cold, and distant in his behaviour. . . . I have never seen a man more elaborately serene, self-confident, and commanding.

I shall never forget the first weeks I spent at the country house. The weather was magnificent; we left town on the 9th of May, on St. Nicholas's day. I used to walk about in our garden, in the Neskutchny gardens, and beyond the town gates; I would take some book with me—Keidanov's Course, for instance—but I rarely looked into it, and more often than anything declaimed verses aloud; I knew a great deal of poetry by heart; my blood was in a ferment and my heart ached—so sweetly and absurdly; I was all hope and anticipation, was a little frightened of something, and full of wonder at everything, and was on the tiptoe of expectation; my imagination played continually, fluttering rapidly about the same fancies, like martins about a bell-tower at dawn; I dreamed, was sad, even wept; but through the tears and through the sadness, inspired by a musical verse, or the beauty of evening, shot up like grass in spring the delicious sense of youth and effervescent life.

FIRST LOVE

I had a horse to ride; I used to saddle it myself and set off alone for long rides, break into a rapid gallop and fancy myself a knight at a tournament. How gaily the wind whistled in my ears! or turning my face towards the sky, I would absorb its shining radiance and blue into my soul, that opened wide to welcome it.

I remember that at that time the image of woman, the vision of love, scarcely ever arose in definite shape in my brain; but in all I thought, in all I felt, lay hidden a half-conscious, shamefaced presentiment of something new, unutterably sweet, feminine. . . .

This presentiment, this expectation, permeated my whole being; I breathed in it, it coursed through my veins with every drop of blood . . . it was destined to be soon fulfilled.

The place, where we settled for the summer, consisted of a wooden manor-house with columns and two small lodges; in the lodge on the left there was a tiny factory for the manufacture of cheap wall-papers. . . . I had more than once strolled that way to look at about a dozen thin and dishevelled boys with greasy smocks and worn faces, who were perpetually jumping on to wooden levers, that pressed down the square blocks of the press, and so by the weight of their feeble bodies struck off the variegated patterns of the wall-papers. The lodge on the right stood empty, and was to let, One day—three weeks after the 9th of May—the blinds in the windows of this lodge were drawn up, women's faces appeared at them—some family had installed themselves in it. I remember the same day at dinner, my mother inquired of the butler who were our new neighbours, and hearing the name of the Princess Zasyekin, first observed with some respect, 'Ah! a princess!' . . . and then added, 'A poor one, I suppose?'

'They arrived in three hired flies,' the butler remarked deferentially, as he handed a dish: 'they don't keep their own carriage, and the furniture's of the poorest.'

'Ah,' replied my mother, 'so much the better.'

My father gave her a chilly glance; she was silent.

Certainly the Princess Zasyekin could not be a rich woman; the lodge she had taken was so dilapidated and small and low-pitched that people, even moderately well-off in the world, would hardly have consented to occupy it At the time, however, all this went in at one ear and out at the other. The princely title had very little effect on me; I had just been reading Schiller's *Robbers*.

FIRST LOVE

II

I was in the habit of wandering about our garden every evening on the look-out for rooks. I had long cherished a hatred for those wary, sly, and rapacious birds. On the day of which I have been speaking, I went as usual into the garden, and after patrolling all the walks without success (the rooks knew me, and merely cawed spasmodically at a distance), I chanced to go close to the low fence which separated our domain from the narrow strip of garden stretching beyond the lodge to the right, and belonging to it I was walking along, my eyes on the ground. Suddenly I heard a voice; I looked across the fence, and was thunderstruck. . . . I was confronted with a curious spectacle.

A few paces from me on the grass between the green raspberry bushes stood a tall slender girl in a striped pink dress, with a white kerchief on her head; four young men were close round her, and she was slapping them by turns on the forehead with those small grey flowers, the name of which I don't know, though they are well known to children; the flowers form little bags, and burst open with a pop when you strike them against anything hard. The young men presented their foreheads so eagerly, and in the gestures of the girl (I saw her in profile), there was something so fascinating, imperious, caressing, mocking, and charming, that I almost cried out with admiration and delight, and would, I thought, have given everything in the world on the spot only to have had those exquisite fingers strike me on the forehead. My gun slipped on to the grass, I forgot everything, I devoured with my eyes the graceful shape and neck and lovely arms and the slightly disordered fair hair under the white kerchief, and the half-closed clever eye, and the eyelashes and the soft cheek beneath them. . . .

'Young man, hey, young man,' said a voice suddenly near me: 'is it quite permissible to stare so at unknown young ladies?'

I started, I was struck dumb. . . . Near me, the other side of the fence, stood a man with close-cropped black hair, looking ironically at me. At the same instant the girl too turned towards me. . . . I caught sight of big grey eyes in a bright mobile face, and the whole face suddenly quivered and laughed, there was a flash of white teeth, a droll lifting of the eyebrows. . . . I crimsoned, picked up my gun from the ground, and pursued by a musical but not ill-natured laugh, fled to my own room, flung myself on the bed, and hid my face in my hands. My heart was fairly leaping; I was greatly ashamed and overjoyed; I felt an excitement I had never known before.

After a rest, I brushed my hair, washed, and went downstairs to tea. The image of the young girl floated before me, my heart was no longer leaping, but was full of a sort of sweet oppression.

'What's the matter?' my father asked me all at once: 'have you killed a rook?'

I was on the point of telling him all about it, but I checked myself, and merely smiled to myself. As I was going to bed, I rotated—I don't know why—three times on one leg, pomaded my hair, got into bed, and slept like a top all night. Before morning I woke up for an instant, raised my head, looked round me in ecstasy, and fell asleep again.

III

'How can I make their acquaintance?' was my first thought when I waked in the morning. I went out in the garden before morning tea, but I did not go too near the fence, and saw no one. After drinking tea, I walked several times up and down the street before the house, and looked into the windows from a distance.

FIRST LOVE

. . . I fancied her face at a curtain, and I hurried away in alarm.

'I must make her acquaintance, though,' I thought, pacing distractedly about the sandy plain that stretches before Neskutchny park . . . 'but how, that is the question.' I recalled the minutest details of our meeting yesterday; I had for some reason or other a particularly vivid recollection of how she had laughed at me. . . . But while I racked my brains, and made various plans, fate had already provided for me.

In my absence my mother had received from her new neighbour a letter on grey paper, sealed with brown wax, such as is only used in notices from the post-office or on the corks of bottles of cheap wine. In this letter, which was written in illiterate language and in a slovenly hand, the princess begged my mother to use her powerful influence in her behalf; my mother, in the words of the princess, was very intimate with persons of high position, upon whom her fortunes and her children's fortunes depended, as she had some very important business in hand. 'I address myself to you,' she wrote, 'as one gentlewoman to another gentlewoman, and for that reason am glad to avail myself of the opportunity.' Concluding, she begged my mother's permission to call upon

FIRST LOVE

her. I found my mother in an unpleasant state of indecision; my father was not at home, and she had no one of whom to ask advice. Not to answer a gentlewoman, and a princess into the bargain, was impossible. But my mother was in a difficulty as to how to answer her. To write a note in French struck her as unsuitable, and Russian spelling was not a strong point with my mother herself, and she was aware of it, and did not care to expose herself. She was overjoyed when I made my appearance, and at once told me to go round to the princess's, and to explain to her by word of mouth that my mother would always be glad to do her excellency any service within her powers, and begged her to come to see her at one o'clock. This unexpectedly rapid fulfilment of my secret desires both delighted and appalled me. I made no sign, however, of the perturbation which came over me, and as a preliminary step went to my own room to put on a new necktie and tail coat; at home I still wore short jackets and lay-down collars, much as I abominated them.

IV

In the narrow and untidy passage of the lodge, which I entered with an involuntary tremor in all my limbs, I was met by an old grey-headed servant with a dark copper-coloured face, surly little pig's eyes, and such deep furrows on his forehead and temples as I had never beheld in my life. He was carrying a plate containing the spine of a herring that had been gnawed at; and shutting the door that led into the room with his foot, he jerked out, 'What do you want?'

'Is the Princess Zasyekin at home?' I inquired.

'Vonifaty!' a jarring female voice screamed from within.

The man without a word turned his back on me, exhibiting as he did so the extremely threadbare hindpart of his livery with a solitary reddish heraldic button on it; he put the plate down on the floor, and went away.

'Did you go to the police station?' the same female voice called again. The man muttered something in reply. 'Eh. . . . Has some one come?' I heard again. . . . 'The young gentleman from next door. Ask him in, then.'

'Will you step into the drawing-room?' said the servant, making his appearance once more, and picking up the plate from the floor. I mastered my emotions, and went into the drawing-room.

I found myself in a small and not over clean

apartment, containing some poor furniture that looked as if it had been hurriedly set down where it stood. At the window in an easy-chair with a broken arm was sitting a woman of fifty, bareheaded and ugly, in an old green dress, and a striped worsted wrap about her neck. Her small black eyes fixed me like pins.

I went up to her and bowed.

'I have the honour of addressing the Princess Zasyekin?'

'I am the Princess Zasyekin; and you are the son of Mr. V.?'

'Yes. I have come to you with a message from my mother.'

'Sit down, please. Vonifaty, where are my keys, have you seen them?'

I communicated to Madame Zasyekin my mother's reply to her note. She heard me out, drumming with her fat red fingers on the window-pane, and when I had finished, she stared at me once more.

'Very good; I'll be sure to come,' she observed at last. 'But how young you are! How old are you, may I ask?'

'Sixteen,' I replied, with an involuntary stammer.

The princess drew out of her pocket some greasy papers covered with writing, raised them right up to her nose, and began looking through them.

'A good age,' she ejaculated suddenly, turning round restlessly on her chair. 'And do you, pray, make yourself at home. I don't stand on ceremony.'

'No, indeed,' I thought, scanning her unprepossessing person with a disgust I could not restrain.

At that instant another door flew open quickly, and in the doorway stood the girl I had seen the previous evening in the garden. She lifted her hand, and a mocking smile gleamed in her face.

'Here is my daughter,' observed the princess, indicating her with her elbow. 'Zinotchka, the son of our neighbour, Mr. V. What is your name, allow me to ask?'

'Vladimir,' I answered, getting up, and stuttering in my excitement.

'And your father's name?'

'Petrovitch.'

'Ah! I used to know a commissioner of police whose name was Vladimir Petrovitch too. Vonifaty! don't look for my keys; the keys are in my pocket.'

The young girl was still looking at me with the same smile, faintly fluttering her eyelids, and putting her head a little on one side.

FIRST LOVE

'I have seen Monsieur Voldemar before,' she began. (The silvery note of her voice ran through me with a sort of sweet shiver.) 'You will let me call you so?'

'Oh, please,' I faltered.

'Where was that?' asked the princess.

The young princess did not answer her mother,

'Have you anything to do just now?' she said, not taking her eyes off me.

'Oh, no.'

'Would you like to help me wind some wool? Come in here, to me.'

She nodded to me and went out of the drawing-room. I followed her.

In the room we went into, the furniture was a little better, and was arranged with more taste. Though, indeed, at the moment, I was scarcely capable of noticing anything; I moved as in a dream and felt all through my being a sort of intense blissfulness that verged on imbecility.

The young princess sat down, took out a skein of red wool and, motioning me to a seat opposite her, carefully untied the skein and laid it across my hands. All this she did in silence with a sort of droll deliberation and with the same bright sly smile on her slightly parted lips. She began to wind the wool on a bent card, and all at once she dazzled me with a glance so brilliant and rapid, that I could not help dropping my eyes. When her eyes, which were generally half closed, opened to their full extent, her face was completely transfigured; it was as though it were flooded with light

'What did you think of me yesterday, M'sieu Voldemar?' she asked after a brief pause. 'You thought ill of me, I expect?'

'I . . . princess . . . I thought nothing . . . how can I? . . .' I answered in confusion.

'Listen,' she rejoined. 'You don't know me yet. I'm a very strange person; I like always to be told the truth. You, I have just heard, are sixteen, and I am twenty-one: you see I'm a great deal older than you, and so you ought always to tell me the truth . . . and to do what I tell you,' she added. 'Look at me: why don't you look at me?'

I was still more abashed; however, I raised my eyes to her. She smiled, not her former smile, but a smile of approbation. 'Look at me,' she said, dropping her voice caressingly: 'I don't dislike that . . . I like your face; I have a presentiment we shall be friends. But do you like me?' she added slyly.

'Princess. . . .' I was beginning.

'In the first place, you must call me Zinaïda

Alexandrovna, and in the second place it's a bad habit for children'—(she corrected herself) 'for young people—not to say straight out what they feel. That's all very well for grown-up people. You like me, don't you?'

Though I was greatly delighted that she talked so freely to me, still I was a little hurt. I wanted to show her that she had not a mere boy to deal with, and assuming as easy and serious an air as I could, I observed, 'Certainly. I like you very much, Zinaïda Alexandrovna; I have no wish to conceal it.'

She shook her head very deliberately. 'Have you a tutor?' she asked suddenly.

'No; I've not had a tutor for a long, long while.'

I told a lie; it was not a month since I had parted with my Frenchman.

'Oh! I see then—you are quite grown-up.'

She tapped me lightly on the fingers. 'Hold your hands straight!' And she applied herself busily to winding the ball.

I seized the opportunity when she was looking down and fell to watching her, at first stealthily, then more and more boldly. Her face struck me as even more charming than on the previous evening; everything in it was so delicate, clever, and sweet. She was sitting with her back to a window covered with a white blind, the sunshine, streaming in through the blind, shed a soft light over her fluffy golden curls, her innocent neck, her sloping shoulders, and tender untroubled bosom. I gazed at her, and how dear and near she was already to me! It seemed to me I had known her a long while and had never known anything nor lived at all till I met her. . . . She was wearing a dark and rather shabby dress and an apron; I would gladly, I felt, have kissed every fold of that dress and apron. The tips of her little shoes peeped out from under her skirt; I could have bowed down in adoration to those shoes. . . . 'And here I am sitting before her,' I thought; 'I have made acquaintance with her . . . what happiness, my God!' I could hardly keep from jumping up from my chair in ecstasy, but I only swung my legs a little, like a small child who has been given sweetmeats.

I was as happy as a fish in water, and I could have stayed in that room for ever, have never left that place.

Her eyelids were slowly lifted, and once more her clear eyes shone kindly upon me, and again she smiled.

'How you look at me!' she said slowly, and she held up a threatening finger.

I blushed . . . 'She understands it all, she

sees all,' flashed through my mind. 'And how could she fail to understand and see it all?'

All at once there was a sound in the next room—the clink of a sabre.

'Zina!' screamed the princess in the drawing-room, 'Byelovzorov has brought you a kitten.'

'A kitten!' cried Zinaïda, and getting up from her chair impetuously, she flung the ball of worsted on my knees and ran away.

I too got up and, laying the skein and the ball of wool on the window-sill, I went into the drawing-room and stood still, hesitating. In the middle of the room, a tabby kitten was lying with outstretched paws; Zinaïda was on her knees before it, cautiously lifting up its little face. Near the old princess, and filling up almost the whole space between the two windows, was a flaxen curly-headed young man, a hussar, with a rosy face and prominent eyes.

'What a funny little thing!' Zinaïda was saying; 'and its eyes are not grey, but green, and what long ears! Thank you, Viktor Yegoritch! you are very kind.'

The hussar, in whom I recognised one of the young men I had seen the evening before, smiled and bowed with a clink of his spurs and a jingle of the chain of his sabre.

'You were pleased to say yesterday that you wished to possess a tabby kitten with long ears . . . so I obtained it. Your word is law.' And he bowed again.

The kitten gave a feeble mew and began sniffing the ground.

'It's hungry!' cried Zinaïda. 'Vonifaty, Sonia! bring some milk.'

A maid, in an old yellow gown with a faded kerchief at her neck, came in with a saucer of milk and set it before the kitten. The kitten started, blinked, and began lapping.

'What a pink little tongue it has!' remarked Zinaïda, putting her head almost on the ground and peeping at it sideways under its very nose.

The kitten having had enough began to purr and move its paws affectedly. Zinaïda got up, and turning to the maid said carelessly, 'Take it away.'

'For the kitten—your little hand,' said the hussar, with a simper and a shrug of his strongly-built frame, which was tightly buttoned up in a new uniform.

'Both,' replied Zinaïda, and she held out her hands to him. While he was kissing them, she looked at me over his shoulder.

I stood stockstill in the same place and did not know whether to laugh, to say something, or to be silent Suddenly through the open door into the passage I caught sight of our footman, Fyodor. He was making signs to me. Mechanically I went out to him.

'What do you want?' I asked.

'Your mamma has sent for you,' he said in a whisper. 'She is angry that you have not come back with the answer.'

'Why, have I been here long?'

'Over an hour.'

'Over an hour!' I repeated unconsciously, and going back to the drawing-room I began to make bows and scrape with my heels.

'Where are you off to?' the young princess asked, glancing at me from behind the hussar.

'I must go home. So I am to say,' I added, addressing the old lady, 'that you will come to us about two.'

'Do you say so, my good sir.'

The princess hurriedly pulled out her snuff-box and took snuff so loudly that I positively jumped. 'Do you say so,' she repeated, blinking tearfully and sneezing.

I bowed once more, turned, and went out of the room with that sensation of awkwardness in my spine which a very young man feels when he knows he is being looked at from behind.

'Mind you come and see us again, M'sieu Voldemar,' Zinaïda called, and she laughed again.

'Why is It she's always laughing?' I thought, as I went back home escorted by Fyodor, who said nothing to me, but walked behind me with an air of disapprobation. My mother scolded me and wondered what ever I could have been doing so long at the princess's. I made her no reply and went off to my own room. I felt suddenly very sad. . . . I tried hard not to cry. . . . I was jealous of the hussar.

V

THE princess called on my mother as she had promised and made a disagreeable impression on her. I was not present at their interview, but at table my mother told my father that this Prince Zasyekin struck her as a *femme très vulgaire*, that she had quite worn her out begging her to interest Prince Sergei in their behalf, that she seemed to have no end of lawsuits and affairs on hand—*de vilaines affaires d'argent*—and must be a very troublesome and litigious person. My mother added, however, that she had asked her and her daughter to dinner the next day (hearing the word 'daughter' I buried my nose in my plate), for after all she was a neighbour and a person of title. Upon this my father informed my mother that he remembered now who this lady was; that he had in his youth known the deceased Prince Zasyekin, a very well-bred, but frivolous and absurd person; that he had been nicknamed in society *'le Parisien,'* from having lived a long while in Paris; that he had been very rich, but had gambled away all his property; and for some unknown reason, probably for money, though indeed he might have chosen better, if so, my father added with a cold smile, he had married the daughter of an agent, and after his marriage had entered upon speculations and ruined himself utterly.

'If only she doesn't try to borrow money,' observed my mother.

that's exceedingly possible, 'my father responded tranquilly.' Does she speak French?'

'Very badly.'

'H'm. It's of no consequence anyway. I think you said you had asked the daughter too; some one was telling me she was a very charming and cultivated girl.'

'Ah! Then she can't take after her mother.'

'Nor her father either.' rejoined my father. 'He was cultivated indeed, but a fool.'

My mother sighed and sank into thought. My father said no more. I felt very uncomfortable during this conversation.

After dinner I went into the garden, but without my gun. I swore to myself that I would not go near the Zasyekins' garden, but an irresistible force drew me thither, and not in vain. I had hardly reached the fence when I caught sight of Zinaïda. This time she was alone. She held a book in her hands, and was coming slowly along the path. She did not notice me.

I almost let her pass by; but all at once I changed my mind and coughed.

She turned round, but did not stop, pushed back with one hand the broad blue ribbon of her round straw hat, looked at me, smiled slowly, and again bent her eyes on the book.

I took off my cap, and after hesitating a moment, walked away with a heavy heart. *'Que suis-je pour elle?'* I thought (God knows why) in French.

Familiar footsteps sounded behind me; I looked round, my father came up to me with his light, rapid walk.

'Is that the young princess?' he asked me.

'Yes.'

'Why, do you know her?'

'I saw her this morning at the princess's.'

My father stopped, and, turning sharply on his heel, went back. When he was on a level with Zinaïda, he made her a courteous bow.

She, too, bowed to him, with some astonishment on her face, and dropped her book. I saw how she looked after him. My father was always irreproachably dressed, simple and in a style of his own; but his figure had never struck me as more graceful, never had his grey hat sat more becomingly on his curls, which were scarcely perceptibly thinner than they had once been.

I bent my steps toward Zinaïda, but she did not even glance at me; she picked up her book again and went away.

VI

The whole evening and the following day I spent in a sort of dejected apathy. I remember I tried to work and took up Keidanov, but the boldly printed lines and pages of the famous text-book passed before my eyes in vain. I read ten times over the words: 'Julius Caesar was distinguished by warlike courage.' I did not understand anything and threw the book aside. Before dinner-time I pomaded myself once more, and once more put on my tail-coat and necktie.

'What's that for?' my mother demanded. 'You're not a student yet, and God knows whether you'll get through the examination. And you've not long had a new jacket! You can't throw it away!'

'There will be visitors,' I murmured almost in despair.

'What nonsense! fine visitors indeed!'

I had to submit. I changed my tail-coat for my jacket, but I did not take off the necktie. The princess and her daughter made their appearance half an hour before dinner-time; the old lady had put on, in addition to the green dress with which I was already acquainted, a yellow shawl, and an old-fashioned cap adorned with flame-coloured ribbons. She began talking at once about her money difficulties, sighing, complaining of her poverty, and imploring assistance, but she made herself at home; she took snuff as noisily, and fidgeted and lolled about in her chair as freely as ever. It never seemed to have struck her that she was a princess. Zinaïda on the other hand was rigid, almost haughty in her demeanour, every inch a princess. There was a cold immobility and dignity in her face. I should not have recognised it; I should not have known her smiles, her glances, though I thought her exquisite in this new aspect too. She wore a light barége dress with pale blue flowers on it; her hair fell in long curls down her cheek in the English fashion; this style went well with the cold expression of her face. My father sat beside her during dinner, and entertained his neighbour with the finished and serene courtesy peculiar to him. He glanced at her from time to time, and she glanced at him, but so strangely, almost with hostility. Their conversation was carried on in French; I was surprised, I remember, at the purity of Zinaïda's accent. The princess, while we were at table, as before made no ceremony; she ate a great deal, and praised the dishes. My mother was obviously bored by her, and answered her with a sort of weary indifference; my father faintly frowned now and then. My mother did not like Zinaïda either. 'A conceited minx,' she said next day. 'And fancy, what she has to be conceited about, *avec sa mine de grisette*!'

'It's clear you have never seen any grisettes,' my father observed to her.

'Thank God, I haven't!'

'Thank God, to be sure . . . only how can you form an opinion of them, then?'

To me Zinaïda had paid no attention whatever. Soon after dinner the princess got up to go.

'I shall rely on your kind offices, Maria Nikolaevna and Piotr Vassilitch,' she said in a doleful sing-song to my mother and father. 'I've no help for it! There were days, but they are over. Here I am, an excellency, and a poor honour it is with nothing to eat!'

My father made her a respectful bow and escorted her to the door of the hall. I was standing there in my short jacket, staring at the floor, like a man under sentence of death. Zinaïda's treatment of me had crushed me utterly. What was my astonishment, when, as she passed me, she whispered quickly with her former kind expression in her eyes: 'Come to see us at eight, do you hear, be sure. . . .' I simply threw up my hands, but already she was gone, flinging a white scarf over her head.

VII

At eight o'clock precisely, in my tail-coat and with my hair brushed up into a tuft on my head, I entered the passage of the lodge, where the princess lived. The old servant looked crossly at me and got up unwillingly from his bench. There was a sound of merry voices in the drawing-room. I opened the door and fell back in amazement. In the middle of the room was the young princess, standing on a chair, holding a man's hat in front of her;

round the chair crowded some half a dozen men. They were trying to put their hands into the hat, while she held it above their heads, shaking it violently. On seeing me, she cried, 'Stay, stay, another guest, he must have a ticket too,' and leaping lightly down from the chair she took me by the cuff of my coat. 'Come along,' she said, 'why are you standing still? *Messieurs,* let me make you acquainted: this is M'sieu Voldemar, the son of our neighbour. And this,' she went on, addressing me, and indicating her guests in turn, 'Count Malevsky, Doctor Lushin, Meidanov the poet, the retired captain Nirmatsky, and Byelovzorov the hussar, whom you've seen already. I hope you will be good friends.'

I was so confused that I did not even bow to any one; in Doctor Lushin I recognised the dark man who had so mercilessly put me to shame in the garden; the others were unknown to me.

'Count!' continued Zinaïda, 'write M'sieu Voldemar a ticket.'

'That's not fair,' was objected in a slight Polish accent by the count, a very handsome and fashionably dressed brunette, with expressive brown eyes, a thin little white nose, and delicate little moustaches over a tiny mouth. 'This gentleman has not been playing forfeits with us.'

'It's unfair,' repeated in chorus Byelovzorov and the gentleman described as a retired captain, a man of forty, pock-marked to a hideous degree, curly-headed as a negro, round-shouldered, bandy-legged, and dressed in a military coat without epaulets, worn un-buttoned.

'Write him a ticket I tell you,' repeated the young princess. 'What's this mutiny? M'sieu Voldemar is with us for the first time, and there are no rules for him yet. It's no use grumbling—write it, I wish it.'

The count shrugged his shoulders but bowed submissively, took the pen in his white, ring-bedecked fingers, tore off a scrap of paper and wrote on it.

'At least let us explain to Mr. Voldemar what we are about,' Lushin began in a sarcastic voice, 'or else he will be quite lost. Do you see, young man, we are playing forfeits? the princess has to pay a forfeit, and the one who draws the lucky lot is to have the privilege of kissing her hand. Do you understand what I've told you?'

I simply stared at him, and continued to stand still in bewilderment, while the young princess jumped up on the chair again, and again began waving the hat, They all stretched up to her, and I went after the rest

'Meidanov,' said the princess to a tall young man with a thin face, little dim-sighted eyes, and exceedingly long black hair, 'you as a poet ought to be magnanimous, and give up your number to M'sieu Voldemar so that he may have two chances instead of one.'

But Meidanov shook his head in refusal, and tossed his hair. After all the others I put my hand into the hat, and unfolded my lot . . . Heavens! what was my condition when I saw on it the word, Kiss!

'Kiss!' I could not help crying aloud.

'Bravo! he has won it,' the princess said quickly. 'How glad I am!' She came down from the chair and gave me such a bright sweet look, that my heart bounded. 'Are you glad?' she asked me.

'Me?' . . . I faltered.

'Sell me your lot,' Byelovzorov growled suddenly just in my ear. 'I'll give you a hundred roubles.'

I answered the hussar with such an indignant look, that Zinaïda clapped her hands, while Lushin cried, 'He's a fine fellow!'

'But, as master of the ceremonies,' he went on, 'it's my duty to see that all the rules are kept. M'sieu Voldemar, go down on one knee. That is our regulation.'

Zinaïda stood in front of me, her head a

little on one side as though to get a better look at me; she held out her hand to me with dignity. A mist passed before my eyes; I meant to drop on one knee, sank on both, and pressed my lips to Zinaïda's fingers so awkwardly that I scratched myself a little with the tip of her nail.

'Well done!' cried Lushin, and helped me to get up.

The game of forfeits went on. Zinaïda sat me down beside her. She invented all sorts of extraordinary forfeits! She had among other things to represent a 'statue,' and she chose as a pedestal the hideous Nirmatsky, told him to bow down in an arch, and bend his head down on his breast The laughter never paused for an instant. For me, a boy constantly brought up in the seclusion of a dignified manor-house, all this noise and uproar, this unceremonious, almost riotous gaiety, these relations with unknown persons, were simply intoxicating. My head went round, as though from wine. I began laughing and talking louder than the others, so much so that the old princess, who was sitting in the next room with some sort of clerk from the Tversky gate, invited by her for consultation on business, positively came in to look at me. But I felt so happy that I did not mind anything, I didn't care a straw for any one's jeers, or dubious looks. Zinaïda continued to show me a preference, and kept me at her side. In one forfeit, I had to sit by her, both hidden under one silk handkerchief: I was to tell her *my secret*. I remember our two heads being all at once in a warm, half-transparent, fragrant darkness, the soft, close brightness of her eyes in the dark, and the burning breath from her parted lips, and the gleam of her teeth and the ends of her hair tickling me and setting me on fire. I was silent. She smiled slyly and mysteriously, and at last whispered to me, 'Well, what is it?' but I merely blushed and laughed, and turned away, catching my breath. We got tired of forfeits—we began to play a game with a string. My God! what were my transports when, for not paying attention, I got a sharp and vigorous slap on my fingers from her, and how I tried afterwards to pretend that I was absent-minded, and she teased me, and would not touch the hands I held out to her! What didn't we do that evening! We played the piano, and sang and danced and acted a gypsy encampment. Nirmatsky was dressed up as a bear, and made to drink salt water. Count Malevsky showed us several sorts of card tricks, and finished, after shuffling the cards, by dealing himself all the trumps at whist, on which Lushin 'had the honour of congratulating him.' Meidanov recited portions from his poem 'The Manslayer' (romanticism was at its height at this period), which he intended to bring out in a black cover with the title in blood-red letters; they stole the clerk's cap off his knee, and made him dance a Cossack dance by way of ransom for it; they dressed up old Vonifaty in a woman's cap, and the young princess put on a man's hat. . . . I could not enumerate all we did. Only Byelovzorov kept more and more in the background, scowling and angry. . . . Sometimes his eyes looked bloodshot, he flushed all over, and it seemed every minute as though he would rush out upon us all and scatter us like shavings in all directions; but the young princess would glance at him, and shake her finger at him, and he would retire into his corner again.

We were quite worn out at last Even the old princess, though she was ready for anything, as she expressed it, and no noise wearied her, felt tired at last, and longed for peace and quiet. At twelve o'clock at night, supper was served, consisting of a piece of stale dry cheese, and some cold turnovers of minced ham, which seemed to me more delicious than any pastry I had ever tasted; there was only one bottle of wine, and that was a strange one; a dark-coloured bottle with a wide neck, and the wine in it was of a pink hue; no one drank it, however. Tired out and faint with happiness, I left the lodge; at parting Zinaïda pressed my hand warmly, and again smiled mysteriously.

The night air was heavy and damp in my heated face; a storm seemed to be gathering; black stormclouds grew and crept across the sky, their smoky outlines visibly changing. A gust of wind shivered restlessly in the dark trees, and somewhere, far away on the horizon, muffled thunder angrily muttered as it were to itself.

I made my way up to my room by the back stairs. My old man-nurse was asleep on the floor, and I had to step over him; he waked up, saw me, and told me. that my mother had again been very angry with me, and had wished to send after me again, but that my father had prevented her. (I had never gone to bed without saying good-night to my mother, and asking her blessing. There was no help for it now!)

I told my man that I would undress and go to bed by myself, and I put out the candle But I did not undress, and did not go to bed.

I sat down on a chair, and sat a long while, as though spell-bound. What I was feeling was so new and so sweet. . . . I sat still, hardly looking round and not moving, drew slow breaths, and only from time to time laughed silently at some recollection, or turned cold within at the thought that I was in love, that this was she, that this was love. Zinaïda's face floated slowly before me in the darkness—floated, and did not float away; her lips still wore the same enigmatic smile, her eyes watched me, a little from one side, with a questioning, dreamy, tender look . . . as at the instant of parting from her. At last I got up, walked on tiptoe to my bed, and without undressing, laid my head carefully on the pillow, as though I were afraid by an abrupt movement to disturb what filled my soul. . . . I lay down, but did not even close my eyes. Soon I noticed that faint glimmers of light of some sort were thrown continually into the room. . . . I sat up and looked at the window. The window-frame could be clearly distinguished from the mysteriously and dimly-lighted panes. It is a storm, I thought; and a storm it really was, but it was raging so very far away that the thunder could not be heard; only blurred, long, as it were branching, gleams of lightning flashed continually over the sky; it was not flashing, though, so much as quivering and twitching like the wing of a dying bird. I got up, went to the window, and stood there till morning. . . . The lightning never ceased for an instant; it was what is called among the peasants a *sparrow night* I gazed at the dumb sandy plain, at the dark mass of the Neskutchny gardens, at the yellowish façades of the distant buildings, which seemed to quiver too at each faint flash. . . . I gazed, and could not turn away; these silent lightning flashes, these gleams seemed in response to the secret silent fires which were aglow within me. Morning began to dawn; the sky was flushed in patches of crimson. As the sun came nearer, the lightning grew gradually paler, and ceased; the quivering gleams were fewer and fewer, and vanished at last, drowned in the sobering positive light of the coming day. . . .

And my lightning flashes vanished too. I felt great weariness and peace . . . but Zinaïda's image still floated triumphant over my soul. But it too, this image, seemed more tranquil: like a swan rising out of the reeds of a bog, it stood out from the other unbeautiful figures surrounding it, and as I fell asleep, I flung myself before it in farewell, trusting adoration. . . .

Oh, sweet emotions, gentle harmony, goodness and peace of the softened heart, melting bliss of the first raptures of love, where are they, where are they?

VIII

THE next morning, when I came down to tea, my mother scolded me—less severely, however, than I had expected—and made me tell her how I had spent the previous evening. I answered her in few words, omitting many details, and trying to give the most innocent air to everything.

'Anyway, they're people who're not *comme il faut*,' my mother commented, 'and you've no business to be hanging about there, instead of preparing yourself for the examination, and doing your work.'

As I was well aware that my mother's anxiety about my studies was confined to these few words, I did not feel it necessary to make any rejoinder; but after morning tea was over, my father took me by the arm, and turning into the garden with me, forced me to tell him all I had seen at the Zasyekins'.

A curious influence my father had over me, and curious were the relations existing between us. He took hardly any interest in my education, but he never hurt my feelings; he respected my freedom, he treated me—if I may so express it—with courtesy, . . . only he never let me be really close to him. I loved him, I admired

FIRST LOVE

him, he was my ideal of a man—and Heavens! how passionately devoted I should have been to him, if I had not been continually conscious of his holding me off! But when he liked, he could almost instantaneously, by a single word, a single gesture, call forth an unbounded confidence in him. My soul expanded, I chattered away to him, as to a wise friend, a kindly teacher . . . then he as suddenly got rid of me, and again he was keeping me off, gently and affectionately, but still he kept me off.

Sometimes he was in high spirits, and then he was ready to romp and frolic with me, like a boy (he was fond of vigorous physical exercise of every sort); once—it never happened a second time!—he caressed me with such tenderness that I almost shed tears. . . . But high spirits and tenderness alike vanished completely, and what had passed between us, gave me nothing to build on for the future—it was as though I had dreamed it all. Sometimes I would scrutinise his clever handsome bright face . . . my heart would throb, and my whole being yearn to him . . . he would seem to feel what was going on within me, would give me a passing pat on the cheek, and go away, or take up some work, or suddenly freeze all over as only he knew how to freeze, and I shrank into myself at once, and turned cold too. His rare fits of friendliness to me were never called forth by my silent, but intelligible entreaties: they always occurred unexpectedly. Thinking over my father's character later, I have come to the conclusion that he had no thoughts to spare for me and for family life; his heart was in other things, and found complete satisfaction elsewhere. 'Take for yourself what you can, and don't be ruled by others; to belong to oneself —the whole savour of life lies in that,' he said to me one day. Another time, I, as a young democrat, fell to airing my views on liberty (he was 'kind,' as I used to call it, that day; and at such times I could talk to him as I liked). 'Liberty,' he repeated; 'and do you know what can give a man liberty?'

'What?'

'Will, his own will, and it gives power, which is better than liberty. Know how to will, and you will be free, and will lead.'

My father, before all, and above all, desired to live, and lived. . . . Perhaps he had a presentiment that he would not have long to enjoy the 'savour' of life; he died at forty-two.

I described my evening at the Zasyekins' minutely to my father. Half attentively, half carelessly, he listened to me, sitting on a garden seat, drawing in the sand with his cane. Now and then he laughed, shot bright, droll glances

FIRST LOVE

at me, and spurred me on with short questions and assents. At first I could not bring myself even to utter the name of Zinaïda, but I could not restrain myself long, and began singing her praises. My father still laughed; then he grew thoughtful, stretched, and got up.

I remembered that as he came out of the house he had ordered his horse to be saddled. He was a splendid horseman, and, long before Rarey, had the secret of breaking in the most vicious horses.

'Shall I come with you, father?' I asked.

'No,' he answered, and his face resumed its ordinary expression of friendly indifference. 'Go alone, if you like; and tell the coachman I'm not going.'

He turned his back on me and walked rapidly away. I looked after him; he disappeared through the gates. I saw his hat moving along beside the fence; he went into the Zasyekins'.

He stayed there not more than an hour, but then departed at once for the town, and did not return home till evening.

After dinner I went myself to the Zasyekins'. In the drawing-room I found only the old princess. On seeing me she scratched her head under her cap with a knitting-needle, and suddenly asked me, could I copy a petition for her.

'With pleasure,' I replied, sitting down on the edge of a chair.

'Only mind and make the letters bigger,' observed the princess, handing me a dirty sheet of paper; 'and couldn't you do it to-day, my good sir?'

'Certainly, I will copy it to-day.'

The door of the next room was just opened, and in the crack I saw the face of Zinaïda, pale and pensive, her hair flung carelessly back; she stared at me with big chilly eyes, and softly closed the door.

'Zina, Zina!' the old lady. Zinaïda made no response. I took home the old lady's petition and spent the whole evening over it.

IX

My 'passion' dated from that day. I felt at that time, I recollect, something like what a man must feel on entering the service: I had ceased now to be simply a young boy; I was in love. I have said that my passion dated from that day; I might have added that my sufferings too dated from the same day. Away from Zinaïda I pined; nothing was to my mind; everything went wrong with me; I

FIRST LOVE

spent whole days thinking intensely about her . . . I pined when away, . . . but in her presence I was no better off. I was jealous; I was conscious of my insignificance; I was stupidly sulky or stupidly abject, and, all the same, an invincible force drew me to her, and I could not help a shudder of delight whenever I stepped through the doorway of her room. Zinaïda guessed at once that I was in love with her, and indeed I never even thought of concealing it. She amused herself with my passion, made a fool of me, petted and tormented me. There is a sweetness in being the sole source, the autocratic and irresponsible cause of the greatest joy and profoundest pain to another, and I was like wax in Zinaïda's hands; though, indeed, I was not the only one in love with her. All the men who visited the house were crazy over her, and she kept them all in leading-strings at her feet. It amused her to arouse their hopes and then their fears, to turn them round her finger (she used to call it knocking their heads together), while they never dreamed of offering resistance and eagerly submitted to her. About her whole being, so full of life and beauty, there was a peculiarly bewitching mixture of slyness and carelessness, of artificiality and simplicity, of composure and frolicsomeness; about everything she did or said, about every action of hers, there clung a delicate, fine charm, in which an individual power was manifest at work. And her face was ever changing, working too; it expressed, almost at the same time, irony, dreaminess, and passion. Various emotions, delicate and quick-changing as the shadows of clouds on a sunny day of wind, chased one another continually over her lips and eyes.

Each of her adorers was necessary to her. Byelovzorov, whom she sometimes called 'my wild beast,' and sometimes simply 'mine,' would gladly have flung himself into the fire for her sake. With little confidence in his intellectual abilities and other qualities, he was for ever offering her marriage, hinting that the others were merely hanging about with no serious intention. Meidanov responded to the poetic fibres of her nature; a man of rather cold temperament, like almost all writers, he forced himself to convince her, and perhaps himself, that he adored her, sang her praises in endless verses, and read them to her with a peculiar enthusiasm, at once affected and sincere. She sympathised with him, and at the same time jeered at him a little; she had no great faith in him, and after listening to his outpourings, she would make him read Pushkin, as she said, to clear the air. Lushin, the ironical doctor, so cynical in words, knew her better than any of them, and loved her more than all, though he abused her to her face and behind her back. She could not help respecting him, but made him smart for it, and at times, with a peculiar, malignant pleasure, made him feel that he too was at her mercy. 'I'm a flirt, I'm heartless, I'm an actress in my instincts,' she said to him one day in my presence; 'well and good! Give me your hand then; I'll stick this pin in it, you'll be ashamed of this young man's seeing it, it will hurt you, but you'll laugh for all that, you truthful person.' Lushin crimsoned, turned away, bit his lips, but ended by submitting his hand. She pricked it, and he did in fact begin to laugh, . . . and she laughed, thrusting the pin in pretty deeply, and peeping into his eyes, which he vainly strove to keep in other directions. . . .

I understood least of all the relations existing between Zinaïda and Count Malevsky. He was handsome, clever, and adroit, but something equivocal, something false in him was apparent even to me, a boy of sixteen, and I marvelled that Zinaïda did not notice it. But possibly she did notice this element of falsity really and was not repelled by it. Her irregular education, strange acquaintances and habits, the constant presence of her mother, the poverty and disorder in their house, everything, from the very liberty the young girl enjoyed, with the consciousness of her superiority to the people around her, had developed in her a sort of half-contemptuous carelessness and lack of fastidiousness. At any time anything might happen; Vonifaty might announce that there was no sugar, or some revolting scandal would come to her ears, or her guests would fall to quarrelling among themselves—she would only shake her curls, and say, 'What does it matter?' and care little enough about it.

But my blood, anyway, was sometimes on fire with indignation when Malevsky approached her, with a sly, fox-like action, leaned gracefully on the back of her chair, and began whispering in her ear with a self-satisfied and ingratiating little smile, while she folded her arms across her bosom, looked intently at him and smiled too, and shook her head.

'What induces you to receive Count Malevsky?' I asked her one day.

'He has such pretty moustaches,' she answered. 'But that's rather beyond you.'

'You needn't think I care for him,' she said to me another time. 'No; I can't care for people I have to look down upon. I must have some one who can master me. . . . But, merciful heavens, I hope I may never come

FIRST LOVE

across any one like that! I don't want to be caught in any one's claws, not for anything.'

'You'll never be in love, then?'

'And you? Don't I love you?' she said, and she flicked me on the nose with the tip of her glove.

Yes, Zinaïda amused herself hugely at my expense. For three weeks I saw her every day, and what didn't she do with me! She rarely came to see us, and I was not sorry for it; in our house she was transformed into a young lady, a young princess, and I was a little overawed by her. I was afraid of betraying myself before my mother; she had taken a great dislike to Zinaïda, and kept a hostile eye upon us. My father I was not so much afraid of; he seemed not to notice me. He talked little to her, but always with special cleverness and significance. I gave up working and reading; I even gave up walking about the neighbourhood and riding my horse. Like a beetle tied by the leg, I moved continually round and round my beloved little lodge. I would gladly have stopped there altogether, it seemed . . . but that was impossible. My mother scolded me, and sometimes Zinaïda herself drove me away. Then I used to shut myself up in my room, or go down to the very end of the garden, and climbing into what was left of a tall stone greenhouse, now in ruins, sit for hours with my legs hanging over the wall that looked on to the road, gazing and gazing and seeing nothing. White butterflies flitted lazily by me, over the dusty nettles; a saucy sparrow settled not far off on the half crumbling red brickwork and twittered irritably, incessantly twisting and turning and preening his tail-feathers; the still mistrustful rooks cawed now and then, sitting high, high up on the bare top of a birch-tree; the sun and wind played softly on its pliant branches; the tinkle of the bells of the Don monastery floated across to me from time to time, peaceful and dreary; while I sat, gazed, listened, and was filled full of a nameless sensation in which all was contained: sadness and joy and the foretaste of the future, and the desire and dread of life. But at that time I understood nothing of it, and could have given a name to nothing of all that was passing at random within me, or should have called it all by one name—the name of Zinaïda.

Zinaïda continued to play cat and mouse with me. She flirted with me, and I was all agitation and rapture; then she would suddenly thrust me away, and I dared not go near her —dared not look at her.

I remember she was very cold to me for

FIRST LOVE

several days together; I was completely crushed, and creeping timidly to their lodge, tried to keep close to the old princess, regardless of the circumstance that she was particularly scolding and grumbling just at that time; her financial affairs had been going badly, and she had already had two 'explanations' with the police officials.

One day I was walking in the garden beside the familiar fence, and I caught sight of Zinaïda; leaning on both arms, she was sitting on the grass, not stirring a muscle. I was about to make off cautiously, but she suddenly raised her head and beckoned me imperiously. My heart failed me; I did not understand her at first. She repeated her signal. I promptly jumped over the fence and ran joyfully up to her, but she brought me to a halt with a look, and motioned me to the path two paces from her. In confusion, not knowing what to do, I fell on my knees at the edge of the path. She was so pale, such bitter suffering, such intense weariness, was expressed in every feature of her face, that it sent a pang to my heart, and I muttered unconsciously, 'What is the matter?'

Zinaïda stretched out her head, picked a blade of grass, bit it and flung it away from her.

'You love me very much?' she asked at last. 'Yes.'

I made no answer—indeed, what need was there to answer?

'Yes,' she repeated, looking at me as before. 'That's so. The same eyes,'—she went on; sank into thought, and hid her face in her hands. 'Everything's grown so loathsome to me,' she whispered, 'I would have gone to the other end of the world first—I can't bear it, I can't get over it. . . . And what is there before me! . . . Ah, I am wretched. . . . My God, how wretched I am!'

'What for?' I asked timidly.

Zinaïda made no answer, she simply shrugged her shoulders. I remained kneeling, gazing at her with intense sadness. Every word she had uttered simply cut me to the heart. At that instant I felt I would gladly have given my life, if only she should not grieve. I gazed at her—and though I could not understand why she was wretched, I vividly pictured to myself, how in a fit of insupportable anguish, she had suddenly come out into the garden, and sunk to the earth, as though mown down by a scythe. It was all bright and green about her; the wind was whispering in the leaves of the trees, and swinging now and then a long branch of a raspberry bush over Zinaïda's head. There was a sound of the cooing of doves, and the bees hummed, flying low over the scanty grass.

FIRST LOVE

Overhead the sun was radiantly blue—while I was so sorrowful. . . .

'Read me some poetry,' said Zinaïda in an undertone, and she propped herself on her elbow; 'I like your reading poetry. You read it in sing-song, but that's no matter, that comes of being young. Read me "On the Hills of Georgia." Only sit down first.'

I sat down and read 'On the Hills of Georgia.'

'"That the heart cannot choose but love,"' repeated Zinaïda. 'That's where poetry's so fine; it tells us what is not, and what's not only better than what is, but much more like the truth, "cannot choose but love,"—it might want not to, but it can't help it.' She was silent again, then all at once she started and got up. 'Come along. Meidanov's indoors with mamma, he brought me his poem, but I deserted him. His feelings are hurt too now . . . I can't help it! you'll understand it all some day . . . only don't be angry with me!'

Zinaïda hurriedly pressed my hand and ran on ahead. We went back into the lodge. Meidanov set to reading us his 'Manslayer,' which had just appeared in print, but I did not hear him. He screamed and drawled his four-foot iambic lines, the alternating rhythms jingled like little bells, noisy and meaningless, while I still watched Zinaïda and tried to take in the import of her last words.

> 'Perchance some unknown rival
> Has surprised and mastered thee?'

Meidanov bawled suddenly through his nose—and my eyes and Zinaïda's met. She looked down and faintly blushed. I saw her blush, and grew cold with terror. I had been jealous before, but only at that instant the idea of her being in love flashed upon my mind. 'Good God! she is in love!'

X

My real torments began from that instant. I racked my brains, changed my mind, and changed it back again, and kept an unremitting, though, as far as possible, secret watch on Zinaïda. A change had come over her, that was obvious. She began going walks alone—and long walks. Sometimes she would not see visitors; she would sit for hours together in her room. This had never been a habit of hers till now. I suddenly became—or fancied I had become—extraordinarily penetrating.

'Isn't it he? or isn't it he?' I asked myself, passing in inward agitation from one of her admirers to another. Count Malevsky secretly struck me as more to be feared than the others, though, for Zinaïda's sake, I was ashamed to confess it to myself.

My watchfulness did not see beyond the end of my nose, and its secrecy probably deceived no one; any way, Doctor Lushin soon saw through me. But he, too, had changed of late; he had grown thin, he laughed as often, but his laugh seemed more hollow, more spiteful, shorter, an involuntary nervous irritability took the place of his former light irony and assumed cynicism.

'Why are you incessantly hanging about here, young man?' he said to me one day, when we were left alone together in the Zasyekins' drawing-room. (The young princess had not come home from a walk, and the shrill voice of the old princess could be heard within; she was scolding the maid.) 'You ought to be studying, working—while you're young—and what are you doing?'

'You can't tell whether I work at home,' I retorted with some haughtiness, but also with some hesitation.

'A great deal of work you do! that's not what you're thinking about! Well, I won't find fault with that . . . at your age that's in the natural order of things. But you've been awfully unlucky in your choice. Don't you see what this house is?'

'I don't understand you,' I observed.

'You don't understand? so much the worse for you. I regard it as a duty to warn you. Old bachelors, like me, can come here, what harm can it do us! we're tough, nothing can hurt us, what harm can it do us; but your skin's tender yet—this air is bad for you—believe me, you may get harm from it.'

'How so?'

'Why, are you well now? Are you in a normal condition? Is what you're feeling—beneficial to you—good for you?'

'Why, what am I feeling?' I said, while in my heart I knew the doctor was right.

'Ah, young man, young man,' the doctor went on with an intonation that suggested that something highly insulting to me was contained in these two words, 'what's the use of your prevaricating, when, thank God, what's in your heart is in your face, so far? But there, what's the use of talking? I shouldn't come here myself, if . . . (the doctor compressed his lips). . . . if I weren't such a queer fellow. Only this is what surprises me; how it is, you, with your intelligence, don't see what is going on around you?'

'And what is going on?' I put in, all on the alert.

FIRST LOVE

The doctor looked at me with a sort of ironical compassion.

'Nice of me!' he said as though to himself, 'as if he need know anything of it. In fact, I tell you again,' he added, raising his voice, 'the atmosphere here is not fit for you. You like being here, but what of that! it's nice and sweet-smelling in a greenhouse—but there's no living in it. Yes! do as I tell you, and go back to your Keidanov.'

The old princess came in, and began complaining to the doctor of her toothache. Then Zinaïda appeared.

'Come,' said the old princess, 'you must scold her, doctor. She's drinking iced water all day long; is that good for her, pray, with her delicate chest?'

'Why do you do that?' asked Lushin.

'Why, what effect could it have?'

'What effect? You might get a chill and die.'

'Truly? Do you mean it? Very well—so much the better.'

'A fine idea!' muttered the doctor. The old princess had gone out.

'Yes, a fine idea,' repeated Zinaïda. 'Is life such a festive affair? Just look about you, . . . Is it nice, eh? Or do you imagine I don't understand it, and don't feel it? It gives me pleasure—drinking iced water; and can you seriously assure me that such a life is worth too much to be risked for an instant's pleasure—happiness I won't even talk about.'

'Oh, very well,' remarked Lushin, 'caprice and irresponsibility. . . . Those two words sum you up; your whole nature's contained in those two words.'

Zinaïda laughed nervously.

'You're late for the post, my dear doctor. You don't keep a good look-out; you're behind the times. Put on your spectacles. I'm in no capricious humour now. To make fools of you, to make a fool of myself . . . much fun there is in that!—and as for irresponsibility . . . M'sieu Voldemar,' Zinaïda added suddenly, stamping, 'don't make such a melancholy face. I can't endure people to pity me.' She went quickly out of the room.

'It's bad for you, very bad for you, this atmosphere, young man,' Lushin said to me once more.

XI

ON the evening of the same day the usual guests were assembled at the Zasyekins'. I was among them.

The conversation turned on Meidanov's poem.

Zinaïda expressed genuine admiration of it. 'But do you know what?' she said to him. 'If I were a poet, I would choose quite different subjects. Perhaps it's all nonsense, but strange ideas sometimes come into my head, especially when I'm not asleep in the early morning, when the sky begins to turn rosy and grey both at once. I would, for . . . instance . . . You won't laugh at me?'

'No, no!' we all cried, with one voice.

'I would describe,' she went on, folding her arms across her bosom and looking away, 'a whole company of young girls at night in a great boat, on a silent river. The moon is shining, and they are all in white, and wearing garlands of white flowers, and singing, you know, something in the nature of a hymn.'

'I see—I see; go on,' Meidanov commented with dreamy significance.

'All of a sudden, loud clamour, laughter, torches, tambourines on the bank. . . . It's a troop of Bacchantes dancing with songs and cries. It's your business to make a picture of it, Mr. Poet; . . . only I should like the torches to be red and to smoke a great deal, and the Bacchantes' eyes to gleam under their wreaths, and the wreaths to be dusky Don't forget the tiger-skins, too, and goblets and gold—lots of gold. . . .'

'Where ought the gold to be?' asked Meidanov, tossing back his sleek hair and distending his nostrils.

'Where? on their shoulders and arms and legs—everywhere. They say in ancient times women wore gold rings on their ankles. The Bacchantes call the girls in. the boat to them. The girls have ceased singing their hymn—they cannot go on with it, but they do not stir, the river carries them to the bank. And suddenly one of them slowly rises. . . . This you must describe nicely: how she slowly gets up in the moonlight, and how her companions are afraid. . . . She steps over the edge of the boat, the Bacchantes surround her, whirl her away into night and darkness. . . . Here put in smoke in clouds and everything in confusion. There is nothing but the sound of their shrill cry, and her wreath left lying on the bank.'

Zinaïda ceased. ('Oh! she is in love!' I thought again.)

'And is that all?' asked Meidanov.

'That's all.'

'That can't be the subject of a whole poem,' he observed pompously, 'but I will make use of your idea for a lyrical fragment.'

'In the romantic style?' queried Malevsky.

'Of course, in the romantic style—Byronic.'

'Well, to my mind, Hugo beats Byron,' the

young count observed negligently; 'he's more interesting.'

'Hugo is a writer of the first class,' replied Neidanov; 'and friend, Tonkosheev, in his Spanish romance, *El Trovador* . . .'

'Ah! is that the book with the question-marks turned upside down?' Zinaïda interrupted.

'Yes. That's the custom with the Spanish. I was about to observe that Tonkosheev . . .'

'Come! you're going to argue about classicism and romanticism again,' Zinaïda interrupted him a second time. 'We'd much better play . . .'

'Forfeits?' put in Lushin.

'No, forfeits are a bore; at comparisons.' (This game Zinaïda had invented herself. Some object was mentioned, every one tried to compare it with something, and the one who chose the best comparison got a prize.)

She went up to the window. The sun was just setting; high up in the sky were large red clouds.

'What are those clouds like?' questioned Zinaïda; and without waiting for our answer, she said, 'I think they are like the purple sails on the golden ship of Cleopatra, when she sailed to meet Antony. Do you remember, Neidanov, you were telling me about it not long ago?'

All of us, like Polonius in *Hamlet,* opined

that the clouds recalled nothing so much as those sails, and that not one of us could discover a better comparison.

'And how old was Antony then?' inquired Zinaïda.

'A young man, no doubt,' observed Malevsky.

'Yes, a young man,' Meidanov chimed in in confirmation.

'Excuse me,' cried Lushin, 'he was over forty.'

'Over forty' repeated Zinaïda, giving him a rapid glance. . . .

I soon went home. 'She is in love,' my lips unconsciously repeated. . . . 'But with whom?'

XII

THE days passed by. Zinaïda became stranger and stranger, and more and more incomprehensible. One day I went over to her, and saw her sitting in a basket-chair, her head pressed to the sharp edge of the table. She drew herself up . . . her whole face was wet with tears.

'Ah, you!' she said with a cruel smile. 'Come here.'

I went up to her. She put her hand on my head, and suddenly catching hold of my hair began pulling it.

'It hurts me,' I said at last.

'Ah! does it? And do you suppose nothing hurts me?' she replied.

'Ai!' she cried suddenly, seeing she had pulled a little tuft of hair out. 'What have I done? Poor M'sieu Voldemar!'

She carefully smoothed the hair she had torn out, stroked it round her finger, and twisted it into a ring.

'I shall put your hair in a locket and wear it round my neck,' she said, while the tears still glittered in her eyes. 'That will be some small consolation to you, perhaps . . . and now good-bye.'

I went home, and found an unpleasant state of things there. My mother was having a scene with my father; she was reproaching him with something, while he, as his habit was, maintained a polite and chilly silence, and soon left her. I could not hear what my mother was talking of, and indeed I had no thought to spare for the subject; I only remember that when the interview was over, she sent for me to her room, and referred with great displeasure to the frequent visits I paid the princess, who was, in her words, *une femme capable de tout.* I kissed her hand (this was what I always did when I wanted to cut short a conversation) and went off to my room. Zinaïda's tears had completely overwhelmed me; I positively did not know what to think, and was ready to cry myself; I was a child after all, in spite of my sixteen years. I had now given up thinking about Malevsky, though Byelovzorov looked more and more threatening every day, and glared at the wily count like a wolf at a sheep; but I thought of nothing and of no one. I was lost in imaginings, and was always seeking seclusion and solitude. I was particularly fond of the ruined greenhouse. I would climb up on the high wall, and perch myself, and sit there, such an unhappy, lonely, and melancholy youth, that I felt sorry for myself—and how consolatory where those mournful sensations, how I revelled in them! . . .

One day I was sitting on the wall looking into the distance and listening to the ringing of the bells. . . . Suddenly something floated up to me—not a breath of wind and not a shiver, but as it were a whiff of fragrance—as it were, a sense of some one's being near. . . . I looked down. Below, on the path, in a light greyish gown, with a pink parasol on her shoulder, was Zinaïda, hurrying along. She caught sight of me, stopped, and pushing back the brim of her straw hat, she raised her velvety eyes to me.

'What are you doing up there at such a height?' she asked me with a rather queer

FIRST LOVE

smile. 'Come,' she went on, 'you always declare you love me; jump down into the road to me if you really do love me.'

Zinaïda had hardly uttered those words when I flew down, just as though some one had given me a violent push from behind. The wall was about fourteen feet high. I reached the ground on my feet, but the shock was so great that I could not keep my footing; I fell down, and for an instant fainted away. When I came to myself again, without opening my eyes, I felt Zinaïda beside me. 'My dear boy,' she was saying, bending over me, and there was a note of alarmed tenderness in her voice, 'how could you do it, dear; how could you obey? . . . You know I love you . . . Get up.'

Her bosom was heaving close to me, her hands were caressing my head, and suddenly —what were my emotions at that moment— her soft, fresh lips began covering my face with kisses . . . they touched my lips. . . . But then Zinaïda probably guessed by the expression of my face that I had regained consciousness, though I still kept my eyes closed, and rising rapidly to her feet, she said: 'Come, get up, naughty boy, silly, why are you lying in the dust?' I got up. 'Give me my parasol,' said Zinaïda, 'I threw it down somewhere, and don't stare at me like that . . .

what ridiculous nonsense! you're not hurt, are you? stung by the nettles, I daresay? Don't stare at me, I tell you. . . . But he doesn't understand, he doesn't answer.' she added, as though to herself. . . . 'Go home, M'sieu' Voldemar, brush yourself, and don't dare to follow me, or I shall be angry, and never again . . .'

She did not finish her sentence, but walked rapidly away, while I sat down by the side of the road . . . my legs would not support me. The nettles had stung my hands, my back ached, and my head was giddy; but the feeling of rapture I experienced then has never come a second time in my life. It turned to a sweet ache in all my limbs and found expression at last in joyful hops and skips and shouts. Yes, I was still a child.

XIII

I WAS so proud and light-hearted all that day, I so vividly retained on my face the feeling of Zinaïda's kisses, with such a shudder of delight I recalled every word she had uttered, I so hugged my unexpected happiness that I felt positively afraid, positively unwilling to see her, who had given rise to these new sensations. It seemed to me that now I. could ask nothing more of fate, that now I ought to 'go,and draw a deep

FIRST LOVE

last sigh and die.' But, next day, when I went into the lodge, I felt great embarrassment, which I tried to conceal under a show of modest confidence, befitting a man who wishes to make it apparent that he knows how to keep a secret. Zinaïda received me very simply, without any emotion, she simply shook her finger at me and asked me, whether I wasn't black and blue? All my modest confidence and air of mystery vanished instantaneously and with them my embarrassment. Of course, I had not expected anything particular, but Zinaïda's composure was like a bucket of cold water thrown over me. I realised that in her eyes I was a child, and was extremely miserable! Zinaïda walked up and down the room, giving me a quick smile, whenever she caught my eye, but her thoughts were far away, I saw that clearly. . . . 'Shall I begin about what happened yesterday myself,' I pondered; 'ask her, where she was hurrying off so fast, so as to find out once for all' . . . but with a gesture of despair, I merely went and sat down in a corner.

Byelovzorov came in; I felt relieved to see him.

'I've not been able to find you a quiet horse,' he said in a sulky voice; 'Freitag warrants one, but I don't feel any confidence in it, I am afraid.'

'What are you afraid of?' said Zinaïda; 'allow me to inquire?'

'What am I afraid of? Why, you don't know how to ride. Lord save us, what might happen! What whim is this has come over you all of a sudden?'

'Come, that's my business, Sir Wild Beast. In that case I will ask Piotr Vassilievitch.'. . . (My father's name was Piotr Vassilievitch. I was surprised at her mentioning his name so lightly and freely, as though she were confident of his readiness to do her a service.)

'Oh, indeed, 'retorted Byelovzorov,' you mean to go out riding with him then?'

'With him or with some one else is nothing to do with you. Only not with you, anyway.'

'Not with me,' repeated Byelovzorov. 'As you wish. Well, I shall find you a horse.'

'Yes, only mind now, don't send some old cow. I warn you I want to gallop.'

'Gallop away by all means . . . with whom is it, with Malevsky, you are going to ride?'

'And why not with him, Mr. Pugnacity? Come, be quiet,' she added, 'and don't glare. I'll take you too. You know that to my mind now Malevsky's—ugh!' She shook her head.

'You say that to console me,' growled Byelovzorov.

Zinaïda half closed her eyes. 'Does that

FIRST LOVE

console you? O . . . O . . . O . . . Mr. Pugnacity!' she said at last, as though she could find no other word. 'And you, M'sieu' Voldemar, would you come with us?'

'I don't care to . . . in a large party,' I muttered, not raising my eyes.

'You prefer a *tête-à-téte*? . . . Well, freedom to the free, and heaven to the saints,' she commented with a sigh. 'Go along, Byelovzorov, and bestir yourself. I must have a horse for to-morrow.'

Oh, and where's the money to come from?' put in the old princess.

Zinaïda scowled.

'I won't ask you for it; Byelovzorov will trust me.'

'He'll trust you, will he?' . . . grumbled the old princess, and all of a sudden she screeched at the top of her voice, 'Duniashka!'

'Maman, I have given you a bell to ring,' observed Zinaïda.

'Duniashka!' repeated the old lady.

Byelovzorov took leave; I went away with him. Zinaïda did not try to detain me.

XIV

THE next day I got up early, cut myself a stick, and set off beyond the town-gates. I thought I would walk off my sorrow. It was a lovely day, bright and not too hot, a fresh sportive breeze roved over the earth with temperate rustle and frolic, setting all things a-flutter and harassing nothing. I wandered a long while over hills and through woods; I had not felt happy, I had left home with the intention of giving myself up to melancholy, but youth, the exquisite weather, the fresh air, the pleasure of rapid motion, the sweetness of repose, lying on the thick grass in a solitary nook, gained the upper hand; the memory of those never-to-be-forgotten words, those kisses, forced itself once more upon my soul. It was sweet to me to think that Zinaïda could not, anyway, fail to do justice to my courage, my heroism. . . . 'Others may seem better to her than I,' I mused, 'let them! But others only say what they would do, while I have done it And what more would I not do for her?' My fancy set to work. I began picturing to myself how I would save her from the hands of enemies; how, covered with blood I would tear her by force from prison, and expire at her feet. I remembered a picture hanging in our drawing-room—Malek-Adel bearing away Matilda—but at that point my attention was absorbed by the appearance of a speckled woodpecker who climbed busily up the slender stem of a birch-tree and peeped out uneasily from behind it, first to the right, then to the left, like a musician behind the bass-viol.

Then I sang 'Not the white snows,' and passed from that to a song well known at that period: 'I await thee, when the wanton zephyr,' then I began reading aloud Yermak's address to the stars from Homyakov's tragedy. I made an attempt to compose something myself in a sentimental vein, and invented the line which was to conclude each verse: 'O Zinaïda, Zinaïda!' but could get no further with it. Meanwhile it was getting on towards dinner-time. I went down into the valley; a narrow sandy path winding through it led to the town. I walked along this path. . . . The dull thud of horses' hoofs resounded behind me. I looked round instinctively, stood still and took off my cap. I saw my father and Zinaïda. They were riding side by side. My father was saying something to her, bending right over to her, his hand propped on the horses' neck, he was smiling. Zinaïda listened to him in silence, her eyes severely cast down, and her lips tightly pressed together. At first I saw them only; but a few instants later, Byelovzorov came into sight round a bend in the glade, he was wearing a hussar's uniform with a pelisse, and riding a foaming black horse. The gallant horse tossed its head, snorted and pranced from side to side, his rider was at once holding him in and spurring him on. I stood aside. My father gathered up the reins, moved away from Zinaïda, she slowly raised her eyes to him, and both galloped off. . . . Byelovzorov flew after them, his sabre clattering behind him. 'He's as red as a crab,' I reflected, 'while she . . . why's she so pale? out riding the whole morning, and pale?'

I redoubled my pace, and got home just at dinner-time. My father was already sitting by my mother's chair, dressed for dinner, washed and fresh; he was reading an article from the *Journal des Débats* in his smooth musical voice; but my mother heard him without attention, and when she saw me, asked where I had been to all day long, and added that she didn't like this gadding about God knows where, and God knows in what company. 'But I have been walking alone,' I was on the point of replying, but I looked at my father, and for some reason or other held my peace.

XV

FOR the next five or six days I hardly saw Zinaïda; she said she was ill, which did not, however, prevent the usual visitors from calling

FIRST LOVE

at the lodge to pay—as they expressed it, their duty—all, that is, except Meidanov, who promptly grew dejected and sulky when he had not an opportunity of being enthusiastic. Byelovzorov sat sullen and red-faced in a corner, buttoned up to the throat; on the refined face of Malevsky there flickered continually an evil smile; he had really fallen into disfavour with Zinaïda, and waited with special assiduity on the old princess, and even went with her in a hired coach to call on the Governor-General. This expedition turned out unsuccessful, however, and even led to an unpleasant experience for Malevsky; he was reminded of some scandal to do with certain officers of the engineers, and was forced in his explanations to plead his youth and inexperience at the time. Lushin came twice a day, but did not stay long; I was rather afraid of him after our last unreserved conversation, and at the same time felt a genuine attraction to him. He went a walk with me one day in the Neskutchny gardens, was very good-natured and nice, told me the names and properties of various plants and flowers, and suddenly, *à propos* of nothing at all, cried, hitting himself on his forehead, 'And I, poor fool, thought her a flirt! it's clear self-sacrifice is sweet for some people!'

'What do you mean by that?' I inquired.

'I don't mean to tell you anything.' Lushin replied abruptly.

Zinaïda avoided me; my presence—I could not help noticing it—affected her disagreeably. She involuntarily turned away from me . . . involuntarily; that was what was so bitter, that was what crushed me! But there was no help for it, and I tried not to cross her path, and only to watch her from a distance, in which I was not always successful. As before, something incomprehensible was happening to her; her face was different, she was different altogether. I was specially struck by the change that had taken place in her one warm still evening. I was sitting on a low garden bench under a spreading elderbush; I was fond of that nook; I could see from there the window of Zinaïda's room. I sat there; over my head a little bird was busily hopping about in the darkness of the leaves; a grey cat, stretching herself at full length, crept warily about the garden, and the first beetles were heavily droning in the air, which was still clear, though it was not light. I sat and gazed at the window, and waited to see if it would open; it did open, and Zinaïda appeared at it She had on a white dress, and she herself, her face, shoulders, and arms, were pale to whiteness. She stayed a long while without moving, and looked out straight before her from under her knitted brows. I had never known such a look on her. Then she clasped her hands tightly, raised them to her lips, to her forehead, and suddenly pulling her fingers apart, she pushed back her hair behind her ears, tossed it, and with a sort of determination nodded her head, and slammed-to the window.

Three days later she met me in the garden. I was turning away, but she stopped me of herself.

'Give me your arm,' she said to me with her old affectionateness, 'it's a long while since we have had a talk together.'

I stole a look at her; her eyes were full of a soft light, and her face seemed as it were smiling through a mist.

'Are you still not well?' I asked her.

'No, that's all over now,' she answered, and she picked a small red rose. 'I am a little tired, but that too will pass off.'

'And will you be as you used to be again?' I asked.

Zinaïda put the rose up to her face, and I fancied the reflection of its bright petals had fallen on her cheeks. 'Why, am I changed?' she questioned me.

'Yes, you are changed,' I answered in a low voice.

'I have been cold to you, I know,' began Zinaïda, 'but you mustn't pay attention to that . . . I couldn't help it . . . Come, why talk about it!'

'You don't want me to love you, that's what it is!' I cried gloomily, in an involuntary outburst.

'No, love me, but not as you did.'

'How then?'

'Let us be friends—come now!' Zinaïda gave me the rose to smell. 'Listen, you know I'm much older than you—I might be your aunt, really; well, not your aunt, but an older sister. And you . . .'

'You think me a child,' I interrupted.

'Well, yes, a child, but a dear, good clever one, whom I love very much. Do you know what? From this day forth I confer on you the rank of page to me; and don't you forget that pages have to keep close to their ladies. Here is the token of your new dignity,' she added, sticking the rose in the buttonhole of my jacket, 'the token of my favour.'

'I once received other favours from you,' I muttered.

'Ah!' commented Zinaïda, and she gave me a sidelong look, 'What a memory he has! Well? I'm quite ready now . . . .' And stooping to me, she imprinted on my forehead a pure, tranquil kiss.

FIRST LOVE

I only looked at her, while she turned away, and saying, 'Follow me, my page,' went into the lodge. I followed her—all in amazement. 'Can this gentle, reasonable girl,' I thought, 'be the Zinaïda I used to know?' I fancied her very walk was quieter, her whole figure statelier and more graceful . . .

And, mercy! with what fresh force love burned within me!

XVI

After dinner the usual party assembled again at the lodge, and the young princess came out to them. All were there in full force, just as on that first evening which I never forgot; even Nirmatsky had limped to see her; Meidanov came this time earliest of all, he brought some new verses. The games of forfeits began again, but without the strange pranks, the practical jokes and noise—the gipsy. element had vanished. Zinaïda gave a different tone to the proceedings. I sat beside her by virtue of my office as page. Among other things, she proposed that any one who had to pay a forfeit should tell his dream; but this was not successful. The dreams were either uninteresting

(Byelovzorov had dreamed that he fed his mare on carp, and that she had a wooden head), or unnatural and invented. Meidanov regaled us with a regular romance; there were sepulchres in it, and angels with lyres, and talking flowers and music wafted from afar. Zinaïda did not let him finish. 'If we are to have compositions,' she said, 'let every one tell something made up, and no pretence about it.' The first who had to speak was again Byelovzorov.

The young hussar was confused. 'I can't make up anything!' he cried.

'What nonsense!' said Zinaïda. 'Well, imagine, for instance, you are married, and tell us how you would treat your wife. Would you lock her up?'

'Yes, I should lock her up.'

'And would you stay with her yourself?'

'Yes, I should certainly stay with her myself.'

'Very good. Well, but if she got sick of that, and she deceived you?'

'I should kill her.'

'And if she ran away?'

'I should catch her up and kill her all the same.'

'Oh. And suppose now I were your wife, what would you do then?'

FIRST LOVE

Byelovzorov was silent a minute. 'I should kill myself....'

Zinaïda laughed. 'I see yours is not a long story.'

The next forfeit was Zinaïda's. She looked at the ceiling and considered. 'Well, listen, she began at last, 'what I have thought of.... Picture to yourselves a magnificent palace, a summer night, and a marvellous ball. This ball is given by a young queen. Everywhere gold and marble, crystal, silk, lights, diamonds, flowers, fragrant scents, every caprice of luxury.'

'You love luxury?' Lushin interposed.

'Luxury is beautiful,' she retorted; 'I love everything beautiful.'

'More than what is noble?' he asked.

'That's something clever, I don't understand it. Don't interrupt me. So the ball is magnificent. There are crowds of guests, all of them are young, handsome, and brave, all are frantically in love with the queen.'

'Are there no women among the guests?' queried Malevsky.

'No—or wait a minute—yes, there are some.'

'Are they all ugly?'

'No, charming. But the men are all in love with the queen. She is tall and graceful; she has a little gold diadem on her black hair.'

I looked at Zinaïda, and at that instant she

seemed to me so much above all of us, there was such bright intelligence, and such power about her unruffled brows, that I thought: 'You are that queen!'

'They all throng about her,' Zinaïda went on, 'and all lavish the most flattering speeches upon her.'

'And she likes flattery?' Lushin queried.

'What an intolerable person! he keeps interrupting . . . who doesn't like flattery?'

'One more last question,' observed Malevsky, has the queen a husband?'

'I hadn't thought about that. No, why should she have a husband?'

'To be sure,' assented Malevsky, 'why should she have a husband?'

'*Silence!*' cried Meidanov in French,-which he spoke very badly.

'*Merci!*' Zinaïda said to him. 'And so the queen hears their speeches, and hears the music, but does not look at one of the guests. Six windows are open from top to bottom, from floor to ceiling, and beyond them is a dark sky with big stars, a dark garden with big trees. The queen gazes out into the garden. Out there among the trees is a fountain; it is white in the darkness, and rises up tall, tall as an apparition. The queen hears, through the talk and the music, the soft splash of its waters.

FIRST LOVE

She gazes and thinks: you are all, gentlemea noble, clever, and rich, you crowd round me, you treasure every word I utter, you are all ready to die at my feet, I hold you in my power . . . but out there, by the fountain, by that splashing water, stands and waits he whom I love, who holds me in his power. He has neither rich raiment nor precious stones, no one knows him, but he awaits me, and is certain I shall come—and I shall come—and there is no power that could stop me when I want to go out to him, and to stay with him, and be lost with him out there in the darkness of the garden, under the whispering of the trees, and the splash of the fountain . . .' Zinaïda ceased.

'Is that a made-up story?' Malevsky inquired slyly. Zinaïda did not even look at him.

'And what should we have done, gentlemen?' Lushin began suddenly, 'if we had been among the guests, and had known of the lucky fellow at the fountain?'

'Stop a minute, stop a minute,' interposed Zuiaïda, 'I will tell you myself what each of you would have done. You, Byelovzorov, would have challenged him to a duel; you, Meidanov, would have written an epigram on him. . . . No, though, you can't write epigrams, you would have made up a long poem on him in the style of Barbier, and would have inserted your production in the *Telegraph*. You, Nirmatsky, would have borrowed . . . no, you would have lent him money at high interest; you, doctor . . .' she stopped. 'There, I really don't know what you would have done. . . .'

'In the capacity of court physician,' answered Lushin, 'I would have advised the queen not to give balls when she was not in the humour for entertaining her guests. . . .'

'Perhaps you would have been right And you, Count? . . .'

'And I?' repeated Malevsky with his evil smile. . . .

'You would offer him a poisoned sweetmeat.'

Malevsky's face changed slightly, and assumed for an instant a Jewish expression, but he laughed directly.

'And as for you, Voldemar, . . .' Zinaïda went on, 'but that's enough, though; let us play another game.'

'M'sieu Voldemar, as the queen's page, would have held up her train when she ran into the garden,' Malevsky remarked malignantly.

I was crimson with anger, but Zinaïda hurriedly laid a hand on my shoulder, and getting up, said in a rather shaky voice: 'I have never given your excellency the right to be rude, and therefore I will ask you to leave us.' She pointed to the door.

'Upon my word, princess,' muttered Malevsky, and he turned quite pale.

'The princess is right,' cried Byelovzorov, and he too rose.

'Good God, I'd not the least idea,' Malevsky went on, 'in my words there was nothing, I think, that could . . . I had no notion of offending you. . . . Forgive me.'

Zinaïda looked him up and down coldly, and coldly smiled. 'Stay, then, certainly,' she pronounced with a careless gesture of her arm. 'M'sieu Voldemar and I were needlessly incensed. It is your pleasure to sting . . . may it do you good.'

'Forgive me,' Malevsky repeated once more; while I, my thoughts dwelling on Zinaïda's gesture, said to myself again that no real queen could with greater dignity have shown a presumptuous subject to the door.

The game of forfeits went on for a short time after this little scene; every one felt rather ill at ease, not so much on account of this scene, as from another, not quite definite, but oppressive feeling. No one spoke of it, but every one was conscious of it in himself and in his neighbour. Meidanov read us his verses; and Malevsky praised them with exaggerated warmth. 'He wants to show how good he is now,' Lushin whispered to me. We soon broke up. A mood of reverie seemed to have come upon Zinaïda; the old princess sent word that she had a headache; Nirmatsky began to complain of his rheumatism. . . .

I could not for a long while get to sleep. I had been impressed by Zinaïda's story. 'Can there have been a hint in it?' I asked myself: 'and at whom and at what was she hinting? And if there really is anything to hint at . . . how is one to make up one's mind? No, no, it can't be,' I whispered, turning over from one hot cheek on to the other. . . . But I remembered the expression of Zinaïda's face during her story. . . . I remembered the exclamation that had broken from Lus hin in the Neskutchny gardens, the sudden change in her behaviour to me, and I was lost in conjectures. 'Who is he?' These three words seemed to stand before my eyes traced upon the darkness; a lowering malignant cloud seemed hanging over me, and I felt its oppressiveness, and waited for it to break. I had grown used to many things of late; I had learned much from what I had seen at the Zasyekins; their disorderly ways, tallow candle-ends, broken knives and forks, grumpy Vonifaty, arid shabby maid-servants, the manners of the old princess—all their strange mode of life no longer struck me. . . . But what I was dimly discerning now in

FIRST LOVE

Zinaïda, I could never get used to. . . . 'An adventuress!' my mother had said of her one day. An adventuress—she, my idol, my divinity? This word stabbed me, I tried to get away from it into my pillow, I was indignant—and at the same time what would I not have agreed to, what would I not have given only to be that lucky fellow at the fountain! . . . My blood was on fire and boiling within me. 'The garden . . . the fountain,' I mused. . . . 'I will go into the garden.' I dressed quickly and slipped out of the house. The night was dark, the trees scarcely whispered, a soft chill air breathed down from the sky, a smell of fennel trailed across from the kitchen garden. I went through all the walks; the light sound of my own footsteps at once confused and emboldened me; I stood still, waited and heard my heart beating fast and loudly. At last I went up to the fence and leaned against the thin bar. Suddenly, or was it my fancy, a woman's figure flashed by, a few paces from me . . . I strained my eyes eagerly into the darkness, I held my breath. What was that? Did I hear steps, or was it my heart beating again? 'Who is here?' I faltered, hardly audibly. What was that again, a smothered laugh . . . or a rustling in the leaves . . . or a sigh just at my ear? I felt afraid . . . 'Who is here?' I repeated still more softly.

The air blew in a gust for an instant; a streak of fire flashed across the sky; it was a star falling. 'Zinaïda?' I wanted to call, but the word died away on my lips. And all at once everything became profoundly still around, as is often the case in the middle of the night. . . . Even the grasshoppers ceased their churr in the trees—only a window rattled somewhere. I stood and stood, and then went back to my room, to my chilled bed. I felt a strange sensation; as though I had gone to a tryst, and had been left lonely, and had passed close by another's happiness.

XVII

THE following day I only had a passing glimpse of Zinaïda: she was driving somewhere with the old princess in a cab. But I saw Lushin, who, however, barely vouchsafed me a greeting, and Malevsky. The young count grinned, and began affably talking to me. Of all those who visited at the lodge, he alone had succeeded in forcing his way into our house, and had favourably impressed my mother. My father did not take to him, and treated him with a civility almost insulting.

'Ah, *monsieur le page*,' began Malevsky, 'delighted to meet you. What is your lovely queen doing?'

His fresh handsome face was so detestable to me at that moment, and he looked at me with such contemptuous amusement that I did not answer him at all.

'Are you still angry?' he went on. 'You've no reason to be. It wasn't I who called you a page, you know, and pages attend queens especially. But allow me to remark that you perform your duties very badly.'

'How so?'

'Pages ought to be inseparable from their mistresses; pages ought to know everything they do, they ought, indeed, to watch over them,' he added, lowering his voice, 'day and night.'

'What do you mean?'

'What do I mean? I express myself pretty clearly, I fancy. Day and night. By day it's not so much matter; it's light, and people are about in the daytime; but by night, then look out for misfortune. I advise you not to sleep at nights and to watch, watch with all your energies. You remember, in the garden, by night, at the fountain, that's where there's need to look out You will thank me.'

Malevsky laughed and turned his back on me. He, most likely, attached no great importance to what he had said to me, he had a reputation for mystifying, and was noted for his power of taking people in at masquerades, which was greatly augmented by the almost unconscious falsity in which his whole nature was steeped. . . . He only wanted to tease me; but every word he uttered was a poison that ran through my veins. The blood rushed to my head. 'Ah! so that's it!' I said to myself; 'good! So there was reason for me to feel drawn into the garden! That shan't be so!' I cried aloud, and struck myself on the chest with my fist, though precisely what should not be so I could not have said. 'Whether Malevsky himself goes into the garden,' I thought (he was bragging, perhaps; he has insolence enough for that), 'or some one else (the fence of our garden was very low, and there was no difficulty in getting over it), anyway, if any one falls into my hands, it will be the worse for him! I don't advise any one to meet me! I will prove to all the world and to her, the traitress (I actually used the word 'traitress') that I can be revenged!'

I returned to my own room, took out of the writing-table an English knife I had recently bought, felt its sharp edge, and knitting my brows with an air of cold and concentrated

FIRST LOVE

determination, thrust it into my pocket, as though doing such deeds was nothing out of the way for me, and not the first time. My heart heaved angrily, and felt heavy as a stone. All day long I kept a scowling brow and lips tightly compressed, and was continually walking up and down, clutching, with my hand in my pocket, the knife, which was warm from my grasp, while I prepared myself beforehand for something terrible. These new unknown sensations so occupied and even delighted me, that I hardly thought of Zinaïda herself. I was continually haunted by Aleko, the young gipsy—'Where art thou going, young handsome man? Lie there,' and then, 'thou art all besprent with blood. . . . Oh, what hast thou done? . . . Naught!' With what a cruel smile I repeated that 'Naught!' My father was not at home; but my mother, who had for some time past been in an almost continual state of dumb exasperation, noticed my gloomy and heroic aspect, and said to me at supper, 'Why are you sulking like a mouse in a meal-tub?' I merely smiled condescendingly in reply, and thought, 'If only they knew!' It struck eleven; I went to my room, but did not undress; I waited for midnight; at last it struck. 'The time has come!' I muttered between my teeth; and buttoning myself up to the throat, and even pulling my sleeves up, I went into the garden.

I had already fixed on the spot from which to keep watch. At the end of the garden, at the point where the fence, separating our domain from the Zasyekins,' joined the common wall, grew a pine-tree, standing alone. Standing under its low thick branches, I could see well, as far as the darkness of the night permitted, what took place around. Close by, ran a winding path which had always seemed mysterious to me; it coiled like a snake under the fence, which at that point bore traces of having been climbed over, and led to a round arbour formed of thick acacias. I made my way to the pine-tree, leaned my Back against its trunk, and began my watch.

The night was as still as the night before, but there were fewer clouds in the sky, and the outlines of bushes, even of tail flowers, could be more distinctly seen. The first moments of expectation were oppressive, almost terrible. I had made up my mind to everything. I only debated how to act; whether to thunder, 'Where goest thou? Stand! show thyself—or death!' or simply to strike. . . . Every sound, every whisper and rustle, seemed to me portentous and extraordinary. . . . I prepared myself. . . . I bent forward. . . . But half-an-

FIRST LOVE

hour passed, an hour passed; my blood had grown quieter, colder; the consciousness that I was doing all this for nothing, that I was even a little absurd, that Malevsky had been making fun of me, began to steal over me. I left my ambush, and walked all about the garden. As if to taunt me, there was not the smallest sound to be heard anywhere; everything was at rest. Even our dog was asleep, curled up into a ball at the gate. I climbed up into the ruins of the greenhouse, saw the open country far away before me, recalled my meeting with Zinaïda, and fell to dreaming. . . .

I started. . . . I fancied I heard the creak of a door opening, then the faint crack of a broken twig. In two bounds I got down from the ruin, and stood still, all aghast. Rapid, light, but cautious footsteps sounded distinctly in the garden. They were approaching me. 'Here he is . . . here he is, at last!' flashed through my heart. With spasmodic haste, I pulled the knife out of my pocket; with spasmodic haste, I opened it. Flashes of red were whirling before my eyes; my hair stood up on my head in my fear and fury. . . . The steps were coming straight towards me; I bent—I craned forward to meet him. . . . A man came into view. . . . My God! it was my father!

I recognised him at once, though he was all

muffled up in a dark cloak, and his hat was pulled down over his face. On tip-toe he walked by. He did not notice me, though nothing concealed me; but I was so huddled up and shrunk together that I fancy I was almost on the level of the ground. The jealous Othello, ready for murder, was suddenly transformed into a school-boy. . . . I was so taken aback by my father's unexpected appearance that for the first moment I did not notice where he had come from or in what direction he, disappeared. I only drew myself up, and thought, 'Why is it my father is walking about in the garden at night?' when everything was still again. In my horror I had dropped my knife in the grass, but I did not even attempt to look for it; I was very much ashamed of myself. I was completely sobered at once. On my way to the house, however, I went up to my seat under the elder-tree, and looked up at Zinaïda's window. The small slightly-convex panes of the window shone dimly blue in the faint light thrown on them by the night sky. All at once—their colour began to change. . . . Behind them—I saw this, saw it distinctly—softly and cautiously a white blind was let down, let down right to the window-frame, and so stayed.

'What is that for?' I said aloud almost

involuntarily when I found myself once more in my room. 'A dream, a chance, or . . .' The suppositions which suddenly rushed into my head were so new and strange that I did not dare to entertain them.

XVIII

I GOT up in the morning with a headache. My emotion of the previous day had vanished. It was replaced by a dreary sense of blankness and a sort of sadness I had not known till then, as though something had died in me.

'Why is it you're looking like a rabbit with half its brain removed?' said Lushin on meeting me. At lunch I stole a look first at my father, then at my mother: he was composed, as usual; she was, as usual, secretly irritated. I waited to see whether my father would make some friendly remarks to me, as he sometimes did. . . . But he did not even bestow his everyday cold greeting upon me. 'Shall I tell Zinaïda all?' I wondered. . . . 'It's all the same, anyway; all is at an end between us.' I went to see her, but told her nothing, and, indeed, I could not even have managed to get a talk with her if I had wanted to. The old princess's son, a cadet of twelve years old, had come from Petersburg for his holidays; Zinaïda at once handed her brother over to me. 'Here,' she said, 'my dear Volodya,'—it was the first time she had used this pet-name to me—'is a companion for you. His name is Volodya, too. Please, like him; he is still shy, but he has a good heart. Show him Neskutchny gardens, go walks with him, take him under your protection. You'll do that, won't you? you're so good, too!' She laid both her hands affectionately on my shoulders, and I was utterly bewildered. The presence of this boy transformed me, too, into a boy. I looked in silence at the cadet, who stared as silently at me. Zinaïda laughed, and pushed us towards each other. 'Embrace each other, children!' We embraced each other. 'Would you like me to show you the garden?' I inquired of the cadet. 'If you please,' he replied, in the regular cadet's hoarse voice, Zinaïda laughed again. . . . I had time to notice that she had never had such an exquisite colour in her face before. I set off with the cadet There was an old-fashioned swing in our garden. I sat him down on the narrow plank seat, and began swinging him. He sat rigid in his new little uniform of stout cloth, with its broad gold braiding, and kept tight hold of the cords. 'You'd better unbutton your collar,' I said to him. 'It's all right; we're used to it,' he said, and cleared his throat He was like his sister. The eyes especially recalled her. I liked being nice to him; and at the same time an aching sadness was gnawing at my heart. 'Now I certainly am a child,' I thought; 'but yesterday. . . .' I remembered where I had dropped my knife the night before, and looked for it. The cadet asked me for it, picked a thick stalk of wild parsley, cut a pipe out of it, and began whistling. Othello whistled too.

But in the evening how he wept, this Othello, in Zinaïda's arms, when, seeking him out in a corner of the garden, she asked him why he was so depressed. My tears flowed with such violence that she was frightened. 'What is wrong with you? What is it, Volodya?' she repeated; and seeing I made no answer, and did not cease weeping, she was about to kiss my wet cheek. But I turned away from her, and whispered through my sobs, 'I know all. Why did you play with me? . . . What need had you of my love?'

'I am to blame, Volodya . . .' said Zinaïda. 'I am very much to blame . . .' she added, wringing her hands. 'How much there is bad and black and sinful in me! . . . But I am not playing with you now. I love you; you don't even suspect why and how. . . . But what is it you know?'

What could I say to her? She stood facing me, and looked at me; and I belonged to her altogether from head to foot directly she looked at me. . . . A quarter of an hour later I was running races with the cadet and Zinaïda. I was not crying, I was laughing, though my swollen eyelids dropped a tear or two as I laughed. I had Zinaïda's ribbon round my neck for a cravat, and I shouted with delight whenever I succeeded in catching her round the waist. She did just as she liked with me.

XIX

I SHOULD be in a great difficulty, if I were forced to describe exactly what passed within me in the course of the week after my unsuccessful midnight expedition. It was a strange feverish time, a sort of chaos, in which the most violently opposed feelings, thoughts, suspicions, hopes, joys, and sufferings, whirled together in a kind of hurricane. I was afraid to look into myself, if a boy of sixteen ever can look into himself; I was afraid to take stock of anything; I simply hastened to live through every day till evening; and at night I slept . . . the light-heartedness of childhood came to my aid. I did not want to know whether I was

FIRST LOVE

loved, and I did not want to acknowledge to myself that I was not loved; my father I avoided—but Zinaïda I could not avoid. . . . I burnt as in a fire in her presence . . . but what did I care to know what the fire was in which I burned and melted—it was enough that it. was sweet to burn and melt. I gave myself up to all my passing sensations, and cheated myself, turning away from memories, and shutting my eyes to what I foreboded before me. . . . This weakness would not most likely have lasted long in any case . . . a thunderbolt cut it all short in a moment, and flung me into a new track altogether.

Coming in one day to dinner from a rather long walk, I learnt with amazement that I was to dine alone, that my father had gone away and my mother was unwell, did not want any dinner, and had shut herself up in her bedroom. From the faces of the footmen, I surmised that something extraordinary had taken place. . . . I did not dare to cross-examine them, but I had a friend in the young waiter Philip, who was passionately fond of poetry, and a performer on the guitar. I addressed myself to him. From him I learned that a terrible scene had taken place between my father and mother (and every word had been overheard in the maids' room; much of it had been in French, but Masha the lady's-maid had lived five years' with a dressmaker from Paris, and she understood it all); that my mother had reproached my father with infidelity, with an intimacy with the young lady next door, that my father at first had defended himself, but afterwards had lost his temper, and he too had said something cruel, 'reflecting on her age,' which had made my mother cry; that my mother too had alluded to some loan-which it seemed had been made to the old princess, and had spoken very ill of her and of the young lady too, and that then my father had threatened her. 'And all the mischief,' continued Philip, 'came from an anonymous letter; and who wrote it, no one knows, or else there'd have been no reason whatever for the matter to have come out at all.'

'But was there really any ground,' I brought out with difficulty, while my hands and feet went cold, and a sort of shudder ran through my inmost being.

Philip winked meaningly. 'There was. There's no hiding those things; for all that your father was careful this time—but there, you see, he'd, for instance, to hire a carriage or something . . . no getting on without servants, either.'

I dismissed Philip, and fell on to my bed. I

FIRST LOVE

did not sob, I did not give myself up to despair; I did not ask myself when and how this had happened; I did not wonder how it was I had not guessed it before, long ago; I did not even upbraid my father. . . . What I had learnt was more than I could take in; this sudden revelation stunned me. . . . All was at an end. All the fair blossoms of my heart were roughly plucked at once, and lay about me, flung on the ground, and trampled underfoot

XX

My mother next day announced her intention of returning to the town. In the morning my father had gone into her bedroom, and stayed there a long while alone with her. No one had overheard what he said to her; but my mother wept no more; she regained her composure, and asked for food, but did not make her appearance nor change her plans. I remember I wandered about the whole day, but did not go into the garden, and never once glanced at the lodge, and in the evening I was the spectator of an amazing occurrence: my father conducted Count Malevsky by the arm through the dining-room into the hall, and, in the presence of a footman, said icily to him: 'A few days ago your excellency was shown the door in our house; and now I am not going to enter into any kind of explanation with you, but I have the honour to announce to you that if you ever visit me again, I shall throw you out of window. I don't like your handwriting.' The count bowed, bit his lips, shrank away, and vanished.

Preparations were beginning for our removal to town, to Arbaty Street, where we had a house. My father himself probably no longer cared to remain at the country house; but clearly he had succeeded in persuading my mother not to make a public scandal. Everything was done quietly, without hurry; my mother even sent her compliments to the old princess, and expressed her regret that she was prevented by indisposition from seeing her again before her departure. I wandered about like one possessed, and only longed for one thing, for it all to be over as soon as possible. One thought I could not get out of my head: how could she, a young girl, and a princess too, after all, bring herself to such a step, knowing that my father was not a free man, and having an opportunity of marrying, for instance, Byelovzorov? What did she hope for? How was it she was not afraid of ruining her whole future? Yes, I thought, this is love, this is passion, this is devotion . . . and . . . Lushin's words came back

FIRST LOVE

to me: to sacrifice oneself for some people is sweet. I chanced somehow to catch sight of something white in one of the windows of the lodge. . . . 'Can it be Zinaïda's face?' I thought . . . yes, it really was her face. I could not restrain myself. I could not part from her without saying a last good-bye to her. I seized a favourable instant, and went into the lodge.

In the drawing-room the old princess met me with her usual slovenly and careless greetings.

'How's this, my good man, your folks are off in such a hurry?' she observed, thrusting snuff into her nose. I looked at her, and a load was taken off my heart. The word 'loan,' dropped by Philip, had been torturing me. She had no suspicion . . . at least I thought so then. Zinaïda came in from the next room, pale, and dressed in black, with her hair hanging loose; she took me by the hand without a word, and drew me away with her.

'I heard your voice,' she began, 'and came out at once. Is it so easy for you to leave us, bad boy?'

'I have come to say good-bye to you, princess,' I answered, 'probably for ever. You have heard, perhaps, we are going away.'

Zinaïda looked intently at me.

'Yes, I have heard. Thanks for coming. I

was beginning to think I should not see you again. Don't remember evil against me. I have sometimes tormented you, but all the same I am not what you imagine me.'

She turned away, and leaned against the window.

'Really, I am not like that I know you have a bad opinion of me.'

'I?'

'Yes, you . . . you.'

'I ?' I repeated mournfully, and my heart throbbed as of old under the influence of her overpowering, indescribable fascination. 'I? Believe me, Zinaïda Alexandrovna, whatever you did, however you tormented me, I should love and adore you to the end of my days.'

She turned with a rapid motion to me, and flinging wide her arms, embraced my head, and gave me a warm and passionate kiss. God knows whom that long farewell kiss was seeking, but I eagerly tasted its sweetness. I knew that it would never be repeated. 'Good-bye, good-bye,' I kept saying . . .

She tore herself away, and went out And I went away. I cannot describe the emotion with which I went away. I should not wish it ever to come again; but I should think myself unfortunate had I never experienced such an emotion

FIRST LOVE

We went back to town. I did not quickly shake off the past; I did not quickly get to work. My wound slowly began to heal; but I had no ill-feeling against my father. On the contrary he had, as it were, gained in my eyes . . . let psychologists explain the contradiction as best they can. One day I was walking along a boulevard, and to my indescribable delight, I came across Lushin. I liked him for his straightforward and unaffected character, and besides he was dear to me for the sake of the memories he aroused in me. I rushed up to him. 'Aha!' he said, knitting his brows, 'so it's you, young man. Let me have a look at you. You're still as yellow as ever, but yet there's not the same nonsense in your eyes. You look like a man, not a lap-dog. That's good. Well, what are you doing? working?'

I gave a sigh. I did not like to tell a lie, while I was ashamed to tell the truth.

'Well, never mind,' Lushin went on, 'don't be shy. The great thing is to lead a normal life, and not be the slave of your passions. What do you get if not? Wherever you are carried by the tide—it's all a bad look-out; a man must stand on his own feet, if he can get nothing but a rock to stand on. Here, I've got a cough . . . and Byelovzorov—have you heard anything of him?'

'No. What is it?'

'He's lost, and no news of him; they say he's gone away to the Caucasus. A lesson to you, young man. And it's all from not knowing how to part in time, to break out of the net. You seem to have got off very well. Mind you don't fall into the same snare again. Good-bye.'

'I shan't,' I thought. . . . 'I shan't see her again,' But I was destined to see Zinaïda once more.

XXI

My father used every day to ride out on horseback. He had a splendid English mare, a chestnut piebald, with a long slender neck and long legs, an inexhaustible and vicious beast. Her name was Electric. No one could ride her except my father. One day he came up to me in a good humour, a frame of mind in which I had not seen him for a long while; he was getting ready for his ride, and had already put on his spurs. I began entreating him to take me with him.

'We'd much better have a game of leap-frog,' my father replied. 'You'll never keep up with me on your cob.'

FIRST LOVE

'Yes, I will; I'll put on spurs too.'

'All right, come along then.'

We set off. I had a shaggy black horse, strong, and fairly spirited. It is true it had to gallop its utmost, when Electric went at full trot, still I was not left behind. I have never seen any one ride like my father; he had such a fine carelessly easy seat, that it seemed that the horse under him was conscious of it, and proud of its rider. We rode through all the boulevards, reached the 'Maidens' Field,' jumped several fences (at first I had been afraid to take a leap, but my father had a contempt for cowards, and I soon ceased to feel fear), twice crossed the river Moskva, and I was under the impression that we were on our way home, especially as my father of his own accord observed that my horse was tired, when suddenly he turned off away from me at the Crimean ford, and galloped along the river-bank. I rode after him. When he had reached a high stack of old timber, he slid quickly off Electric, told me to dismount, and giving me his horse's bridle, told me to wait for him there at the timber-stack, and, turning off into a small street, disappeared. I began walking up and down the river-bank, leading the horses, and scolding Electric, who kept pulling, shaking her head, snorting and neighing as she went; and when

I stood still, never failed to paw the ground, and whining, bite my cob on the neck; in fact she conducted herself altogether like a spoilt thorough-bred. My father did not come back. A disagreeable damp mist rose from the river; a fine rain began softly blowing up, and spotting with tiny dark flecks the stupid grey timber-stack, which I kept passing and repassing, and was deadly sick of by now. I was terribly bored, and still my father did not come. A sort of sentry-man, a Fin, grey all over like the timber, and with a huge old-fashioned shako, like a pot, on his head, and with a halberd (and how ever came a sentry, if you think of it, on the banks of the Moskva!) drew near, and turning his wrinkled face, like an old woman's, towards me, he observed, 'What are you doing here with the horses, young master? Let me hold them.'

I made him no reply. He asked me for tobacco. To get rid of him (I was in a fret of impatience, too), I took a few steps in the direction in which my father had disappeared, then walked along the little street to the end, turned the corner, and stood still. In the street, forty paces from me, at the open window of a little wooden house, stood my father, his back turned to me; he was leaning forward over the window-sill, and in the house, half hidden by a curtain, sat a woman in a dark dress talking to my father; this woman was Zinaïda.

I was petrified. This, I confess, I had never expected. My first impulse was to run away. 'My father will look round,' I thought, 'and I am lost . . .' but a strange feeling—a feeling stronger than curiosity, stronger than jealousy, stronger even than fear—held me there. I began to watch; I strained my ears to listen. It seemed as though my father were insisting on something. Zinaïda would not consent. I seem to see her face now—mournful, serious, lovely, and with an inexpressible impress of devotion, grief, love, and a sort of despair—I can find no other word for it. She uttered monosyllables, not raising her eyes, simply smiling—submissively, but without yielding. By that smile alone, I should have known my Zinaïda of old days. My father shrugged his shoulders, and straightened his hat on his head, which was always a sign of impatience with him. . . . Then I caught the words: '*Vous devez vous séparer de cette* . . .' Zinaïda sat up, and stretched out her arm. . . . Suddenly, before my very eyes, the impossible happened. My father suddenly lifted the whip, with which he had been switching the dust off his coat, and I heard a sharp blow on that arm, bare to the elbow. I could scarcely restrain myself from crying out; while Zinaïda shuddered, looked without a word at my father, and slowly raising her arm to her lips, kissed the streak of red upon it. My father flung away the whip, and running quickly up the steps, dashed into the house. . . . Zinaïda turned round, and with outstretched arms and downcast head, she too moved away from the window.

My heart sinking with panic, with a sort of awe-struck horror, I rushed back, and running down the lane, almost letting go my hold of Electric, went back to the bank of the river. I could not think clearly of anything. I knew that my cold and reserved father was sometimes seized by fits of fury; and all the same, I could never comprehend what I had just seen. . . . But I felt at the time that, however long I lived, I could never forget the gesture, the glance, the smile, of Zinaïda; that her image, this image so suddenly presented to me, was imprinted for ever on my memory. I stared vacantly at the river, and never noticed that my tears were streaming. 'She is beaten,' I was thinking, . . . 'beaten . . . beaten. . . .'

'Hullo! what are you doing? Give me the mare!' I heard my father's voice saying behind me.

Mechanically I gave him the bridle. He leaped on to Electric . . . the mare, chill with

FIRST LOVE

standing, reared on her haunches, and leaped ten feet away . . . but my father soon subdued her; he drove the spurs into her sides, and gave her a blow on the neck with his fist. . . . 'Ah, I've no whip,' he muttered.

I remembered the swish and fall of the whip, heard so short a time before, and shuddered.

'Where did you put it?' I asked my father, after a brief pause.

My father made no answer, and galloped on ahead. I overtook him. I felt that I must see his face.

'Were you bored waiting for me?' he muttered through his teeth.

'A little. Where did you drop your whip?' I asked again.

My father glanced quickly at me. 'I didn't drop it,' he replied; 'I threw it away.' He sank into thought, and dropped his head . . . and then, for the first, and almost for the last time, I saw how much tenderness and pity his stern features were capable of expressing.

He galloped on again, and this time I could not overtake him; I got home a quarter-of-an-hour after him.

'That's love,' I said to myself again, as I sat at night before my writing-table, on which books and papers had begun to make their appearance; 'that's passion! . . . To think of not revolting, of bearing a blow from any one whatever . . . even the dearest hand! But it seems one can, if one loves. . . . While I . . . I imagined . . .'

I had grown much older during the last month; and my love, with all its transports and sufferings, struck me myself as something small and childish and pitiful beside this other unimagined something, which I could hardly fully grasp, and which frightened me like an unknown, beautiful, but menacing face, which one strives in vain to make out clearly in the half-darkness. . . .

A strange and fearful dream came to me that same night. I dreamed I went into a low dark room. . . . My father was standing with a whip in his hand, stamping with anger; in the corner crouched Zinaïda, and not on her arm, but on her forehead, was a stripe of red . . . while behind them both towered Byelovzorov, covered with blood; he opened his white lips, and wrathfully threatened my father.

Two months later, I entered the university; and within six months my father died of a stroke in Petersburg, where he had just moved with my mother and me. A few days before his death he received a letter from Moscow which threw him into a violent agitation. . . . He went to my mother to beg some favour of her: and, I was told, he positively shed tears—he, my father! On the very morning of the day when he was stricken down, he had begun a letter to me in French. 'My son,' he wrote to me, 'fear the love of woman; fear that bliss, that poison. . . .' After his death, my mother sent a considerable sum of money to Moscow.

XXII

Four years passed. I had just left the university, and did not know exactly what to do with myself, at what door to knock; I was hanging about for a time with nothing to do. One fine evening I met Meidanov at the theatre. He had got married, and had entered the civil service; but I found no change in him. He fell into ecstasies in just the same superfluous way, and just as suddenly grew depressed again.

'You know,' he told me among other things, 'Madame Dolsky's here.'

'What Madame Dolsky?'

'Can you have forgotten her?—the young Princess Zasyekin whom we were all in love with, and you too. Do you remember at the country-house near Neskutchny gardens?'

'She married a Dolsky?'

'Yes.'

'And is she here, in the theatre?'

'No: but she's in Petersburg. She came here a few days ago. She's going abroad.'

'What sort of fellow is her husband?' I asked.

'A splendid fellow, with property. He's a colleague of mine in Moscow. You can well understand—after the scandal . . . you must know all about it . . .' (Meidanov smiled significantly) 'it was no easy task for her to make a good marriage; there were consequences . . . but with her cleverness, everything is possible. Go and see her; she'll be delighted to see you. She's prettier than ever.'

Meidanov gave me Zinaïda's address. She was staying at the Hotel Demut. Old memories were astir within me. . . . I determined next day to go to see my former 'flame.' But some business happened to turn up; a week passed, and then another, and when at last I went to the Hotel Demut and asked for Madame Dolsky, I learnt that four days before, she had died, almost suddenly, in childbirth.

I felt a sort of stab at my heart. The thought that I might have seen her, and had not seen her, and should never see her—that bitter thought stung me with all the force of overwhelming reproach. 'She is dead! I repeated,

FIRST LOVE

staring stupidly at the hall-porter. I slowly made my way back to the street, and walked on without knowing myself where I was going. All the past swam up and rose at once before me. So this was the solution, this was the goal to which that young, ardent, brilliant life had striven, all haste and agitation! I mused on this; I fancied those dear features, those eyes, those curls—in the narrow box, in the damp underground darkness—lying here, not far from me—while I was still alive, and, maybe, a few paces from my father. . . . I thought all this; I strained my imagination, and yet all the while the lines:

> 'From lips indifferent of her death I heard,
> Indifferently I listened to it, too,'

were echoing in my heart. O youth, youth! little dost thou care for anything; thou art master, as it were, of all the treasures of the universe—even sorrow gives thee pleasure, even grief thou canst turn to thy profit; thou art self-confident and insolent; thou sayest, 'I alone am living—look you!'—but thy days fly by all the while, and vanish without trace or reckoning; and everything in thee vanishes, like wax in the sun, like snow. . . . And, perhaps, the whole secret of thy charm lies, not in being able to do anything, but in being able to think thou wilt do anything; lies just in thy throwing to the winds, forces which thou couldst not make other use of; in each of us gravely regarding himself as a prodigal, gravely supposing that he is justified in saying, 'Oh, what might I not have done if I had not wasted my time!'

I, now . . . what did I hope for, what did I expect, what rich future did I foresee, when the phantom of my first love, rising up for an instant, barely called forth one sigh, one mournful sentiment?

And what has come to pass of all I hoped for? And now, when the shades of evening begin to steal over my life, what have I left fresher, more precious, than the memories of the storm—so soon over—of early morning, of spring?

But I do myself injustice. Even then, in those light-hearted young days, I was not deaf to the voice of sorrow, when it called upon me, to the solemn strains floating to me from beyond the tomb. I remember, a few days after I heard of Zinaïda's death, I was present, through a peculiar, irresistible impulse, at the death of a poor old woman who lived in the same house as we. Covered with rags, lying on hard boards, with a sack under her head, she died hardly and painfully. Her whole life had been passed in the bitter struggle with daily want;

she had known no joy, had not tasted the honey of happiness. One would have thought, surely she would rejoice at death, at her deliverance, her rest. But yet, as long as her decrepit body held out, as long as her breast still heaved in agony under the icy hand weighing upon it, until her last forces left her, the old woman crossed herself, and kept whispering, 'Lord, forgive my sins'; and only with the last spark of consciousness, vanished from her eyes the look of fear, of horror of the end. And I remember that then, by the death-bed of that poor old woman, I felt aghast for Zinaïda, and longed to pray for her, for my father—and for myself.

MUMU

In one of the outlying streets of Moscow, in a grey house with white columns and a balcony, warped all askew, there was once living a lady, a widow, surrounded by a numerous household of serfs. Her sons were in the government service at Petersburg; her daughters were married; she went out very little, and in solitude lived through the last years of her miserly and dreary old age. Her day, a joyless and gloomy day, had long been over; but the evening of her life was blacker than night.

Of all her servants, the most remarkable personage was the porter, Gerasim, a man full twelve inches over the normal height, of heroic build, and deaf and dumb from his birth. The lady, his owner, had brought him up from the village where he lived alone in a little hut, apart from his brothers, and was reckoned about the most punctual of her peasants in the payment of the seignorial dues. Endowed with extraordinary strength, he did the work of four men; work flew apace under his hands, and it was a pleasant sight to see him when he was ploughing, while, with his huge palms pressing hard upon the plough, he seemed alone, unaided by his poor horse, to cleave the yielding bosom of the earth, or when, about St. Peter's Day, he plied his scythe with a furious energy that might have mown a young birch copse up by the roots, or swiftly and untiringly wielded a flail over two yards long; while the hard oblong muscles of his shoulders rose and fell like a lever. His perpetual silence lent a solemn dignity to his unwearying labour. He was a splendid peasant, and, except for his affliction, any girl would have been glad to marry him. . . . But now they had taken Gerasim to Moscow, bought him boots, had him made a full-skirted coat for summer, a sheepskin for winter, put into his hand a broom and a spade, and appointed him porter.

At first he intensely disliked his new mode of life. From his childhood he had been used to field labour, to village life. Shut off by his affliction from the society of men, he had grown up, dumb and mighty, as a tree grows on a fruitful soil. When he was transported to the town, he could not understand what was being done with him; he was miserable and stupefied, with the stupefaction of some strong young bull, taken straight from the meadow, where the rich grass stood up to his belly, taken and put in the truck of a railway train, and there, while smoke and sparks and gusts of steam puff out upon the sturdy beast, he is whirled onwards, whirled along with loud roar and whistle, whither—God knows! What Gerasim had to do in his new duties seemed a mere trifle to him after his hard toil as a peasant; in half-an-hour, all his work was done, and he would once more stand stock-still in the middle of the courtyard, staring open-mouthed at all the passers-by, as though trying to wrest from them the explanation of his perplexing position; or he would suddenly go off into some corner, and flinging a long way off the broom or the spade, throw himself on his face on the ground, and lie for hours together without stirring, like a caged beast But man gets used to anything, and Gerasim got used at last to living in town. He had little work to do; his whole duty consisted in keeping the courtyard clean, bringing in a barrel of water twice a day, splitting and dragging in wood for the kitchen and the house, keeping out strangers, and watching at night. And it must be said he did his duty zealously. In his courtyard there was never a shaving lying about, never a speck of dust; if sometimes, in the muddy season, the wretched nag, put under his charge for fetching water, got stuck in the road, he would simply give it a shove with his shoulder, and set not only the cart but the horse itself moving. If he set to chopping wood, the axe fairly rang like glass, and chips and chunks flew in all directions. And as for strangers, after he had one night caught two thieves and knocked their heads together—knocked them so that there was not the slightest need to take them to the police-station afterwards—every one in the neighbourhood began to feel a great respect for him; even those who came in the day-time, by no means robbers, but simply unknown persons, at the sight of the terrible porter, waved and shouted to him as though he could hear their shouts. With all the rest of the servants, Gerasim was on terms, hardly friendly—they were afraid of him—but familiar; he regarded them as his fellows. They explained themselves to him by signs, and he understood them, and exactly carried out all orders, but knew his own rights too, and soon no one dared to take his seat at the table. Gerasim was altogether of a strict and serious temper, he liked order in everything; even the cocks did not dare to fight in his presence, or woe betide them! directly he caught sight of them, he would seize them by the legs, swing them ten times round in the air like a wheel, and throw them in different directions. There were geese, too, kept in the yard; but the goose, as is well known, is a dignified and reasonable bird; Gerasim felt a respect for them, looked after them, and fed them; he was himself not unlike a gander of the steppes. He was assigned a little garret over the kitchen; he arranged it himself to his own liking, made a bedstead in it of oak boards on four stumps of wood for legs—a truly Titanic bedstead; one might have put a ton or two on it—it would not have bent under the load; under the bed was a solid chest; in a corner stood a little table of the same strong kind, and near the table, a three-legged stool, so solid and squat that Gerasim himself would sometimes pick it up and drop it again with a smile of delight. The garret was locked up by means of a padlock that looked like a kalatch or basket-shaped loaf, only black; the key of this padlock Gerasim always carried about him in his girdle. He did not like people to come to his garret.

So passed a year, at the end of which a little incident befell Gerasim.

The old lady, in whose service he lived as porter, adhered in everything to the ancient ways, and kept a large number of servants. In her house were not only laundresses, sempstresses, carpenters, tailors and tailoresses, there was even a harness-maker—he was reckoned as a veterinary surgeon, too,—and a doctor for the servants; there was a household doctor for the mistress; there was, lastly, a shoemaker, by name Kapiton Klimov, a sad drunkard. Klimov regarded himself as an injured creature, whose merits were unappreciated, a cultivated man from Petersburg, who ought not to be living in Moscow without occupation—in the wilds, so to speak; and if he drank, as he himself expressed it emphatically, with a blow on his chest, it was sorrow drove him to it. So one day his mistress had a conversation about him with her head steward, Gavrila, a man whom, judging solely from his little yellow eyes and nose like a duck's beak, fate itself, it seemed, had marked out as a person in authority. The lady expressed her regret at the corruption of the morals of Kapiton, who had, only theevening before, been picked up somewhere in the street.

'Now, Gavrila,' she observed, all of a sudden, 'now, if we were to marry him, what do you think, perhaps he would be steadier?'

'Why not marry him, indeed,'m? He could be married,'m,' answered Gavrila, 'and it would be a very good thing, to be sure,'m.'

'Yes; only who is to marry him?'

'Ay,'m. But that's at your pleasure,'m.

MUMU

He may, any way, so to say, be wanted for something; he can't be turned adrift altogether.'

'I fancy he likes Tatiana.'

Gavrila was on the point of making some reply, but he shut his lips tightly.

'Yes! . . . let him marry Tatiana,' the lady decided, taking a pinch of snuff complacently, 'Do you hear?'

'Yes,'m,' Gavrila articulated, and he withdrew.

Returning to his own room (it was in a little lodge, and was almost filled up with metal-bound trunks), Gavrila first sent his wife away, and then sat down at the window and pondered. His mistress's unexpected arrangement had clearly put him in a difficulty. At last he got up and sent to call Kapiton. Kapiton made his appearance . . . But before reporting their conversation to the reader, we consider it not out of place to relate in few words who was this Tatiana, whom it was to be Kapiton's lot to marry, and why the great lady's order had disturbed the steward.

Tatiana, one of the laundresses referred to above (as a trained and skilful laundress she was in charge of the fine linen only), was a woman of twenty-eight, thin, fair-haired, with moles on her left cheek. Moles on the left cheek are regarded as of evil omen in Russia—

a token of unhappy life. . . . Tatiana could not boast of her good luck. From her earliest youth she had been badly treated; she had done the work of two, and had never known affection; she had been poorly clothed and had received the smallest wages. Relations she had practically none; an uncle she had once had, a butler, left behind in the country as useless, and other uncles of hers were peasants—that was all. At one time she had passed for a beauty, but her good looks were very soon over. In disposition, she was very meek, or, rather, scared; towards herself, she felt perfect indifference; of others, she stood in mortal dread; she thought of nothing but how to get her work done in good time, never talked to any one, and trembled at the very name of her mistress, though the latter scarcely knew her by sight. When Gerasim was brought from the country, she was ready to die with fear on seeing his huge figure, tried all she could to avoid meeting him, even dropped her eyelids when sometimes she chanced to run past him, hurrying from the house to the laundry. Gerasim at first paid no special attention to her, then he used to smile when she came his way, then he began even to stare admiringly at her, and at last he never took his eyes off her. She took his fancy, whether by the mild expression of her face or the timidity of her movements, who can tell? So one day she was stealing across the yard, with a starched dressing-jacket of her mistress's carefully poised on her outspread fingers . . . some one suddenly grasped her vigorously by the elbow; she turned round and fairly screamed; behind her stood Gerasim. With a foolish smile, making inarticulate caressing grunts, he held out to her a gingerbread cock with gold tinsel on his tail and wings. She was about to refuse it, but he thrust it forcibly into her hand, shook his head, walked away, and turning round, once more grunted something very affectionately to her. From that day forward he gave her no peace; wherever she went, he was on the spot at once, coming to meet her, smiling, grunting, waving his hands; all at once he would pull a ribbon out of the bosom of his smock and put it in her hand, or would sweep the dust out of her way. The poor girl simply did not know how to behave or what to do. Soon the whole household knew of the dumb porter's wiles; jeers, jokcs, sly hints were showered upon Tatiana. At Gerasim, however, it was not every one who would dare to scoff; he did not like jokes; indeed, in his presence, she, too, was left in peace. Whether she liked it or not, the girl found herself to be under his protection. Like all deaf-mutes, he was very suspicious, and very readily perceived when they were laughing at him or at her. One day, at dinner, the wardrobe-keeper, Tatiana's superior, fell to nagging, as it is called, at her, and brought the poor thing to such a state that she did not know where to look, and was almost crying with vexation. Gerasim got up all of a sudden, stretched out his gigantic hand, laid it on the wardrobe-maid's head, and looked into her face with such grim ferocity that her head positively flopped upon the table. Every one was still. Gerasim took up his spoon again and went on with his cabbage-soup. 'Look at him, the dumb devil, the wood-demon!' they all muttered in under-tones, while the ward robe-maid got up and went out into the maids' room. Another time, noticeing that Kapiton—the same Kapiton who was the subject of the conversation reported above—was gossiping somewhat too attentively with Tatiana, Gerasim beckoned him to him, led him into the cartshed, and taking up a shaft that was standing in a corner by one end, lightly, but most significantly, menaced him with it Since then no one addressed a word to Tatiana. And all this cost him nothing. It is true the wardrobe-maid, as soon as she reached the maids' room, promptly fell into a fainting-fit, and behaved altogether so skilfully

MUMU

that Gerasim's rough action reached his mistress's knowledge the same day. But the capricious old lady only laughed, and several times, to the great offence of the wardrobe-maid, forced her to repeat 'how he bent your head down with his heavy hand,' and next day she sent Gerasim a rouble. She looked on him with favour as a strong and faithful watchman. Gerasim stood in considerable awe of her, but, all the same, he had hopes of her favour, and was preparing to go to her with a petition for leave to marry Tatiana. He was only waiting for a new coat, promised him by the steward, to present a proper appearance before his mistress, when this same mistress suddenly took it into her head to marry Tatiana to Kapiton.

The reader will now readily understand the perturbation of mind that overtook the steward Gavrila after his conversation with his mistress. 'My lady,' he thought, as he sat at the window, 'favours Gerasim, to be sure'—(Gavrila was well aware of this, and that was why he himself looked on him with an indulgent eye)—'still he is a speechless creature. I could not, indeed, put it before the mistress that Gerasim's courting Tatiana. But, after all, it's true enough; he's a queer sort of husband. But on the other hand, that devil, God forgive me, has only got to find out they're marrying Tatiana to Kapiton, he'll smash up everything in the house,' pon my soul! There's no reasoning with him; why, he's such a devil, God forgive my sins, there's no getting over him no how . . .' pon my soul!'

Kapiton's entrance broke the thread of Gavrila's reflections. The dissipated shoemaker came in, his hands behind him, and lounging carelessly against a projecting angle of the wall, near the door, crossed his right foot in front of his left, and tossed his head, as much as to say, 'What do you want?'

Gavrila looked at Kapiton, and drummed with his fingers on the window-frame. Kapiton merely screwed up his leaden eyes a little, but he did not look down, he even grinned slightly, and passed his hand over his whitish locks which were sticking up in all directions. 'Well, here I am. What is it?'

'You're a pretty fellow,' said Gavrila, and paused. 'A pretty fellow you are, there's no denying!'

Kapiton only twitched his little shoulders. 'Are you any better, pray?' he thought to himself.

'Just look at yourself, now, look at yourself,' Gavrila went on reproachfully; 'now, what ever do you look like?'

MUMU

Kapiton serenely surveyed his shabby tattered coat, and his patched trousers, and with special attention stared at his burst boots, especially the one on the tip-toe of which his right foot so gracefully poised, and he fixed his eyes again on the steward.

'Well?'

'Well?' repeated Gavrila. 'Well? And then you say well? You look like old Nick himself, God forgive my saying so, that's what you look like.'

Kapiton blinked rapidly.

'Go on abusing me, go on, if you like, Gavrila Andreitch,' he thought to himself again.

'Here you've been drunk again,' Gavrila began, 'drunk again, haven't you? Eh? Come, answer me!'

'Owing to the weakness of my health, I have exposed myself to spirituous beverages, certainly,' replied Kapiton.

'Owing to the weakness of your health! . . . They let you off too easy, that's what it is; and you've been apprenticed in Petersburg. . . . Much you learned in your apprenticeship! You simply eat your bread in idleness.'

'In that matter, Gavrila Andreitch, there is one to judge me, the Lord God Himself, and no one else. He also knows what manner of man I be in this world, and whether I eat my bread in idleness. And as concerning your contention regarding drunkenness, in that matter, too, I am not to blame, but rather a friend; he led me into temptation, but was diplomatic and got away, while I . . .'

'While you were left, like a goose, in the street. Ah, you're a dissolute fellow! But that's not the point,' the steward went on, 'I've something to tell you. Our lady. . . .' here he paused a minute, 'it's our lady's pleasure that you should be married. Do you hear? She imagines you may be steadier when you're married. Do you understand?'

'To be sure I do.'

'Well, then. For my part I think it would be better to give you a good hiding. But there —it's her business. Well? are you agreeable?'

Kapiton grinned.

'Matrimony is an excellent thing for any one, Gavrila Andreitch; and, as far as I am concerned, I shall be quite agreeable.'

'Very well, then,' replied Gavrila, while he reflected to himself: 'there's no denying the man expresses himself very properly. Only there's one thing,' he pursued aloud: 'the wife our lady's picked out for you is an unlucky choice.'

'Why, who is she, permit me to inquire?'

'Tatiana.'

'Tatiana?'

And Kapiton opened his eyes, and moved a little away from the wall.

'Well, what are you in such a taking for? . . . Isn't she to your taste, hey?'

'Not to my taste, do you say, Gavrila Andreitch! She's right enough, a hard-working steady girl. . . . But you know very well yourself, Gavrila Andreitch, why that fellow, that wild man of the woods, that monster of the steppes, he's after her, you know. . . .'

'I know, mate, I know all about it,' the butler cut him short in a tone of annoyance: 'but there, you see . . .'

'But upon my soul, Gavrila Andreitch! why, he'll kill me, by God, he will, he'll crush me like some fly; why, he's got a fist—why, you kindly look yourself what a fist he's got; why, he's simply got a fist like Minin Pozharsky's. You see he's deaf, he beats and does not hear how he's beating! He swings his great fists, as if he's asleep. And there's no possibility of pacifying him; and for why? Why, because, as you know yourself, Gavrila Andreitch, he's deaf, and what's more, has no more wit than the heel of my foot Why, he's a sort of beast, a heathen idol, Gavrila Andreitch, and worse . . . a block of wood; what have I done that I should have to suffer from him now? Sure it is, it's all over with me now; I've knocked about, I've had enough to put up with, I've been battered like an earthenware pot, but still I'm a man, after all, and not a worthless pot.'

'I know, I know, don't go talking away . . .'

'Lord, my God!' the shoemaker continued warmly, 'when is the end? when, O Lord! A poor wretch I am, a poor wretch whose sufferings are endless! What a life, what a life mine's been, come to think of it! In my young days, I was beaten by a German I was 'prentice to; in the prime of life beaten by my own countrymen, and last of all, in ripe years, see what I have been brought to. . . .'

'Ugh, you flabby soul!' said Gavrila Andreitch. 'Why do you make so many words about it?'

'Why, do you say, Gavrila Andreitch? It's not a beating I'm afraid of, Gavrila Andreitch. A gentleman may chastise me in private, but give me a civil word before folks, and I'm a man still; but see now, whom I've to do with. . . .'

'Come, get along,' Gavrila interposed impatiently. Kapiton turned away and staggered off.

'But, if it were not for him,' the steward

shouted after him, 'you would consent for your part?'

'I signify my acquiescence,' retorted Kapiton as he disappeared.

His fine language did not desert him, even in the most trying positions.

The steward walked several times up and down the room.

'Well, call Tatiana now,' he said at last.

A few instants later, Tatiana had come up almost noiselessly, and was standing in the doorway.

'What are your orders, Gavrila Andreitch?' she said in a soft voice.

The steward looked at her intently.

Well, Taniusha,' he said, 'would you like to be married? Our lady has chosen a husband for you.'

'Yes, Gavrila Andreitch. And whom has she deigned to name as a husband for me?' she added falteringly.

'Kapiton, the shoemaker.'

'Yes, sir.'

'He's a feather-brained fellow, that's certain. But it's just for that the mistress reckons upon you.'

'Yes, sir.'

'There's one difficulty . . . you know the deaf man, Gerasim, he's courting you, you sec.

How did you come to bewitch such a bear? But you see, he'll kill you, very like, he's such a bear....'

'He'll kill me, Gavrila Andreitch, he'll kill me, and no mistake.'

'Kill you.... Well, we shall see about that. What do you mean by saying he'll kill you? Has he any right to kill you? tell me yourself.'

'I don't know, Gavrila Andreitch, about his having any right or not.'

'What a woman! why, you've made him no promise, I suppose...'

'What are you pleased to ask of me?'

The steward was silent for a little, thinking, 'You're a meek soul! Well, that's right,' he said aloud; 'we'll have another talk with you later, now you can go, Taniusha; I see you're not unruly, certainly.'

Tatiana turned, steadied herself a little against the doorpost, and went away.

'And, perhaps, our lady will forget all about this wedding by to-morrow,' thought the steward; 'and here am I worrying myself for nothing! As for that insolent fellow, we must tie him down, if it comes to that, we must let the police know'... Ustinya Fyedorovna!' he shouted in a loud voice to his wife, 'heat the samovar, my good... soul....' All that day

MUMU

Tatiana hardly went out of the laundry. At first she had started crying, then she wiped away her tears, and set to work as before. Kapiton stayed till late at night at the ginshop with a friend of his, a man of gloomy appearance, to whom he related in detail how he used to live in Petersburg with a gentleman, who would have been all right, except he was a bit too strict, and he had a slight weakness besides, tie was too fond of drink; and, as to the fair sex, he didn't stick at anything. His gloomy companion merely said yes; but when Kapiton announced at last that, in a certain event, he would have to lay hands on himself to-morrow, his gloomy companion remarked that it was bedtime. And they parted in surly silence.

Meanwhile, the steward's anticipations were lot fulfilled. The old lady was so much taken ap with the idea of Kapiton's wedding, that even in the night she talked of nothing else to one of her companions, who was kept in her nouse solely to entertain her in case of sleeplessness, and, like a night cabman, slept in the day. When Gavrila came to her after morning: cea with his report, her first question was: And how about our wedding—is it getting on all right?' He replied, of course, that it was jetting on first rate, and that Kapiton would appear before her to pay his reverence to her that day. The old lady was not quite well; she did not give much time to business. The steward went back to his own room, and called a council. The matter certainly called for serious consideration. Tatiana would make no difficulty, of course; but Kapiton had declared in the hearing of all that he had but one head to lose, not two or three . . . Gerasim turned rapid sullen looks on every one, would not budge from the steps of the maids 'quarters, and seemed to guess that some mischief was being hatched against him. They met together. Among them was an old sideboard waiter, nicknamed Uncle Tail, to whom every one looked respectfully for counsel, though all they got out of him was, 'Here's a pretty pass! to be sure, to be sure, to be sure!' As a preliminary measure of security, to provide against contingencies, they locked Kapiton up in the lumber-room where the filter was kept; then considered the question with the gravest deliberation It would, to be sure, be easy to have recourse to force. But Heaven save us! there would be an uproar, the mistress would be put out—it would be awful! What should they do? They thought and thought, and at last thought out a solution. It had many a time been observed that Gerasim could not bear drunkards. . . . As he sat at the gates, he would always turn away with disgust when some one passed by intoxicated, with unsteady steps and his cap on one side of his ear. They resolved that Tatiana should be instructed tc pretend to be tipsy, and should pass by Gerasim staggering and reeling about. The poor girl refused for a long while to agree to this, but they persuaded her at last; she saw, too, that it was the only possible way of getting rid of her adorer. She went out. Kapiton was released from the lumber-room; for, all, he had an interest in the affair. Gerasim was sitting on the curb-stone at the gates, scraping the ground with a spade . . . From behind every corner, from behind every window-blind, the others were watching him. . . . The trick succeeded beyond all expectations. On seeing Tatiana, at first, he nodded as usual, making caressing, inarticulate sounds; then he looked carefully at her, dropped his spade, jumped up, went up to her, brought his face close to her face. . . . In her fright she staggered more than ever, and shut her eyes. . . . He took her by the arm, whirled her right across the yard, and going into the room where the council had been sitting, pushed her straight at Kapiton. Tatiana fairly swooned away. . . . Gerasim stood, looked at her, waved his hand, laughed, and went off, stepping heavily, to his garret.

MUMU

. . . For the next twenty-four hours, he did not come out of it. The postillion Antipka said afterwards that he saw Gerasim through a crack in the wall, sitting on his bedstead, his face in his hand. From time to time he uttered soft regular sounds; he was wailing a dirge, that is, swaying backwards and forwards with his eyes shut, and shaking his head as drivers or bargemen do when they chant their melancholy songs. Antipka could not bear it, and he came away from the crack. When Gerasim came out of the garret next day, no particular change could be observed in him. He only seemed, as it were, more morose, and took not the slightest notice of Tatiana or Kapiton. The same evening, they both had to appear before their mistress with geese under their arms, and in a week's time they were married. Even on the day of the wedding Gerasim showed no change of any sort in his behaviour. Only, he came back from the river without water, he had somehow broken the barrel on the road; and at night, in the stable, he washed and rubbed down his horse so vigorously, that it swayed like a blade of grass in the wind, and staggered from one leg to the other under his fists of iron.

All this had taken place in the spring. Another year passed by, during which Kapiton

MUMU

became a hopeless drunkard, and as being absolutely of no use for anything, was sent away with the store waggons to a distant village with his wife. On the day of his departure, he put a very good face on it at first, and declared that he would always be at home, send him where they would, even to the other end of the world; but later on he lost heart, began grumbling that he was being taken to uneducated people, and collapsed so completely at last that he could not even put his own hat on. Some charitable soul stuck it on his forehead, set the peak straight in front, and thrust it on with a slap from above. When everything was quite ready, and the peasants already held the reins in their hands, and were only waiting for the words 'With God's blessing!' to start, Gerasim came out of his garret, went up to Tatiana, and gave her as a parting present a red cotton handkerchief he had bought for her a year ago. Tatiana, who had up to that instant borne all the revolting details of her life with great indifference, could not control herself upon that; she burst into tears, and as she took her seat in the cart, she kissed Gerasim three times like a good Christian. He meant to accompany her as far as the town-barrier, and did walk beside her cart for a while, but he stopped suddenly at the

Crimean ford, waved his hand, and walked away along the riverside.

It was getting towards evening. He walked slowly, watching the water. All of a sudden he fancied something was floundering in the mud close to the bank. He stooped over, and saw a little white-and-black puppy, who, in spite of all its efforts, could not get out of the water; it was struggling, slipping back, and trembling all over its thin wet little body. Gerasim looked at the unlucky little dog, picked it up with one hand, put it into the bosom of his coat, and hurried with long steps homewards. He went into his garret, put the rescued puppy on his bed, covered it with his thick overcoat, ran first to the stable for straw, and then to the kitchen for a cup of milk Carefully folding back the overcoat, and spreading out the straw, he set the milk on the bedstead. The poor little puppy was not more than three weeks old, its eyes were only just open—one eye still seemed rather larger than the other; it did not know how to lap out of a cup, and did nothing but shiver and blink. Gerasim took hold of its head softly with two fingers, and dipped its little nose into the milk. The pup suddenly began lapping greedily, sniffing, shaking itself, and choking. Gerasim watched and watched it, and all at once he laughed

MUMU

outright. . . . All night long he was waiting on it, keeping it covered, and rubbing it dry. He fell asleep himself at last, and slept quietly and happily by its side.

No mother could have looked after her baby as Gerasim looked after his little nursling. At first, she—for the pup turned out to be a bitch—was very weak, feeble, and ugly, but by degrees she grew stronger and improved in looks, and thanks to the unflagging care of her preserver, in eight months' time she was transformed into a very pretty dog of the spaniel breed, with long ears, a bushy spiral tail, and large expressive eyes. She was devotedly attached to Gerasim, and was never a yard from his side; she always followed him about wagging her tail. He had even given her a name—the dumb know that their inarticulate noises call the attention of others. He called her Mumu. All the servants in the house liked her, and called her Mumu, too. She was very intelligent, she was friendly with every one, but was only fond of Gerasim. Gerasim, on his side, loved her passionately, and he did not like it when other people stroked her; whether he was afraid for her, or jealous—God knows! She used to wake him in the morning, pulling at his coat; she used to take the reins in her mouth, and bring him up the old horse that carried the water, with whom she was on very friendly terms. With a face of great importance, she used to go with him to the river; she used to watch his brooms and spades, and never allowed any one to go into his garret. He cut a little hole in his door on purpose for her, and she seemed to feel that only in Gerasim's garret she was completely mistress and at home; and directly she went in, she used to jump with a satisfied air upon the bed. At night she did not sleep at all, but she never barked without sufficient cause, like some stupid house-dog, who, sitting on its hind-legs, blinking, with its nose in the air, barks simply from dulness, at the stars, usually three times in succession. No! Mumu's delicate little voice was never raised without good reason; either some stranger was passing close to the fence, or there was some suspicious sound or rustle somewhere. . . . In fact, she was an excellent watch-dog. It is true that there was another dog in the yard, a tawny old dog with brown spots, called Wolf, but he was never, even at night, let off the chain; and, indeed, he was so decrepit that he did not even wish for freedom. He used to lie curled up in his kennel, and only rarely uttered a sleepy, almost noiseless bark, which broke off at once, as though he were himself aware of its uselessness.

MUMU

Mumu never went into the mistress's house; and when Gerasim carried wood into the rooms, she always stayed behind, impatiently waiting for him at the steps, pricking up her ears and turning her head to right and to left at the slightest creak of the door. . . .

So passed another year. Gerasim went on performing his duties as house-porter, and was very well content with his lot, when suddenly an unexpected incident occurred. . . . One fine summer day the old lady was walking up and down the drawing-room with her dependants. She was in high spirits; she laughed and made jokes. Her servile companions laughed and joked too, but they did not feel particularly mirthful; the household did not much like it, when their mistress was in a lively mood, for, to begin with, she expected from every one prompt and complete participation in her merriment, and was furious if any one showed a face that did not beam with delight, and secondly, these outbursts never lasted long with her, and were usually followed by a sour and gloomy mood. That day she had got up in a lucky hour; at cards she took the four knaves, which means the fulfilment of one's wishes (she used to try her fortune on the cards every morning), and her tea struck her as particularly delicious, for which her maid was rewarded by words of praise, and by twopence in money. With a sweet smile on her wrinkled lips, the lady walked about the drawing-room and went up to the window. A flower-garden had been laid out before the window, and in the very middle bed, under a rose-bush, lay Mumu busily gnawing a bone. The lady caught sight of her.

'Mercy on us!' she cried suddenly; 'what dog is that?'

The companion, addressed by the old lady, hesitated, poor thing, in that wretched state of uneasiness which is common in any person in a dependent position who doesn't know very well what significance to give to the exclamation of a superior.

'I d . . . d . . . don't know,' she faltered: 'I fancy it's the dumb man's dog.'

'Mercy!' the lady cut her short: 'but it's a charming little dog! order it to be brought in. Has he had it long? How is it I've never seen it before? . . . Order it to be brought in.'

The companion flew at once into the hall.

'Boy, boy!' she shouted: 'bring Mumu in at once! She's in the flower-garden.'

'Her name's Mumu then,' observed the lady: 'a very nice name.'

'Oh, very, indeed!' chimed in the companion. 'Make haste, Stepan!'

Stepan, a sturdily-built young fellow, whose

MUMU

duties were those of a footman, rushed headlong into the flower-garden, and tried to capture Mumu, but she cleverly slipped from his fingers, and with her tail in the air, fled full speed to Gerasim, who was at that instant in the kitchen, knocking out and cleaning a barrel, turning it upside down in his hands like a child's drum. Stepan ran after her, and tried to catch her just at her master's feet; but the sensible dog would not let a stranger touch her, and with a bound, she got away. Gerasim looked on with a smile at all this ado; at last, Stepan got up, much amazed, and hurriedly explained to him by signs that the mistress wanted the dog brought in to her. Gerasim was a little astonished; he called Mumu, however, picked her up, and handed her over to Stepan. Stepan carried her into the drawing-room, and put her down on the parquette floor. The old lady began calling the dog to her in a coaxing voice. Mumu, who had never in her life been in such magnificent apartments, was very much frightened, and made a rush for the door, but, being driven back by the obsequious Stepan, she began trembling, and huddled close up against the wall.

'Mumu, Mumu, come to me, come to your mistress,' said the lady; 'come, silly thing . . . don't be afraid.'

'Come, Mumu, come to the mistress,' repeated the companions. 'Come along!'

But Mumu looked round her uneasily, and did not stir.

'Bring her something to eat,' said the old lady. 'How stupid she is! she won't come to her mistress. What's she afraid of?'

'She's not used to your honour yet,' ventured one of the companions in a timid and conciliatory voice.

Stepan brought in a saucer of milk, and set it down before Mumu, but Mumu would not even sniff at the milk, and still shivered, and looked round as before.

'Ah, what a silly you are!' said the lady, and going up to her, she stooped down, and was about to stroke her, but Mumu turned her head abruptly, and showed her teeth. The lady hurriedly drew back her hand. . . .

A momentary silence followed. Mumu gave a faint whine, as though she would complain and apologise. . . . The old lady moved back, scowling. The dog's sudden movement had frightened her.

'Ah!' shrieked all the companions at once, she's not bitten you, has she? Heaven forbid! (Mumu had never bitten any one in her life.) Ah! ah!'

'Take her away,' said the old lady in a

changed voice. 'Wretched little dog! What a spiteful creature!'

And, turning round deliberately, she went towards her boudoir. Her companions looked timidly at one another, and were about to follow her, but she stopped, stared coldly at them, and said, 'What's that for, pray? I've not called you,' and went out.

The companions waved their hands to Stepan in despair. He picked up Mumu, and flung her promptly outside the door, just at Gerasim's feet, and half-an-hour later a profound stillness reigned in the house, and the old lady sat on her sofa looking blacker than a thunder-cloud.

What trifles, if you think of it, will sometimes disturb any one!

Till evening the lady was out of humour; she did not talk to any one, did not play cards, and passed a bad night. She fancied the eau-de-Cologne they gave her was not the same as she usually had, and that her pillow smelt of soap, and she made the wardrobe-maid smell all the bed linen—in fact she was very upset and cross altogether. Next morning she ordered Gavrila to be summoned an hour earlier than usual.

'Tell me, please,' she began, directly the latter, not without some inward trepidation, crossed the threshold of her boudoir, 'what dog was that barking all night in our yard? It wouldn't let me sleep!'

'A dog,'m . . . what dog,'m . . . may be, the dumb man's dog,'m.' he brought out in a rather unsteady voice.

'I don't know whether it was the dumb man's or whose, but it wouldn't let me sleep. And I wonder what we have such a lot of dogs for! I wish to know. We have a yard dog, haven't we?'

'Oh yes,'m, we have,'m. Wolf,'m.'

'Well, why more, what do we want more dogs for? It's simply introducing disorder. There's no one in control in the house— that's what it is. And what does the dumb man want with a dog? Who gave him leave to keep dogs in my yard? Yesterday I went to the window, and there it was lying in the flower-garden; it had dragged in some nastiness it was gnawing, and my roses are planted there. . . .'

The lady ceased.

'Let her be gone from to-day . . . do you hear?'

'Yes,'m.'

'To-day. Now go. I will send for you later for the report.'

Gavrila went away.

MUMU

As he went through the drawing-room, the steward by way of maintaining order moved a bell from one table to another; he stealthily blew his duck-like nose in the hall, and went into the outer-hall. In the outer-hall, on a locker was Stepan asleep in the attitude of a slain warrior in a battalion picture, his bare legs thrust out below the coat which served him for a blanket. The steward gave him a shove, and whispered some instructions to him, to which Stepan responded with something between a yawn and a laugh. The steward went away, and Stepan got up, put on his coat and his boots, went out and stood on the steps. Five minutes had hot passed before Gerasim made his appearance with a huge bundle of hewn logs on his back, accompanied by the inseparable Mumu. (The lady had given orders that her bedroom and boudoir should be heated at times even in the summer.) Gerasim turned sideways before the door, shoved it open with his shoulder, and staggered into the house with his load. Mumu, as usual, stayed behind to wait for him. Then Stepan, seizing his chance, suddenly pounced on her, like a kite on a chicken, held her down to the ground, gathered her up in his arms, and without even putting on his cap, ran out of the yard with her, got into the first fly he met, and galloped off to a market-place. There he soon found a purchaser, to whom he sold her for a shilling, on condition that he would keep her for at least a week tied up; then he returned at once. But before he got home, he got off the fly, and going right round the yard, jumped over the fence into the yard from a back street. He was afraid to go in at the gate for fear of meeting Gerasim.

His anxiety was unnecessary, however; Gerasim was no longer in the yard. On coming out of the house he had at once missed Mumu. He never remembered her failing to wait for his return, and began running up and down, looking for her, and calling her in his own way. . . . He rushed up to his garret, up to the hay-loft, ran out into the street, this way and that. . . . She was lost! He turned to the other serfs, with the most despairing signs, questioned them about her, pointing to her height from the ground, describing her with his hands. . . . Some of them really did not know what had become of Mumu, and merely shook their heads, others did know, and smiled to him for all response, while the steward assumed an important air, and began scolding the coachmen. Then Gerasim ran right away out of the yard.

It was dark by the time he came back.

MUMU

From his worn-out look, his unsteady walk, and his dusty clothes, it might be surmised that he had been running over half Moscow. He stood still opposite the windows of the mistress' house, took a searching look at the steps where a group of house-serfs were crowded together, turned away, and uttered once more his inarticulate 'Mumu.' Mumu did not answer. He went away. Every one looked after him, but no one smiled or said a word, and the inquisitive postillion Antipka reported next morning in the kitchen that the dumb man had been groaning all night.

All the next day Gerasim did not show himself, so that they were obliged to send the coachman Potap for water instead of him, at which the coachman Potap was anything but pleased. The lady asked Gavrila if her orders had been carried out. Gavrila replied that they had. The next morning Gerasim came out of his garret, and went about his work. He came in to his dinner, ate it, and went out again, without a greeting to any one. His face, which had always been lifeless, as with all deaf-mutes, seemed now to be turned to stone. After dinner he went out of the yard again, but not for long; he came back, and went straight up to the hay-loft. Night came on, a clear moonlight night. Gerasim lay breathing heavily, and incessantly turning from side to side. Suddenly he felt something pull at the skirt of his coat. He started, but did not raise his head, and even shut his eyes tighter. But again there was a pull, stronger than before; he jumped up . . . before him, with an end of string round her neck, was Mumu, twisting and turning. A prolonged cry of delight broke from his speechless breast; he caught up Mumu, and hugged her tight in his arms, she licked his nose and eyes, and beard and moustache, all in one instant. . . . He stood a little, thought a minute, crept cautiously down from the hay-loft, looked round, and having satisfied himself that no one could see him, made his way successfully to his garret Gerasim had guessed before that his dog had not got lost by her own doing, that she must have been taken away by the mistress' orders; the servants had explained to him by signs that his Mumu had snapped at her, and he determined to take his own measures. First he fed Mumu with a bit of bread, fondled her. and put her to bed, then he fell to meditating, and spent the whole night long in meditating how he could best conceal her. At last he decided to leave her all day in the garret, and only to come in now and then to see her, and to take her out at night. The hole in the door

MUMU

he stopped up effectually with his old overcoat, and almost before it was light he was already in the yard, as though nothing had happened, even—innocent guile!—the same expression of melancholy on his face. It did not even occur to the poor deaf man that Mumu would betray herself by her whining; in reality, every one in the house was soon aware that the dumb man's dog had come back, and was locked up in his garret, but from sympathy with him and with her, and partly, perhaps, from dread of him, they did not let him know that they had found out his secret. The steward scratched his hand, and gave a despairing wave of his hand, as much as to say, 'Well, well, God have mercy on him! If only it doesn't come to the mistress' ears!'

But the dumb man had never shown such energy as on that day; he cleaned and scraped the whole courtyard, pulled up every single weed with his own hand, tugged up every stake in the fence of the flower-garden, to satisfy himself that they were strong enough, and unaided drove them in again; in ract, he toiled and laboured so that even the old lady noticed his zeal. Twice in the course of the day Gerasim went stealthily in to see his prisoner; when night came on, he lay down to sleep with her in the garret, not in the hay-loft, and only at two o'clock in the night he went out to take her a turn in the fresh air. After walking about the courtyard a good while with her, he was just turning back, when suddenly a rustle was heard behind the fence on the side of the back street. Mumu pricked up her ears, growled—went up to the fence, sniffed, and gave vent to a loud shrill bark. Some drunkard had thought fit to take refuge under the fence for the night. At that very time the old lady had just fallen asleep after a prolonged fit of 'nervous agitation'; these fits of agitation always overtook her after too hearty a supper. The sudden bark waked her up: her heart palpitated, and she felt faint. 'Girls, girls!' she moaned. 'Girls!' The terrified maids ran into her bedroom. 'Oh, oh, I am dying!' she said, flinging her arms about in her agitation. 'Again, that dog again! . . . Oh, send for the doctor. They mean to be the death of me. . . . The dog, the dog again! Oh!' And she let her head fall back, which always signified a swoon. They rushed for the doctor, that is, for the household physician, Hariton. This doctor, whose whole qualification consisted in wearing soft-soled boots, knew how to feel the pulse delicately. He used to sleep fourteen hours out of the twenty-four, but the rest of the time he was always sighing, and continually dosing

MUMU

the old lady with cherrybay drops. This doctor ran up at once, fumigated the room with burnt feathers, and when the old lady opened her eyes, promptly offered her a wineglass of the hallowed drops on a silver tray. The old lady took them, but began again at once in a tearful voice complaining of the dog, of Gavrila, and of her fate, declaring that she was a poor old woman, and that every one had forsaken her, no one pitied her, every one wished her dead. Meanwhile the luckless Mumu had gone on barking, while Gerasim tried in vain to call her away from the fence. 'There . . . there . . . again,' groaned the old lady, and once more she turned up the whites of her eyes. The doctor whispered to a maid, she rushed into the outer-hall, and shook Stepan, he ran to wake Gavrila, Gavrila in a fury ordered the whole household to get up.

Gerasim turned round, saw lights and shadows moving in the windows, and with an instinct of coming trouble in his heart, put Mumu under his arm, ran into his garret, and locked himself in. A few minutes later five men were banging at his door, but feeling the resistance of the bolt, they stopped. Gavrila ran up in a fearful state of mind, and ordered them all to wait there and watch till morning. Then he flew off himself to the maids' quarter, and through an old companion, Liubov Liubimovna, with whose assistance he used to steal tea, sugar, and other groceries and to falsify the accounts, sent word to the mistress that the dog had unhappily run back from somewhere, but that to-morrow she should be killed, and would the mistress be so gracious as not to be angry and to overlook it. The old lady would probably not have been so soon appeased, but the doctor had in his haste given her fully forty drops instead of twelve. The strong dose of narcotic acted; in a quarter of an hour the old lady was in a sound and peaceful sleep; while Gerasim was lying with a white face on his bed, holding Mumu's mouth, tightly shut.

Next morning the lady woke up rather late. Gavrila was waiting till she should be awake, to give the order for a final assault on Gerasim's stronghold, while he prepared himself to face a fearful storm. But the storm did not come off. The old lady lay in bed and sent for the eldest of her dependent companions.

'Liubov Liubimovna,' she began in a subdued weak voice—she was fond of playing the part of an oppressed and forsaken victim; needless to say, every one in the house was made extremely uncomfortable at such times—'Liubov Liubimovna, you see my position; go, my love to Gavrila Andreitch, and talk to him a little

MUMU

Can he really prize some wretched cur above the repose—the very life—of his mistress? I could not bear to think so,' she added, with an expression of deep feeling. 'Go, my love; be so good as to go to Gavrila Andreitch for me.'

Liubov Liubimovna went to Gavrila's room. What conversation passed between them is not known, but a short time after, a whole crowd of people was moving across the yard in the direction of Gerasim's garret. Gavrila walked in front, holding his cap on with his hand, though there was no wind. The footmen and cooks were close behind him; Uncle Tail was looking out of a window, giving instructions, that is to say, simply waving his hands. At the rear there was a crowd of small boys skipping and hopping along; half of them were outsiders who had run up. On the narrow staircase leading to the garret sat one guard; at the door were standing two more with sticks. They began to mount the stairs, which they entirely blocked up. Gavrila went up to the door, knocked with his fist, shouting, 'Open the door!'

A stifled bark was audible, but there was no answer.

'Open the door, I tell you,' he repeated.

'But, Gavrila Andreitch,' Stepan observed from below, 'he's deaf, you know—he doesn't hear.'

MUMU

They all laughed.

'What are we to do?' Gavrila rejoined from above.

'Why, there's a hole there in the door,' answered Stepan, 'so you shake the stick in there.'

Gavrila bent down.

'He's stuffed it up with a coat or something.'

'Well, you just push the coat in.'

At this moment a smothered bark was heard again.

'See, see—she speaks for herself,' was remarked in the crowd, and again they laughed.

Gavrila scratched his ear.

'No, mate,' he responded at last, 'you can poke the coat in yourself, if you like.'

'All right, let me.'

And Stepan scrambled up, took the stick, pushed in the coat, and began waving the stick about in the opening, saying, 'Come out, come out!' as he did so. He was still waving the stick, when suddenly the door of the garret was flung open; all the crowd flew pell-mell down the stairs instantly, Gavrila first of all. Uncle Tail locked the window.

'Come, come, come,' shouted Gavrila from the yard, 'mind what you're about'

Gerasim stood without stirring in his doorway. The crowd gathered at the foot of the stairs Gerasim, with his arms akimbo, looked

MUMU

down at all these poor creatures in German coats; in his red peasant's shirt he looked like a giant before them. Gavrila took a step forward.

'Mind, mate,' said he,' don't be insolent.'

And he began to explain to him by signs that the mistress insists on having his dog; that he must hand it over at once, or it would be the worse for him.

Gerasim looked at him, pointed to the dog, made a motion with his hand round his neck, as though he were pulling a noose tight, and glanced with a face of inquiry at the steward.

'Yes, yes,' the latter assented, nodding; 'yes, just so.'

Gerasim dropped his eyes, then all of a sudden roused himself and pointed to Mumu, who was all the while standing beside him, innocently wagging her tail and pricking up her ears inquisitively. Then he repeated the strangling action round his neck and significantly struck himself on the breast, as though announcing he would take upon himself the task of killing Mumu.

'But you'll deceive us,' Gavrila waved back in response.

Gerasim looked at him, smiled scornfully, struck himself again on the breast, and slammed-to the door.

They all looked at one another in silence.

'What does that mean?' Gavrila began. 'He's locked himself in.'

'Let him be, Gavrila Andreitch,' Stepan advised; 'he'll do it if he's promised. He's like that, you know. . . . If he makes a promise, it's a certain thing. He's not like us others in that. The truth's the truth with him. Yes, indeed.

'Yes,' they all repeated, nodding their heads, 'yes—that's so—yes.'

Uncle Tail opened his window, and he too said, 'Yes.'

'Well, may be, we shall see,' responded Gavrila; 'any way, we won't take off the guard. Here you, Eroshka!' he added, addressing a poor fellow in a yellow nankeen coat, who considered himself to be a gardener, 'what have you to do? Take a stick and sit here, and if anything happens, run to me at once!'

Eroshka took a stick, and sat down on the bottom stair. The crowd dispersed, all except a few inquisitive small boys, while Gavrila went home and sent word through Liubov Liubimovna to the mistress, that everything had been done, while he sent a postillion for a policeman in case of need. The old lady tied a knot in her handkerchief, sprinkled some eau-de-Cologne on it, sniffed at it, and rubbed her temples with

MUMU

it, drank some tea, and, being still under the influence of the cherrybay drops, fell asleep again.

An hour after all this hubbub the garret door opened, and Gerasim showed himself. He had on his best coat; he was leading Mumu by a string, Eroshka moved aside and let him pass. Gerasim went to the gates. All the small boys in the yard stared at him in silence. He did not even turn round; he only put his cap on in the street. Gavrila sent the same Eroshka to follow him and keep watch on him as a spy. Eroshka, seeing from a distance that he had gone into a cookshop with his dog, waited for him to come out again.

Gerasim was well known at the cookshop, and his signs were understood. He asked for cabbage soup with meat in it, and sat down with his arms on the table. Mumu stood beside his chair, looking calmly at him with her intelligent eyes. Her coat was glossy; one could see she had just been combed down. They brought Gerasim the soup. He crumbled some bread into it, cut the meat up small, and put the plate on the ground. Mumu began eating in her usual refined way, her little muzzle daintily held so as scarcely to touch her food. Gerasim gazed a long while at her; two big tears suddenly rolled from his eyes; one fell on the dog's brow, the other into the soup. He shaded his face with his hand. Mumu ate up half the plateful, and came away from it, licking her lips. Gerasim got up, paid for the soup, and went out, followed by the rather perplexed glances of the waiter. Eroshka, seeing Gerasim, hid round a corner, and letting him get in front, followed him again.

Gerasim walked without haSte, still holding Mumu by a string. When he got to the corner of the street, he stood still as though reflecting, and suddenly set off with rapid steps to the Crimean Ford. On the way he went into the yard of a house, where a lodge was being built, and carried away two bricks under his arm. At the Crimean Ford, he turned along the bank, went to a place where there were two little rowing-boats fastened to stakes (he had noticed them there before), and jumped into one of them with Mumu. A lame old man came out of a shed in the corner of a kitchen-garden and shouted after him; but Gerasim only nodded, and began rowing so vigorously, though against stream, that in an instant he had darted two hundred yards away. The old man stood for a while, scratched his back first with the left and then with the right hand, and went back hobbling to the shed.

MUMU

Gerasim rowed on and on. Moscow was soon left behind. Meadows stretched each side of the bank, market gardens, fields, and copses; peasants' huts began to make their appearance. There was the fragrance of the country. He threw down his oars, bent his head down to Mumu, who was sitting facing him on a dry cross seat—the bottom of the boat was full of water—and stayed motionless, his mighty hands clasped upon her back, while the boat was gradually carried back by the current towards the town. At last Gerasim drew himself up hurriedly, with a sort of sick anger in his face, he tied up the bricks he had taken with string, made a running noose, put it round Mumu's neck, lifted her up over the river, and for the last time looked at her. . . . she watched him confidingly and without any fear, faintly wagging her tail. He turned away, frowned, and wrung his hands. . . . Gerasim heard nothing, neither the quick shrill whine of Mumu as she fell, nor the heavy splash of the water; for him the noisiest day was soundless and silent as even the stillest night is not silent to us. When he opened his eyes again, little wavelets were hurrying over the river, chasing one another; as before they broke against the boat's side, and only far away behind wide circles moved widening to the bank.

Directly Gerasim had vanished from Eroshka's sight, the latter returned home and reported what he had seen.

'Well, then,' observed Stepan, 'he'll drown her. Now we can feel easy about it. If he once promises a thing. . . .'

No one saw Gerasim during the day. He did not have dinner at home. Evening came on; they were all gathered together to supper, except him.

'What a strange creature that Gerasim is!' piped a fat laundrymaid; 'fancy, upsetting himself like that over a dog. . . . Upon my word!'

'But Gerasim has been here,' Stepan cried all at once, scraping up his porridge with a spoon.

'How? when?'

'Why, a couple of hours ago. Yes, indeed! I ran against him at the gate; he was going out again from here; he was coming out of the yard. I tried to ask him about his dog, but he wasn't in the best of humours, I could see. Well, he gave me a shove; I suppose he only meant to put me out of his way, as if he'd say, "Let me go, do!" but he fetched me such a crack on my neck, so seriously, that—oh! oh!' And Stepan, who could not help laughing, shrugged up and rubbed the back of

MUMU

his head. 'Yes,' he added; 'he has got a fist; it's something like a fist, there's no denying that!'

They all laughed at Stepan, and after supper they separated to go to bed.

Meanwhile, at that very time, a gigantic figure with a bag on his shoulders and a stick in his hand, was eagerly and persistently stepping out along the T—— highroad. It was Gerasim. He was hurrying on without looking round; hurrying homewards, to his own village, to his own country. After drowning poor Mumu, he had run back to his garret, hurriedly packed a few things together in an old horsecloth, tied it up in a bundle, tossed it on his shoulder, and so was ready. He had noticed the road carefully when he was brought to Moscow; the village his mistress had taken him from lay only about twenty miles off the highroad. He walked along it with a sort of invincible purpose, a desperate and at the same time joyous determination. He walked, his shoulders thrown back and his chest expanded; his eyes were fixed greedily straight before him. He hastened as though his old mother were waiting for him at home, as though she were calling him to her after long wanderings in strange parts, among strangers. The summer night, that was just drawing in, was still and warm; on one side, where the sun had set, the horizon was still light and faintly flushed with the last glow of the vanished day; on the other side a blue-grey twilight had already risen up. The night was coming up from that quarter. Quails were in hundreds around; corncrakes were calling to one another in the thickets. . . . Gerasim could hot hear them; he could not hear the delicate night-whispering of the trees, by which his strong legs carried him, but he smelt the familiar scent of the ripening rye, which was wafted from the dark fields; he felt the wind, flying to meet him—the wind from home— beat caressingly upon his face, and play with his hair and his beard. He saw before him the whitening road homewards, straight as an arrow. He saw in the sky stars innumerable, lighting up his way, and stepped out, strong and bold as a lion, so that when the rising sun shed its moist rosy light upon the still fresh and unwearied traveller, already thirty miles lay between him and Moscow.

In a couple of days he was at home, in his little hut, to the great astonishment of the soldier's wife who had been put in there. After praying before the holy pictures, he set off at once to the village elder. The village elder was at first surprised; but the haycutting

MUMU

had just begun; Gerasim was a first-rate mower, and they put a scythe into his hand on the spot, and he went to mow in his old way, mowing so that the peasants were fairly astounded as they watched his wide sweeping strokes and the heaps he raked together....

In Moscow the day after Gerasim's flight they missed him. They went to his garret, rummaged about in it, and spoke to Gavrila. He came, looked, shrugged his shoulders, and decided that the dumb man had either run away or had drowned himself with his stupid dog. They gave information to the police, and informed the lady. The old lady was furious, burst into tears, gave orders that he was to be found whatever happened, declared she had never ordered the dog to be destroyed, and, in fact, gave Gavrila such a rating that he could do nothing all day but shake his head and murmur, 'Well!' until Uncle Tail checked him at last, sympathetically echoing 'We-ell!' At last the news came from the country of Gerasim's being there. The old lady was somewhat pacified; at first she issued a mandate for him to be brought back without delay to Moscow; afterwards, however, she declared that such an ungrateful creature was absolutely of no use to her. Soon after this she died herself; and her heirs had no thought to spare for Gerasim; they let their mother's other servants redeem their freedom on payment of an annual rent.

And Gerasim is living still, a lonely man in his lonely hut; he is strong and healthy as before, and does the work of four men as before, and as before is serious and steady. But his neighbours have observed that ever since his return from Moscow he has quite given up the society of women; he will not even look at them, and does not keep even a single dog. 'It's his good luck, though,' the peasants reason; 'that he can get on without female folk; and as for a dog—what need has he of a dog? you wouldn't get a thief to go into his yard for any money!' Such is the fame of the dumb man's Titanic strength

THE END